Scapegoat

Scapegoat

Patrick Marrinan

ROBERT HALE · LONDON

© Patrick Marrinan 2009
First published in Great Britain 2009

ISBN 978-0-7090-8855-4

Robert Hale Limited
Clerkenwell House
Clerkenwell Green
London EC1R 0HT

2 4 6 8 10 9 7 5 3 1

Typeset in 10.25/13pt Sabon
Printed in Great Britain by the MPG Books Group, Bodmin and King's Lynn

one

It was approaching midnight, and a fog hung like a shroud over the centre of Dublin. A blue Toyota Carina slid slowly along Dame Street from the direction of the castle and when it reached the plaza beneath the hanging gardens of the Central Bank, it stopped. This was the gateway to the self-styled cultural quarter of Temple Bar, a warren of narrow, cobblestoned streets that housed lively bars, discos and lap-dancing clubs. The wide flagstoned plaza, a meeting place for young couples and a favoured spot for drug pushers and their clientele, was rocking with activity. A busker strummed his guitar as he sang *California Dreaming* to a small audience of American tourists.

A gaggle of girls, wearing T-shirts declaring them to be from Birmingham and supposedly in search of casual sex, emerged from Temple Bar. Teetering precariously on high heels, they crossed Dame Street, and then staggered off down Georges Street. The car moved off slowly towards the imposing grandeur of Trinity College and swung along Westmorland Street towards O'Connell Street.

Georges Street was lively, its numerous bars bursting with music and drunken laughter. Outside the George, one of the city's oldest and most popular gay bars, meticulously groomed young men smoked and flirted pretentiously with one another. Inside, a group of students sat huddled around a small circular table. Amongst them was Johnny O'Shea, nineteen, and an engineering student at Dublin City University. It was early October and his college friends had gathered to recount tall tales gathered from all corners of the globe during the summer recess. Johnny, pale and slim, wore a white T-shirt and faded denim jeans. Unlike his pals he was straight, though temporarily celibate due to his acute shyness.

As the evening wore on, and the alcohol did its work, Johnny began to feel queasy. After midnight he went outside for a breath of air. It had been a great night, and the *craic* still mighty, so he remained, determined to stay the course. He lit a cigarette and sauntered aimlessly through the throngs of young people on the bustling street. He met the girls from Birmingham, who appeared to be hunting in a pack, and was duly surrounded by them.

'You're a real cutie,' teased one of the girls in the group.

'Give us a kiss,' another said, as the rest of the girls fell into staged laughter.

Johnny bowed his head, politely absorbing their brashness, and walked on.

'Are you a faggot?' one jeered after him.

'Are all you Irish lads bent?' and they all giggled and staggered away.

Johnny appeared mildly amused by the encounter. He stopped at the corner of a dimly lit alleyway, looked around and walked a few paces into the privacy of the darkness and began to urinate in a doorway.

The sound of heavy boots on the cobblestones startled him, and he glanced towards the entrance to the laneway and prematurely pulled up his fly. Silhouetted against the bright yellow streetlights in the background, stood a tall, slim figure wearing a leather jacket. Johnny, eyes narrowed, strained to see a face, but it was cloaked in darkness. Then the figure moved menacingly and silently towards him, hands thrust deep in his pockets. Johnny turned and looked into the blackness of the far end of the alley, but was unsure where it led. He hesitated, and moved towards the sanctuary of Georges Street, hugging the brick wall as he gingerly approached the stranger. The figure drifted closer and settled directly in Johnny's path.

'What do you want?' Johnny called out firmly, trying to disguise the tremor in his voice.

The figure moved closer without speaking. Johnny took a step back.

'I have no money,' he said, fumbling in the pocket of his jeans, 'but you can take this if you want.' He held out his mobile phone in his trembling hand. Suddenly he saw a flash of steel, as the figure lunged at him. There was a strange gurgling sound and a swish of escaping air, like a tyre deflating. Then silence.

Moments later in the communications room in Pearse Street Garda Station, a young guard was examining banks of CCTV monitors. His attention focused on a tall figure leaving Dame Lane. The fog clouded the image, but he observed the figure walk quickly towards Wicklow Street, where it hastily donned a helmet and mounted some class of a large motorbike. He then sped off towards the south of the city.

On Dawson Street opposite the Mansion House, home to the lord mayor, a queue of Dublin's young, rich and beautiful were waiting impatiently to gain admittance to Café En Seine, a fashionable drinking emporium. The blue Toyota was parked across the road under a street lamp. At the wheel sat the giant figure of Detective Sergeant Pat O'Hara and beside him Detective Garda Nicola Murphy. Both armed members of the Emergency Response Unit, they had just come on duty and were waiting to be deployed to the scene of some violent conflict. Tonight, however, was quiet, and O'Hara supped black coffee from a plastic cup in an effort to remain awake.

'Pat, would you look at the state of those young ones,' Nicola said, as she studied some nubile girls, wearing micro minis and little else, joining the long queue outside the bar.

Pat glanced sideways and smiled. 'If their mothers could only see them now,' he said sardonically.

'Sure, their mothers are probably inside, and already half cut,' Nicola retorted.

'Dublin isn't what it used to be and that's for sure,' Pat replied.

'How do you mean, Pat?' she asked earnestly.

'All this wealth has gone to the country's head and we've now lost the plot.'

'In what way?'

'You'll accuse me of being a grumpy old man when I say this, but there's no poetry left.'

'No poetry?' Nicola looked bemused.

Pat was from the village of Ballydavid, as far west as one can travel on the rugged Dingle Peninsula. A place where neighbours collaborated to ward off evil and from time to time gathered together and shared the joys of life. His father, a strict disciplinarian, had taught at the local national school and his mother was known as the finest midwife on the peninsula. Both were a long time deceased. Pat was the eldest of three sons. The youngest, Rory, had departed to Boston in the dark years and ran a successful construction company. Paul, the favoured one, had joined the priesthood and worked in Africa on famine relief. In 1991 whilst attending to sick children in a makeshift hospital on the outskirts of war-torn Mogadishu, he was attacked by machete-wielding Sunni Muslim rebel forces, and savagely hacked to death.

Pat, being over 6ft 5ins and strongly built, was known locally as the 'bear'. From his teenage days he had been told, more than once, that he was born to be a guard.

'What do you mean, Pat, no poetry?'

'I suppose what I really meant to say was romance. We were once a proud romantic race with music in our hearts and dreams to beat the band.'

'And?'

'The euro rules our hearts and minds,' he snapped. 'We've become so European that we have forgotten what made us unique. Why, the might of the British Empire couldn't rob us of our independence or bury our heritage. But look at us now; Dublin could be any city in Europe.'

Pat had played Gaelic football for the kingdom and was deeply proud of his two All Ireland medals. He duly joined An Garda Siochana when he left school and rapidly proved his worth. He was transferred to Dublin in the late 70s and was recruited into the notorious murder squad. He was by then a detective sergeant and already a legend in the force. Though some of the squad's methods of interrogation were highly suspect, the unit ensured that Ireland had an unrivalled detection rate.

'You're right Pat, you are a grumpy old man,' Nicola replied cheekily. 'How the hell did you end up in this unit anyway?'

Pat glanced at Nicola and a broad grin crossed his ruddy face. Nicola was still a rookie, only five years out of the training college in Templemore, and seemingly unaware of Pat's notoriety.

In 1983 Pat had secured a confession of murder from a Provo. Though there had been a conviction, the case haunted him for years as the media took up the cudgels of the terrorist, eventually persuading the public that a miscarriage of justice had occurred. The Provo was pardoned on dubious grounds and because Pat had taken the contro-versial confession, the media hunted him down like jackals. Eventually, under the weight of political pressure, the unit was disbanded. Only a few heads rolled and Pat's was one of them. And so ended his inves-tigative days, and the glory of bringing murderers to justice. He had felt an outcast ever since and rarely socialized with his colleagues in the force, who he felt had hung him out to dry.

The ERU was only marginally more interesting than a desk job. Sure, he had his thirty years done and could retire when he wished, but he hung on in the forlorn hope that someday he would be redeemed. Redemption however was a long time coming.

Just then the radio crackled into life.

'Serious incident, Dame Lane, Georges Street, bravo 3 respond.'

The Toyota tore off down Dawson Street and was at the scene in minutes. A small crowd had gathered as Pat and Nicola leapt from the car. A tramp was lying in a pool of his own vomit at the entrance to the laneway, muttering incoherently. He looked up as Pat approached, and Pat at once recognized him as Dan Pender, from Oliver Bond flats. Once a handy shoplifter and scourge of the fancy department stores on nearby Grafton Street, he had succumbed to heroin and what little quality existed in his already miserable life, evaporated as his addiction consumed him. The Aids virus had left him frail and he resorted to begging to feed his addiction.

Pender's eyes were bloodshot and bleary, but the fear that gripped him was all too obvious to Pat.

'What's the matter?' Nicola asked Pender.

He raised an arm and pointed towards the laneway and then threw up again. Pat pushed his way through the crowd and peered into the blackness. Taking a small torch from the pocket of his tweed sports jacket, he shone it from side to side as he tentatively explored the darkness. He sniffed the air and a sickly smell at once filled his nostrils. It was a smell he knew well and long buried memories came flooding back. He stopped, and turned to Nicola who was at his shoulder.

'Go back to the street and clear away the crowd. They may be trampling on evidence.' Pat said.

'Evidence of what?' Nicola asked.

He glared at her and barked, 'Just do as I say.'

Nicola withdrew reluctantly as Pat cautiously explored further. He shone his torch to the left, and on the brick wall splatters of blood glistened in the torchlight. He glanced down and on the cobblestones he observed a trail of freshly smeared blood. He followed it and, after a few more cautious paces, he stopped, placed his hand to his head and sighed heavily.

A young man was lying motionless on his back, his face grey and drained of life, a gaping wound across his neck, his head almost severed. Pat knelt down on his hunkers and reached out to take a hand to feel for a pulse. Then his body shuddered and a chill passed over him. He looked away, coughed into the palm of his hand and, taking a deep breath, looked back at the body. Both hands were severed at the wrists, the amputated limbs placed neatly beside the corpse. Pat flashed his torch around the area and looked for a weapon. There was none. He then stood up and returned to where Nicola was holding curious onlookers at bay.

'Well what's the story?' she asked.

He shook his head. 'It's not good,' he answered gravely, 'get these folks out of here and get on the radio and call in a homicide.'

She peered over his shoulder.

9

'Can I take a look?' she asked tentatively.

He looked down at her. Her wide brown eyes still bore the innocence of youth.

'I think it's better if you don't.'

Within minutes the area was crawling with Garda cars, which arrived with a fanfare of wailing sirens. Once the scene was secure and taped off, Pat noticed that Pender had vanished into the night. He hurried up towards Wicklow Street and he stopped at the corner. In the distance he saw Pender shuffling towards Grafton Street. He ran and quickly caught up with him.

'And where do you think you're going?' he said, placing a large hand on Pender's shoulder.

Pender was trembling. He took a slug from a bottle of cider, which was wrapped in a brown bag, and looked up at Pat.

'I never did anything, guard, I never touched him,' Pender pleaded.

'I know that, Dan, but you were the first person to find him and we need to have a chat.'

Dan appeared surprised Pat knew his name and his eyes narrowed suspiciously.

'So I found him, what does that matter?' he said defensively.

'We need to get a statement from you; don't look so worried it's merely a formality.'

Pender's face became even more twisted.

'I don't make statements to you pigs, never did, so I ain't about to start now.'

Pat noticed some fresh blood over the left pocket of his grubby coat. Cocking his head, he looked down at Pender.

'Did you take something from the body, Dan?'

Pender stepped back. 'I said I didn't touch him,' he replied aggressively. 'Do you think I'm crazy? I didn't go near him, Gospel.'

'So you won't mind emptying your pockets then,' said Pat, raising a dubious eyebrow.

Dan looked up at him and hesitated. The pig was a giant, no point in resisting. He reached deep into the pocket of his grubby coat, took out a watch and handed it over.

'I copped it lying on the ground near the entrance to the alley when I was leaving.'

Pat placed the watch on a handkerchief he took from the breast pocket of his jacket and inspected it closely. It was solid gold, the face studded with diamonds. The strap was broken.

'But it's covered in blood,' Pat observed.

Pender became agitated. 'I swear to God I found it there,' he protested.

'OK, Dan, calm down, I need you to come down to the station with me to make that statement.'

Pender pulled away. 'I don't make no statements.'

The guard's keen eyes narrowed. 'Do you want to do this the easy way, or the hard way?'

Pender pressed his fingers to his lips. 'OK, OK, but can you get me a drink on the way?'

Pender was escorted back to the scene and placed in the rear of the patrol car. The scene had been cordoned off and a tarpaulin erected over the body. The scenes of crime boys were donning their white overalls as they prepared to dissect the crime scene. A tall man, with greased back dark hair and an air of self-importance, emerged from the alley. A young, smartly dressed detective accompanied him.

'What the hell are you doing here, O'Hara?' the man roared as he spotted Pat.

Pat turned and glared at his nemesis. 'And good evening to you too, Inspector,' he answered sarcastically. 'I was first on the scene.'

'Well, get out of here,' snapped Detective Inspector Brannigan.

Pat considered flooring him on the spot, but instead handed him the handkerchief.

'Better get your boys to place that in an evidence bag, and don't forget to label it,' he said coolly.

The detective inspector examined the watch. 'Where did you get it?' he demanded.

Pat gave him a caustic stare, turned and pointed to the car.

'We have a witness who found it; he might have seen something.'

'Get him out of here, and get someone to take a statement from him at the station,' he barked.

'I'll do it myself,' Pat replied.

The detective inspector shook his head and grinned. 'Oh no you won't. I don't want your filthy paws anywhere near this investigation.'

He handed Pat a student identity card that had been retrieved from the corpse.

'If you want something useful to do, break the news to the family; even you couldn't make a mess of that.'

Pat glared at him, glanced at the photograph and strode away.

two

Pat pulled the car on to the pavement outside a small red-brick terraced house facing the Grand Canal on Whitworth Road in Drumcondra. It was just after 3 a.m. and light rain had washed away the fog. Nicola appeared uncomfortable and was shuffling nervously in her seat.

'What's up with you?' Pat asked.

'I never did this before,' she confessed.

He sighed heavily. 'Well you're not much help then,' he said, as he got out of the car. 'I shouldn't be too long.'

He knocked on the door and saw an upstairs light flicker to life. Then he heard the sound of someone descending the stairs.

'Who is it?' a soft voice came from the small hallway beyond the door.

'It's the Gardai.'

The door was pulled back slightly and Pat felt himself being surveyed. The door closed again and he heard the rattle of the safety chain being removed. When the door was eventually opened, a petite woman wearing a pale-pink nightdress and slippers invited him into the hallway. He asked her if she was Mrs O'Shea and she nodded. He introduced himself and showed her his warrant card. She appeared half asleep and confused as she ushered him into the front parlour. The room, though small, was tastefully furnished. Pat smelt the remnants of a turf fire.

'Is your husband at home, ma'am?' he enquired.

'No, he's away in Spain playing golf with his friends. Why do you ask?'

Her face, within the vivid circle of the overhead lamp, was unquestionably that of a middle-aged woman. Her slightly greying hair drawn back in a bun, a delicate nose set between high cheekbones.

'Are there any other members of the family at home with you?'

Her pale-blue eyes narrowed suspiciously.

'No, I'm alone, but my son should be home shortly. What's wrong, Sergeant? Why are you here?'

Pat hesitated. 'Do you mind if I sit down?'

'Please do.'

Pat took off his jacket and lowered his enormous frame into a small armchair.

'I think you had better sit down too, Mrs O'Shea.'

She did as Pat suggested and looked at him intently. He sat forward, reached across and took hold of her delicate hands in his. She cocked her head, looked down at his gesture and then momentarily appeared puzzled. Then she frowned and a look of fear ghosted across her face.

'It's Johnny, isn't it?' Her voice quivered.

Pat didn't reply but firmed his grip on her trembling hands.

'Has he got himself into trouble?'

Pat didn't answer at first.

'Mrs O'Shea, I'm afraid Johnny has been badly assaulted.'

Her body begin to shake as fear surged within her.

'Is he OK?'

He firmed his grasp on her hand. She pulled away and searched his eyes, which were full of sadness. Closing her eyes she shook her head from side to side.

'God, he's not coming home, is he?'

'No, he's not coming home,' Pat replied, choking on his words.

She threw her head back and began to wail. After a while she lowered her face and stared at Pat. His look of compassion carried a hint of his own solitude. Then her eyes were full of anger and she lashed out at Pat's chest with her clenched fists. He did nothing to stop her. After a few moments, exhausted, she crumpled back into the chair and buried her head deep in her hands and sobbed uncontrollably. Pat moved closer and again tried to console her. At first she pulled away, but then her head was drawn to his chest, where it lay, as she shook as though with fever. He placed his hand on the back of her head and felt her tears seep on to his shirt, as her agony penetrated his soul.

He stroked her hair, and, as her sobbing ebbed and flowed, his eyes wandered around the room. Photographs of Johnny were everywhere – with his father, fishing; with his mother, at his communion; on his own in some photographer's studio. Clearly an only child, adored, even worshipped, by loving decent parents.

He felt a surge of anger, closed his eyes and suddenly they were back: the twisted faces of drunken tinkers as they bludgeoned an elderly

13

farmer to pulp; the bloated face of the smirking headmaster, as he plunged his penis deep into the child's mouth; the calculated laugh of the masked terrorist, as he pumped lead into his kidnapped victim's hooded head. There were many of them, but he knew each by name. And they came to him when anger swamped his reason. And, at that moment, with Johnny's mother's world collapsing before his eyes, he was possessed with a pathological hatred for Johnny's killer.

Eventually Mrs O'Shea's body returned from shock. The trembling subsided but her eyes remained moist. Having composed herself, she pulled away from Pat, stood up and vanished into the kitchen. She returned with two tumblers of whiskey, offered one to Pat, and sat back into her chair opposite him.

'How did it happen?' she asked tentatively.

'He was attacked by someone with a knife.'

'But why?' she burst out in anguish. 'Why my Johnny?'

Tears began to flow over her cheekbones again and for a moment Pat thought he had lost her. Then she stood up, rummaged in her handbag, and took out her mobile phone.

'I had better ring my husband.'

There was no answer. She sat back down, clutching the phone in her hands.

'This is going to kill him you know.'

Pat nodded sympathetically. 'Have you any family who could come and stay with you?' he asked.

'I have a sister in Kilkenny.'

Pat hesitated and then spoke. 'I'm really sorry, Mrs O'Shea, but I have to ask you to come down to the morgue and formally identify Johnny. It's police procedure.'

She looked at him and nodded. She then left the room and returned shortly afterwards wearing a dark-grey tweed suit, with a set of rosary beads hanging from her gloved hands.

Nicola was half asleep in the car and was startled as the rear door opened and Mrs O'Shea climbed into the back. She turned to her and offered her condolences, then glanced at Pat who sat, stone-faced behind the driver's wheel. In the darkness on the short journey to the morgue, they sat in silence listening to the beat of the windscreen wipers and Mrs O'Shea's delicate voice muttering decades of the rosary.

At the morgue, Nicola waited outside as Pat went in to check on the condition of the corpse. A uniformed guard was sitting on a chair in the dimly lit room making sure that no one interfered with the body in advance of the state pathologist arriving to conduct a post-mortem examination. Johnny O'Shea's corpse lay naked on a cold steel trolley. Pat found a white sheet and covered the body, carefully tucking it in around the arms to disguise the amputations. Then he pulled the sheet up to Johnny's chin so that the gaping neck wound was concealed.

Mrs O'Shea came into the room, her steps growing shorter as she approached her son. She took a deep breath and looked down. His face was pale, almost angelic. She bit on her lower lip and fought back the tears and then nodded to Pat. She lowered her trembling body towards her son and kissed his cold forehead. Then she collapsed on to the stone floor.

Back at the house on Whitworth Road, Pat was in the kitchen making tea and toast. He brought the tray into the parlour where Mrs O'Shea was seated on the settee clutching a photograph of her son around which she had wrapped her rosary beads. He listened for hours on end to stories of Johnny's childhood and his many achievements. Of the nice young girl he had recently met in college and how his mother had great hopes for the two of them. Eventually the room fell silent. She looked intently at Pat.

'Have you any children yourself, Sergeant?'

He shook his head. 'I never found a woman who would put up with me.'

From somewhere she mustered a smile. 'I can't believe that,' she replied.

Pat felt her eyes upon him, studying him closely.

'Sergeant, you'll get the man who did this to my son, won't you?'

'We will do our best,' he assured her.

She shook her head. 'No, Sergeant, that's not good enough. I want your word that the bastard who did this will be brought to justice.' There was hardness in her voice, a demand for revenge.

'Do I have your word?' she persisted.

He stood up to leave. As he reached the door he stopped and looked back at her. 'Will you be OK, Mrs O'Shea?' he asked in a near whisper.

She lowered her head. He knew there was no consolation, no joy in revenge. He also knew that there were grim days ahead for her and her husband, as the investigation ebbed and flowed, perhaps even floundered.

'Mrs O'Shea, I promise that we will get him.'

She looked up at him. 'Thank you, Sergeant, you're a good man.'

three

Gerry Hickey sat in the drawing-room of his Georgian terraced house staring vacantly across Dalkey Sound towards the craggy Dalkey Island. The sea, grey and angry, crashed against the rocks below as the cold wind whistled through the gaps in the sash windows. The drawing-room was spacious, but almost barren of furniture. A couple of rickety armchairs and a large settee, the bald patches covered by a velvet throw.

That year Gerry would celebrate his fortieth birthday. And where was he? Sitting in a potentially splendid home in the fashionable village of Dalkey, with rock stars and movie moguls as neighbours. Here he was amongst the self-styled glitterati, a successful criminal barrister, with a beautiful wife and an adorable 10-year-old son. And a mortgage that was strangling the life out of him. Not to mention the leaking roof, rising damp and central-heating boiler that had eventually thrown in the towel.

He picked up the *Sunday Independent* newspaper: GAY MURDERED IN HEART OF PINK DUBLIN. And they had done their research. Feature articles on every case of gay bashing going back to the notorious Fairview Park murder in the 80s. The gay activist, Senator McCrory, was already ascending his pulpit and condemning the latest crime as a scandalous attack on a much beleaguered minority group.

Emily, his wife, called him to the dinner table. She was as delicate as a lily in full bloom. Educated at Mount Anville, a private school for the daughters of the elite, she had a graceful if somewhat distant aura about her. She had first met Gerry in Trinity College, where she was taking a degree in languages, and immediately fell for his boyish good looks and his devilish sense of humour. They were inseparable from the start and their friends referred to them as Mr and Mrs, which they became a year after their graduation. The reception in the Shelbourne Hotel was a lavish affair and occupied several pages of Social and

Personal. Her father, a successful property tycoon, offered to set them up in business, but Gerry remained determined to realize his dream of being a criminal lawyer. After seven years of penury at the Bar, he had begun to make a modest living.

Emily fell in love with the house on Coliemore Road when they first viewed it, and, with some help from her father and a substantial mortgage, they just about managed to outbid the other contenders at the auction. And how Emily loved Dalkey village and her close circle of girlfriends who lunched everyday in the Queens. However, she seemed oblivious to Gerry's continuous struggle to squeeze every euro he could out of the underfunded criminal legal aid scheme to pay for her extravagant lifestyle.

He opened a bottle of Chilean plonk and settled into his chair at the table.

'It's a bit early in the day for that, isn't it?' Emily glanced disapprovingly at the wine.

'I had a tough week and I need to chill out.'

'Why does your idea of chilling out always involve alcohol?'

'Ah, come on, Emily, leave it out, will you?'

'It's setting a bad example for Patrick.' She spoke of their son who was sitting at the table as though he wasn't there.

Gerry poured himself a glass and defiantly knocked it back in one go and then poured himself a second. She ignored his rebellion and sat opposite him at the table, her arms folded.

'Where are we going for Christmas?' she asked provocatively.

He glanced around the room. 'What's wrong with here? That is if we can hang on to the bloody place.'

'Jenny and Fiona are taking their family to Austria skiing; I thought it would be nice if we all went as a group.'

'Not in a million years.' He visibly recoiled at the idea, as she knew he would. 'You know I can't stand their boring husbands and we can't afford it anyway.'

'What do you mean we can't afford it? You always say that, but every time I pick up a newspaper and read about a case you're in it.'

'I told you before, crime doesn't pay.'

'Well, why don't you do some commercial work then?'

'Because it's boring, and anyway you need connections and I don't have them.'

'Then why don't you try to cultivate them? I told you before, Daddy can get you into Fitzwilliam.'

He raised his hand defensively. 'Look, Emily, will you back off? I am trying my best to make ends meet, but, to be perfectly honest, I have enough on my plate without listening to this rubbish.'

An awkward silence descended on the table. After a few minutes Emily appeared to soften.

'Gerry, if things are really that bad I can ask Daddy for some money.'

He looked at her through burning eyes, his teeth grating.

'I told you before we will stand on our own two feet. I won't take a penny from your father and that's that. He always thought I only married you for his money and I sure as hell don't intend to give him the satisfaction of believing he was right.'

They finished the meal in silence.

After lunch Gerry went upstairs to his study. A plethora of bills were laid out across his desk and he didn't remember leaving them there. Angrily he gathered them together, scrunched them into a ball and tossed them into a wastepaper bin.

He picked up a brief that was lying on the desk. The Director of Public Prosecutions v Naguma Borangi. Ms Borangi was a 35-year-old black woman who was detained by customs officers at Dublin Airport. She had flown from Johannesburg to Dublin via Amsterdam. On searching her luggage the customs officials found €75,000 of cannabis resin in vacuum-packed cellophane bags. The customs officers claimed it was a random search, but Gerry knew full well that sniffer dogs had been at work in Schipol airport, detected the drugs, and that Europol had tipped off the Gardai. Anyway, Ms Borangi was in serious trouble and facing a stiff sentence. Gerry put away the brief. He went to light a small cigar, then remembered Emily had banned them from the house. He went outside, walked down the garden and sat on the rocks watching the angry sea. A seagull flapped its wings energetically as it battled against the howling wind. Its progress, if any, appeared indiscernible and Gerry reflected on his own plight. He glanced back at the house. The bleak grey façade blended with the weathered granite rocks. In an upstairs window he caught a glimpse of Emily peering out at him. Why did she hate him so much? OK, he mightn't be the greatest provider on the planet, but they had once been lovers, and she, more than anyone else, should understand that he didn't give a toss for fast cars and fancy houses. What had happened to her?

four

The conference room at Harcourt Square Garda Station was a hive of activity as over fifty experienced detectives assembled for a briefing. Pat O'Hara was standing alone in the corridor outside as Detective Superintendent Cummins and Detective Inspector Brannigan approached. Cummins, a tall man with a cheerful face and unkempt white hair, immediately spotted Pat and approached him. Brannigan hovered at his shoulder. Cummins had been in the murder squad with Pat. He was then only a garda and had somehow avoided the purge. His easy manner and organizational skills ensured that he had moved speedily through the ranks and had become an outstanding commander.

'Hiya Pat,' he said, as he shook Pat's hand warmly, 'what are you doing in this neck of the woods?'

Pat looked at Brannigan and gave him a frosty stare.

'I was first on the scene and the detective inspector tasked me to break the news to the family.'

Cummins's eyes narrowed as he glared at Brannigan.

'And how did you get on with them?'

'The father is returning from Spain tonight, which is just as well because the mother is badly shook.'

'Did you build up any sort of a rapport with her?'

'I would like to think so, Superintendent.'

'That's good. So any ideas on this one?'

Brannigan appeared unhappy and quickly intervened. 'I think the sergeant's job is done; it's better if we let him get back to his unit.'

Cummins rounded on Brannigan. 'This guy was one of the best we ever had, and I just might be interested in his views.' He turned to Pat. 'If you have any of course.'

Pat shrugged his shoulders. 'Not really, but I can tell you one thing.'

'What's that?' asked Cummins.

'This guy is going to kill again, and soon.'

Cummins appeared surprised. 'And what makes you so sure of that?'

'The killer was making a statement, probably anti-gay, and he got it horribly wrong.'

Brannigan intervened again. 'We know that,' he said dismissively.

Pat wasn't easily deterred. 'And what about the small piece of hair that was cut from the victim's head?'

The detective superintendent turned to Brannigan. 'I didn't see anything about that in your briefing document.'

'I don't know what he's talking about,' Brannigan said defensively. 'The pathologist didn't mention anything about it in her report.'

'Have you got the post-mortem photographs?' asked Pat.

Brannigan took a small album of photographs from the folder he was carrying and went to flick through them. Cummins snatched them from him and handed the album to Pat.

'Show me what you're talking about.'

Pat flicked through the album and presented one to Cummins. Just behind the victim's ear, a small patch of hair had been neatly removed. Cummins handed the photograph to Brannigan, inviting his comment.

'He got a bad haircut, so what?' Brannigan responded.

Cummins grabbed the photograph from Brannigan's grasp, put on his glasses and inspected it closely.

'Pat, what's your opinion on this?'

'I think the killer removed it from his victim as some sort of souvenir. And if I'm right about that, I can guarantee you that it's the first of many.'

'That's a load of nonsense, you don't know your arse from your elbow,' Brannigan said, as he turned to walk into the conference room.

Cummins took Pat by the arm and walked him down the corridor. 'Pat, I'm sorry about Brannigan, he seems to have it in for you. I can't think why.'

Pat shrugged his shoulders. 'That stupid ponce doesn't bother me in the slightest; I could never trust a man who manicures his fingernails.'

Cummins laughed.

'So, is there any chance of me being involved in this one?' Pat asked.

Cummins shook his head. 'Pat, I don't need to tell you that with your history you can't be directly involved in this investigation. The commissioner himself has already been on to me and is taking a personal interest. Apparently the Minister for Justice wants results, and fast. But I'll appoint you as liaison officer to the family.'

'What do you mean, Superintendent?'

'Keep the family up to speed on the investigation, that sort of thing. It's all PR, of course, and strictly on a need-to-know basis.'

'I don't understand.'

Cummins winked at him. 'I want you to keep abreast of developments, and if by any chance something occurs to you, bypass Brannigan, and contact me directly.'

Pat's face lit up. 'Thanks, Superintendent, it will be like the old days.'

Cummins raised an arm defensively. 'Jesus, don't say that. I don't want you directly involved in hunting down any suspects. I want that famous nose of yours and nothing else.'

The detective superintendent turned on his heel and walked into the crowded conference-room, where he sat at the top table. Brannigan sat to his right. A large map of the *locus delicti* occupied one wall. Cummins addressed the gathering.

'Good evening, ladies and gentlemen. Before we get underway I want to make a few things crystal clear. The public, the politicians and the media will be breathing down our necks on this one. And when that happens there is a temptation to take shortcuts. But there will be no shortcuts in this investigation. I don't want some tribunal taking us apart in a few years' time and accusing us of a rush to judgment, or of gross negligence. Everything, and I mean absolutely everything, will be done strictly by the book. Do I make myself clear?'

The gathering acknowledged what had been said.

'Young Johnny O'Shea was brutally murdered last night and as yet we don't know why he was killed. There is nothing at the moment to suggest he knew his attacker, and it's highly unlikely that he did. His wallet and mobile phone were found at the scene, so robbery clearly isn't a motive. The location, right in the heart of pink Dublin, strongly suggests that we are dealing with some kind of homophobic psycho. Now that, of course, is mere supposition and we are not going to act on hunches. So, I want every person who was on Georges Street last night identified and interviewed. Furthermore, I want a full profile done on the victim. I want to know everything about him, his friends and, more importantly, his enemies, if he had any. Then we start on the suspects.'

Cummins paused and inspected a spreadsheet in front of him. A wry smile crossed his face.

'You will all be delighted to hear that the confidential lines have been buzzing all day, and the good citizens of Dublin have already nominated a hundred and seventy-five suspects for this crime.'

A titter of laughter engulfed the room but quickly subsided.

'I don't know what you poor bastards are laughing at, because you're going to have to exclude each and every one of them from our inquiries. Maybe, just maybe, one of them might turn out to be genuine. The forensic boys are still at the scene fine-combing everything, but, so far, have come up with zilch. The state pathologist reports that the victim's throat was slit from ear to ear and his hands severed with a degree of precision that suggests our murderer was experienced in such matters, perhaps a butcher, or someone who works in a slaughterhouse. We also have this.'

He turned to Garda Eddie Whelan and asked him to play the CCTV footage, which he did to a hushed audience. When it had finished Cummins resumed his briefing.

'That ladies and gentlemen is our killer. If you were looking closely you will have noticed the wino in the doorway of the travel agents a few doors up from the alley where our suspect emerges. You will also have noticed the wino entering the alley less than a minute later. It was then that he found the victim. So that dark figure leaving the lane is our man. The technical boys have digitally enhanced the tape, and unfortunately that is as good as it gets. But it is enough to tell us that our man is between six feet and six feet three inches in height, has an athletic build and rides a high-powered motor cycle. So there we have it. All leave is cancelled and I want all of you working around the clock. Any questions?'

There was none. The detective superintendent gathered his papers and left the incident-room with Brannigan in tow. As they walked along the corridor Cummins looked worried.

'Jack, something has you rattled,' Brannigan observed.

'There was a time when if you did your homework thoroughly enough on the victim, a list of likely suspects emerged. Motive, Noel, that's what every investigator wants, and a mindless slaughter like this is my worst nightmare.'

five

Heavy dew lingered on the mossy gravestones of Glasnevin Cemetery as a crow squawked and flapped across the dark grey sky. Beneath the gloomy canopy of ancient yews, a small gathering of family and friends encircled the rectangular dark hole where Johnny O'Shea was being laid to rest. Pat and Nicola stood a discreet distance away. Mrs O'Shea's anguish, carried on a cool breeze, resounded in Pat's head, forcing him to momentarily turn away. He spotted a reporter and a photographer perched on the steps of a nearby mausoleum. A surge of anger gripped the detective and he rumbled towards them.

'Give me the camera and get out of here,' he barked.

'And who do you think you are?' asked the reporter.

'Family liaison officer,' Pat declared.

The reporter grinned, and instructed the photographer to continue with his intrusion. Pat's face turned beetroot red and, without further debate, he grabbed the reporter by the lapels of his trench coat with one hand and lifted him off his feet. He then gestured to the photographer to hand over the camera, which he did without hesitation. Nicola, who was standing a short distance away, placed her hand to her brow and shook her head. Pat put the camera in his coat pocket and dropped the reporter, who quickly scurried off, with his sidekick not far behind. Pat returned to where Nicola was standing.

'Vultures, no respect for the dead,' he said sternly.

She looked at him and sighed heavily. 'There will be a complaint to the Garda Complaints Board.'

Pat allowed himself a grin. 'Wouldn't be the first, and won't be the last,' he replied, chuckling to himself.

Nicola rolled her eyes disapprovingly to the heavens.

'Dear God, Pat, will you never learn?'

When the prayers were done Pat approached Mrs O'Shea, who was clutching her husband's arm.

'I'm sorry for your trouble,' he said, as he shook her hand.

'Thank you, Sergeant,' she answered, and turned to her husband. 'This is my husband.'

Mr O'Shea was a low-sized man with brown eyes, a greying beard and little hair beneath the trilby perched on his head. He shook Pat's hand as though he were a long lost cousin and thanked him profusely for helping his wife in her darkest hour. Mrs O'Shea looked over Pat's shoulder at Nicola.

'Did you see what the papers said about my Johnny?' she asked.

Nicola nodded sympathetically.

'My son wasn't gay, you know.' Mrs O'Shea looked to Pat. 'Is there anything we can do about it, Sergeant?'

'I'll get on to our lads in the press office and see what can be done, but it may take a little time.'

She bowed her head, moved to the graveside and threw a solitary lily to her son. She then linked arms with her husband and reluctantly moved away to the sound of soil rustling against the lid of the coffin.

Pat and Nicola sat sipping coffee in the Red Rose Café opposite the Busarus bus depot. Nicola appeared uneasy as she focused on a queue of homeless Eastern Europeans waiting for a hand-out at a mobile soup kitchen.

'Poor bastards,' she muttered.

Pat followed her gaze.

'It's their own choice, coming here without a job lined up and little or no English. Don't worry about them.'

'I'm not worried about them.'

'What's strangling you then?'

She looked across at him. 'You are, Pat.'

He appeared surprised. 'What are you on about?'

'I think you're too close to this one.'

Pat let out a raucous laugh.

'What's so funny?' she asked.

'You are, Nicola. Tell me, have you ever investigated a serious crime?'

'You know rightly I haven't,' she replied, indignantly.

He leant forward resting his elbows on the table. 'Well, if ever you do, and you do it right, it will eat you up day and night until you solve it.'

'That's not the new way, Pat.'

'And what's the new way?'

'Clock in, do what you're told, and then clock out.'

Pat sat back, his eyes narrowed and full of rage. 'That's what I have been doing since I was sidelined and look at me now.'

'What's wrong with you?'

'I'm just a number – Detective Sergeant J 234 reporting for duty, sir.'

'Someone has to do it,' she said quietly, deflecting his anger. She took a sip of her tea and looked across at him.

'Why didn't you ever remarry?'

The question took him by surprise. Pat had married young, to Rosemary, a local beauty and former Rose of Tralee. When they moved to Dublin she was struck down by depression and a longing for the children that Mother Nature denied her. After fifteen years of marriage, overcome with emptiness, she took an overdose of barbiturates and passed away in their three bedroomed semi-detached house in Raheny. Pat went on the batter and remained there too long. The months and years since were a haze.

'I didn't have the guts,' slipped out under his breath.

'It's never too late, you know.'

He looked at her and smiled. Warmly. Nicola's wedding to her childhood sweetheart, who was also a guard, a scene of crimes man, was fast approaching. The bridesmaids' dresses had been a major headache, not to mention the choice of menu in Clontarf Castle. The finer details of the wedding plans had been a source of a continual monologue from Nicola over the last few months, though Pat had long since switched off.

'Aye, must get round to it someday,' he said flippantly.

She cocked her head, squinted her eyes and changed the direction of the conversation.

'So, has Sherlock Holmes cracked the case yet?'

'Nope,' he replied, as he took a self-sealed plastic bag containing a watch from his pocket, 'but this may be a clue.'

She took the watch and examined it closely. 'That's a serious-looking watch; where did you get it?'

'Our friend Mr Pender found it lying not far from the body.'

'So someone lost it,' she said, pointing to the broken clasp.

Pat raised an eyebrow. 'It's smeared in Johnny O'Shea's blood.'

'Perhaps contaminated by Mr Pender,' Nicola countered.

'Nope, he didn't go near the body.'

'Any prints?' she asked, still inspecting the watch.

'Just Pender's.'

'Interesting,' she mused.

Pat sat back twiddling his thumbs. 'Why don't you ask the obvious question?'

'Because a second year student in DCU living on Whitworth Road couldn't afford a watch like that.'

'His mother told me he didn't own a watch anyhow. So, Garda Murphy, where do you suggest we start?'

She stood up. 'I have to collect my wedding bands in Westerns on Grafton Street.'

Pat appeared mystified. She looked down at him, gave him an innocent smile and winked. He felt himself blush as he wondered if she was flirting with him.

'And maybe they can tell us where this watch came from.'

Westerns was a jewellers shop with an elegant façade just off fashionable Grafton Street. Inside a veritable oak-panelled Aladdin's cave. Mr Smythe, the manager, wore a crisp white shirt, burgundy cravat and a blue blazer. His white hair swept back from a proud brow, a pair of gold-rimmed reading glasses dangled from a chain hanging from his neck. Nicola took up the running, sensing Pat's disdain for their source. She enquired about her wedding bands, which were not yet ready, and then produced the watch, placing it carefully on the glass counter. The manager's hawkish eyes settled on it immediately.

'Very nice,' he observed, looking over Nicola's shoulder at Pat, who appeared uncomfortable in the pretentious surroundings.

Nicola produced her warrant card, and showed it to Mr Smythe.

'We're trying to find the owner.'

'May I inspect it? he asked.

She nodded, and he placed the watch on a navy-blue velvet cloth and examined it closely with the aid a small magnifying glass. After some time he turned the watch over and inspected some small letters on the back. He then put away the magnifying glass and leant on the display case looking up at Nicola.

'I can tell you this watch is a genuine Marsau, manufactured in their workshops in Berne, Switzerland, and not one of their standard range.'

'So it was a special order,' Nicola replied.

'Yes,' replied Mr Smythe.

'Is it valuable?' asked Pat.

Mr Smythe looked at Nicola and rolled his eyes to the heavens.

'My dear man, this is an exquisite piece and I would place a value on it of in and around twenty-five thousand euros.'

'For a fecking watch?' Pat snapped incredulously.

'Any way of tracing the owner?' Nicola intervened.

'Yes.' Smythe turned the watch over again and pointed to the letters and numbers SK 1257 engraved on the back. 'The letters are the initials of the watchmaker who assembled the watch and are exclusive to him. If you like I can ring the factory and find out where it was ordered from.'

'That would be very helpful, Mr Smythe.' Nicola gave him a broad smile. 'Can you do it now?'

'Certainly,' he replied, and then vanished behind a solid oak door.

Nicola turned to Pat and gave him the thumbs up. A few minutes later Mr Smythe emerged with a piece of paper, which he shielded from their view.

'The watch was ordered in 2001, Hartley's of Bond Street were the jewellers.' He looked at Pat and smiled. 'I won't tell you the cost. You will have to take the matter up with Hartley's themselves. I am sure they will have a record of the transaction.'

'What makes you so certain?' asked Pat.

'Insurance, my dear man, the owner would more than likely insure such a valuable piece and would need a certificate of valuation from the jeweller.'

Nicola thanked Mr Smythe and they left. Outside on the busy street Nicola felt like doing a jig. Pat, though impressed, gave nothing away.

'So, what do you think?' Nicola asked.

'He's as bent as a bishop's mitre.'

'No, not Mr Smythe; do we make a report out for the incident-room?'

'Not likely,' Pat retorted.

He took his mobile from his pocket and tapped in a number.

'Hello, Arthur, it's Pat O'Hara here.'

'Pat O'Hara, you old scoundrel, are you in town?'

'No, I am in Dublin investigating a murder. Do you remember that scumbag we extradited for you?'

'Sure as hell do, he's still inside.'

'Well, I need a small favour in return and I need it like, yesterday.'

'Fire away and I'll see what I can do.'

Pat gave Arthur all the details, and he promised to deal with the matter immediately. When Pat finished the call, he threw Nicola a sheepish grin.

'An old pal in New Scotland Yard, he owes me one.'

six
_____

It was a bitterly cold evening as Gerry strolled up Constitution Hill towards the women's section of Mountjoy Prison. Dermot Kenny, his instructing solicitor, was already in the consultation-room when he arrived. Dermot was a wiry man in his fifties, with a friendly if somewhat nonchalant air about him. He stood up when Gerry entered the small room, greeted him and then introduced Naguma. As Gerry shook hands with her he noticed her handshake was weak and she stubbornly refused to make eye contact. She looked more than her thirty-five years and spoke softly with her head bowed subserviently.

Gerry spoke in a businesslike way. 'Naguma, I have read the papers in your case and I'm afraid you have been caught red-handed.'

'I know, sir.'

'It appears to me that you have no option but to plead guilty.'

'Yes, guilty, sir, I am guilty.'

'Why did you do it?'

'For the money, sir.'

'You risked everything for two thousand euros?'

She lowered her head as a tear rolled down her cheek.

'Who asked you to do this?' Gerry continued.

'I worked in a hospital as a cleaner in Johannesburg. My mother was a very sick woman. She tried to look after my baby when I was at work, but she couldn't manage. So I finished my job to spend more time at home.'

'Where is the child's father?'

'He gone, sir. When Joy was born he go far away and we never see him again.'

'So what did you live on, social welfare?'

'We have no welfare in South Africa, sir.'

'How did you survive?'

She lowered her head and didn't answer.

'I asked you, how did you survive?' Gerry persisted.

'Why do you want to know this?'

'The judge will want to know how you got involved in all this. Maybe he will take pity on you and be lenient.'

'I see, but what I did was wrong, why should he pity me?'

'Because some people do these things for greed and some out of necessity. I need the full story to be able to present your case. And I can't do that without your co-operation. So please answer my questions.'

There was a long silence and eventually she answered, 'I worked as a prostitute at night for a bad man. He beat me. He beat me real bad. He threatened to kill my mother, and to kill my baby.'

'So he forced you to come to Ireland with the drugs.'

'Yes. I never saw the drugs, but I guessed it had to be drugs.'

'And what happened next?'

'He called to my home with a suitcase. It was already packed. He had a plane ticket, one way to Ireland. I didn't even know where Ireland was. He gave me fifty dollars and a piece of paper with an address to go to when I got to Ireland and a telephone number.'

'And how were you to get home?'

'The man say, someone will come and see me when I get to Ireland, give me my money and a ticket home.'

'And that's it?'

'Yes, that's all I know sir, honestly.'

'And then you got caught at the airport.'

'Yes. I gave the piece of paper to the police. They ask me to go to a hotel in a place called Gardner Street.'

A look of surprise crossed Gerry's face. None of this was contained in the police statements in the Book of Evidence. He started writing in his notebook.

'Tell me more.'

'I went with a policewoman and booked into the hotel.'

'Then what happened?'

'I rang the number on the piece of paper. The policewoman was listening. A Nigerian man answered. He said he would come and collect the drugs. We waited for hours but he never come.'

'What happened then?'

'The police said they had to charge me and then I came here.'

'I see, and have you been in contact with your family?'

Naguma bowed her head and whispered, 'No, they don't know where I am.'

'But surely the welfare people in the prison have made contact with them on your behalf?'

She shook her head. 'I asked them not to. I am ashamed for what I did. I don't want to tell them I am in prison.'

'Who is looking after your child?'

'Probably my mother, maybe my little sister. How long will I be here, sir?'

'It's difficult to say, Naguma. The law says that if the drugs have a street value exceeding thirteen thousand euros you must receive a minimum of ten years in prison.'

Naguma began to tremble, then burst into tears. 'I will never see my baby again.'

She broke down and became hysterical. Dermot put a hand on her shoulder and tried to console her.

'Look, Naguma, ten years is what the law says, but the judge can decide that yours is an exceptional case and in my considerable experience three to five years is the more likely sentence.'

She looked at Gerry, her sad, dark-brown eyes glistening with tears.

'My baby is dying, sir, please do what you can for me.'

'Have you made any friends here?'

She glanced towards a female prison officer who was seated beyond a glass partition reading a copy of the *Evening Herald*.

'They have been very good to me.'

'How do you spend your time?'

'I pray a lot, sir. I also work in the workshop making leather slippers. They pay me twenty euros a week. I already saved two hundred and twenty euros and I will send the money to my mother.'

They both shook hands with her and she shuffled from the visitor's room.

Outside, Gerry turned to Dermot. 'Sad case.'

Dermot grunted, 'If you can believe half of it.'

'Don't be so cynical, Dermot.'

'It goes with the job, you should know that by now.'

seven

The shrill ringing of his mobile woke Pat. He rolled over and glanced at the clock by his bed, it was 3 a.m.

'Pat, sorry to disturb you at this hour, I was wondering if there was any news from your pal across the water.'

'Nicola, I was sound asleep.'

'Sorry for waking you, but have you any news?'

'Yes, as a matter of fact I have. Some fella by the name of Mohamed Barouche ordered the watch.'

'Egyptian?'

'No, he's Saudi.'

'Interesting, and where's he living?'

'He gave an address in Montreal.'

'Any idea of his occupation?' she persisted.

'Yes, he's a doctor.'

There was a long silence.

'So, how did Dr Barouche's watch end up in Dame Lane?' Nicola asked.

'I haven't a clue, Nicola. Now, let me go back to sleep and I'll see you first thing in the morning.'

'OK, Pat, sorry about that, I was just curious.'

'That's OK. Good night, Nicola.'

Pat rolled over in the bed and allowed himself a half smile; had Nicola got the bug? He turned off the light and buried his head in the pillow. All was silent. He tossed in the bed and tried to settle, without success. Eventually he reached for the bedside light and sat up. He picked up his phone and called Nicola's number.

'Yes, Pat,' she said, an air of anticipation in her voice.

'I forgot to tell you something,' he said sheepishly.

'Yes.'

'I did a check with the visa department at the Department of Justice.'

'And?'

'Last year Dr Mohamed Barouche was granted a work permit. He is presently working in St Vincent's Hospital, Elm Park.'

There was a long pause.

'Thanks for sharing that with me, Pat.'

'You're welcome.'

'A doctor from Saudi Arabia, that's very interesting.'

'Sorry, I also forgot to tell you that he has a BMW 600 motor cycle registered in his name.'

'Are you serious?'

'Now would I joke about a thing like that? Do you think we're on the right track?'

'Well, it sounds promising, Pat. Have you any more gems that you want to share with your partner?'

'Nope, that's it.'

'And, of course, you have passed all this information on to Brannigan?'

There was a pregnant pause.

'Nicola, Brannigan gets nothing, is that clear? Anyway we have business to attend to first thing in the morning.'

'What kind of business?'

'Morning prayers at the mosque in Foxrock.'

'Are you looking for divine inspiration?'

'No, for information on the Koran.'

eight

It was 7 a.m. and Gerry appeared gravely worried as he paced up and down the platform of Dalkey station. Remnants of the summer blooms trailed from the hanging baskets that graced the quaint Victorian cut-stone building. The Dart carriage trundled into the station and Gerry, battling against rival commuters, found a seat in the carriage. He glanced around at the soulless faces of the commuters he shared the journey with daily. In the breast pocket of his navy-blue pin-stripe suit, a letter from the Dublin City Sheriff threatened to seize all his worldly goods should he not discharge the considerable debt owed to the Revenue Commissioners within the next ten days. Yet another demeaning visit to his friendly bank manager was called for, but even Mr Smith's considerable patience was wearing thin.

As the Dart sped along the coast, past the port of Dun Loaghaire and over the marshes at Booterstown, he gazed across Dublin Bay towards the east and the Hill of Howth, which rose majestically from the Irish Sea. In the distance Dollymount Strand, a crescent-shaped, white sandy beach, skirted the bay. The only blight, on an otherwise pleasant vista, were the twin stacks of the Pigeon House power plant spewing waste high above the city.

He wondered which judge he was likely to draw for his two cases that morning. It was a bit of a lottery with the day's cases being called on before Judge Colgan in Court 8. Those pleading guilty were dispatched to one of three other judges sitting in court 23, 25 or 29. And each harboured their individual likes and dislikes when it came to sentencing offenders. Judge Maguire, for instance, had been bullied as a child, and was particularly harsh on any sort of assault. Judge Cronin, a cold and humourless woman, who had a thriving commercial practice before she was elevated to the Bench, regarded larceny, no matter how petty, as an attack on the very fabric of society. On the

33

other hand there was Judge Dennehy, formerly a leading prosecutor and a gentle soul, who exhibited a soft spot for what he termed *the unfortunate underdog*. He was a popular man, but his sentences were generally regarded as absurdly lenient and were frequently appealed by the prosecution.

The train pulled into Tara Street station, emptied the masses and Gerry made his way along the quays deep in thought. The meeting with the bank manager loomed large.

A gaggle of American tourists emerged from the Morrison Hotel on Ormond Quay. The Morrison was a *boutique* hotel and an establishment for the rich and famous. Across the road the Boardwalk, a recently constructed wooden promenade, skirted the banks of the River Liffey. The city planners had hoped it would provide a pleasant walkway for Dubliners and tourists alike, but it had quickly become home for the growing number of homeless drug addicts.

On a wooden bench a young man lay huddled under a canopy of damp blankets. His thin frame trembled as the previous night's fix of heroin left his body. He rolled to one side and gazed down at the swollen waters of the river below, washing against the granite banks. Darren Walshe's face was gaunt, and his dark, sunken eyes disguised his youth. His shaky hand lit the butt of his last cigarette. Soon it would be time to call to the Merchants Quay Project drop-in centre for warm soup and the companionship of other addicts.

Darren believed he was destined from birth to be a drug addict. From Mary's Mansions, a slum off O'Connell Street, he was one of five sons. All were drug addicts, and all regular guests at Mountjoy Prison. His mother was a street trader on Moore Street and his father an accomplished pickpocket. The unemployment rate in the area in the eighties when Darren was growing up was over fifty per cent. And there was absolutely nothing to do in the bleak concrete jungle. To alleviate his boredom, he started drinking at 12, was smoking hash at 13, dropping e's at 14 and eventually succumbed to heroin the following year. He had robbed more than once to finance his addiction, though, according to his own moral code, had never used gratuitous violence on his victims. More often than not he got caught by the Gardai and had served numerous short stints in prison. Prison may have deprived him of his liberty and removed a nuisance from the streets, but he found the easy supply of heroin inside comforting and he emerged from prison even more dependent on the drug.

However, imprisonment also deprived him of the companionship of

Suzanne, his childhood sweetheart. As teenagers they first shared their bodies, then their drugs and, as they descended into the blackness of addiction, shared their suffering. Eventually in the small hours of the mornings, huddled together in doorways in the city centre, they also shared their fears. And a bond grew that others, who knew about such things, might call love. He wrote her poetry and always offered her his last butt. She appeared more impressed by the latter.

As the years rolled on, he found he needed Suzanne's companionship more and more. So he was forced to stop robbing. And she was forced to sell her fragile body by the banks of the leafy Grand Canal, near the Pepper Canister Church, to fund their addictions. Her clients knew her as Cindy and they were unaware of Darren lurking in the darkness, watching over her. His heart sank every time she climbed into some anonymous punter's car; the time she was absent an eternity, and he banished thoughts of what she was doing from his mind. And when she returned with her paltry pickings they would rush off to Dolphin's Barn and score more gear.

At first Suzanne disliked Cindy, thought her hard and cold, even disloyal to her partner. Then her dislike turned to hatred and, after one particularly depraved encounter with a drunken punter, she cried her eyes out for hours on end when it dawned on her that she had become Cindy. That cold winter's night Darren held her close, and for the first time told her that he loved her. And they vowed to get help for their addiction.

The next day, full of hope, they joined the queue of addicts outside Pearse Street Clinic. They were put on a methadone maintenance programme and the social worker found them a dingy one bedroomed flat in Summerhill. At least it was a roof over their heads, and for the first time in years they felt secure. Darren even tried to find some work, but without success. The Eastern Europeans and the Chinese seemed to have a monopoly on the unskilled work, so Darren joined the Nigerians on the dole queue. However, Suzanne got a job as a cleaner and life was looking up.

Then, one day on his way back from the clinic, Darren was arrested on an old bench warrant for a robbery he had long forgotten. He was hauled before the court and all appeared lost and their efforts wasted as the heavy steel gates of Mountjoy beckoned.

The next he knew he was sitting in the dock of a crammed court-room listening to a barrister pleading for leniency on his behalf. He wasn't really paying much heed, his eyes fixed on Suzanne who was sitting in the public gallery. But a few of the barrister's words distracted him.

'In this young man, despite his appalling upbringing and horrific addiction, there is a seed of goodness that, if allowed to germinate, may, in time, produce a useful member of the community.'

Darren's heart sank as he watched the judge raise a hand and ward off the barrister's efforts.

'All right Mr Hickey, I have heard enough.'

The barrister sat down and the judge turned to Darren who was trembling in the dock. Looking at him over his half-rimmed glasses, the judge's face was stern and his voice solemn.

'This was an appalling robbery carried out in broad daylight. True, no violence was actually used, but the unfortunate victim, a visitor to our capital city, must have been terrified when you produced your blood-filled syringe and threatened to stab her with it. I have little or no doubt that this lady will never return to these shores and the horror of the attack will live in her memory for years to come. You have a deplorable criminal record, twenty-seven convictions in total, and there is little doubt that you have for many years caused mayhem and terror on the streets of Dublin. I am told you commit these terrible crimes because you need money for drugs. That may well be an explanation for your behaviour, but it is, in my view, no excuse for what you did and offers little comfort to your victims. I believe the appropriate sentence that I should impose in this case is ten years' imprisonment.'

Darren's knees buckled and he reached out to the prison officer beside him for physical support. Ten years and all he'd got were a miserly few euros. He looked around and found Suzanne's angst-ridden face, tears streaming down her soft cheeks.

The judge continued, 'However, every case must be judged on its own merits.'

Was there a ray of hope?

'I have listened very carefully to what Mr Hickey has ably said on your behalf and I have read the detailed probation report. It appears that you may have reached a turning point in your life and are determined at long last to deal with your addiction. I also note you have the support of a young lady who is making similar efforts. I sincerely hope you will help one another. However, you not only need encouragement, but also a significant deterrent from deviating from your good intentions. That's why I am imposing such a lengthy sentence on you. I am, however, going to suspend the sentence for a period of five years. Put bluntly, if you commit another crime in the next five years, no matter how minor, you will be brought back before me and you will go to prison for ten years. Is that clear?'

Darren looked at Judge Dennehy, who somehow appeared less grave, and nodded.

'I asked you, is that clear?' the judge said sternly.

'Yes, Your Honour,' Darren answered quickly. 'You needn't worry, I won't be back here in a hurry and that's for sure.'

The judge gave him a half smile, but appeared unconvinced by Darren's declaration.

And from that moment life got better by the day. They saved some money and bought a television, which they spent their evenings glued to. Then Suzanne thought she might be pregnant. The test was negative but she went to her GP anyway. And he referred her to the Charlemont Clinic where the kind lady consultant told them both in a gentle tone that Suzanne had Aids. She was placed on triple therapy, but the drugs failed to hold the disease at bay. She lost weight and gave up her job. She lost more weight and was soon confined to bed. Her once full lips became thin and her skin taut. She seldom smiled and never laughed, but Darren remained by her side and nursed her day and night. Eventually she caught pneumonia and, as spring approached, she passed away in Darren's arms as he read her one of his poems.

And he was lost without her, empty without her companionship and love. Inevitably he sought refuge from his despair in heroin. Then some children were found playing with discarded needles outside his flat, and an intimidating visit from the local Concerned Parents Action Group followed. It took little persuasion to move him along, and he returned to the streets.

And here he was on the boardwalk, alone. He tossed away the butt as it began to drizzle. He cast an eye over the morning flow of well-heeled professionals wending their way to work – the occasional Prada bag, easy pickings indeed.

In the distance he saw a man in a sharp pin-stripe suit walking in his direction. Darren watched as the man glanced up at the deepening grey sky and opened his umbrella. When he drew nearer, Darren cast aside his blankets and looked around furtively. Then he focused on the man's face. It was Mr Hickey. Darren hauled himself to his feet.

'Good morning, sir,' he greeted Gerry.

Gerry appeared startled and visibly tensed up.

'I'm sorry, I have nothing for you,' he said, as he lowered his umbrella and hurriedly altered course to avoid him.

'But Mr Hickey, do you not remember me?'

Gerry stopped, raised his umbrella and closely examined the wretch standing before him, the sores about his mouth, the tired eyes and matted hair. He appeared to take a step back, as the smell of stale urine wafted under his nose. Instead he took a step closer and held the umbrella so that it sheltered them both.

'Young Darren Walshe from Mary's Mansions,' Gerry declared.

Darren's face lit up at the recognition.

'That's right, Mr Hickey, fair play to you for remembering my name.'

'Darren, I'm really sorry, I heard your girlfriend passed away.'

A look of astonishment crossed Darren's face. 'How did you hear that?'

'I met Sergeant Farrell from Fitzgibbon Street and he told me you were back on the gear, and why.'

'Jesus, I didn't think that he would give a toss.'

'Well he does, and he seemed genuinely concerned about you.'

'Are you serious?'

'Yes, Darren. He doesn't want to have to bring you back in on the ten-year suspended sentence.'

'Get away out of that, why would he care about the likes of me?'

'Apparently he thinks there are a few buckos out there who are more deserving of the free accommodation.'

Darren laughed. 'And what about yourself, Mr Hickey? To be honest you don't look too great.'

Gerry smiled. 'I am fine,' he said as he inspected his watch. 'Best be off, I don't want to be late for court.'

'Just a minute, before you go,' Darren responded.

Gerry dug deep into his pocket for loose change as Darren took a deep breath.

'Mr Hickey, I always thought I was just a number in the system, a prison number, a number on my police record, and a number in court, Bill number 112/05 the Director of Public Prosecutions versus yet another scumbag from the North Inner City. But you showed me respect, man, got me a chance when I didn't deserve it. And I really appreciated it because it gave me a chance to prove my worth to Suzanne, and I would like to thank you for that.'

Gerry dropped the change back into his pocket. He placed his hand on Darren's shoulder.

'Don't give up, Darren. You're still a young man and have everything to live for.'

'I doubt that, Mr Hickey, but thanks anyhow.'

Gerry walked briskly towards the Four Courts as Darren gathered his blankets and trudged off towards the drop-in centre.

nine

Pat and Nicola were parked across the road on the forecourt of a petrol station facing a vast domed edifice. In the bright morning sunlight, the mosque could have been nestling in the heart of Cairo. Only this was middle-class Dublin suburbia. The car-park was bustling with activity as children arrived for school and worshippers gathered for morning prayers. Most of the women wore veils, the men a mixture of white kaftans and modern western dress.

'What about a couple of those outfits for the bridesmaids?' Pat said, as he gestured to two women crossing the road dressed in traditional burkhas. 'No chance of them stealing the show in that get up.'

Nicola was not amused and it showed on her disgruntled face.

'Not that I'm suggesting for one moment that any bridesmaid could compete with your beauty regardless of what she wore,' he added quickly, trying to recover ground.

Nicola gave him a half smile. She had been on the same unit as Pat for the last two years and admired his no-nonsense style. She was a highly trained sharpshooter and could handle herself in most situations. But now and again she felt exposed. Like the night three months earlier when they were called to a row at a bar in Parnell Street, frequented mostly by Russians and Lithuanians. When they arrived, the doorman identified the main troublemaker. He was built like a bull, with no neck, a shaven head and a deep scar that snaked down one of his cheeks. Nicola had approached him, identified herself as a guard, and requested his name. He uttered something, which she didn't understand but took to be an insult, laughed and spat in her face. Production of her firearm wasn't justified in the circumstances and she was unsure of what to do as she wiped the spittle from her face. Then Pat moved in, and it was lights out for Boris, whose heavy frame almost cracked the concrete pavement as he hit it. There were a few disgruntled murmurings from his pals, but they hurried from the scene. An ambulance arrived and Boris was taken to the Mater Hospital, where he remained for two weeks enjoying surgery on his fractured jaw. Nicola's superintendent asked her to file a written report and, to her surprise, Pat hadn't tried to influence the contents. Reasonable force in effecting an arrest, was her conclusion, with a recommendation that Boris not be charged, but merely cautioned for obstructing a police officer. However, she was convinced that Boris would lodge a complaint of assault against Pat with the Garda Complaints Board. Later she became aware that Pat had visited Boris in hospital, and hadn't taken flowers. On his discharge from hospital, Boris vanished from the country. That was Pat all over. No nonsense, act first and pick up the pieces later. But despite his unorthodox methods, she felt safe with him at her shoulder.

Her mobile rang and she answered it. Her mother spoke at length about the guest list for the wedding, the flower arrangements and when she mentioned the bridesmaids' dresses Nicola told her Pat had come up with a good idea, which she would discuss later.

'What next?' she asked when she finished the call.

'You stay here, I am going in on my own, I hear these guys have the good sense not to trust women.'

She was not amused.

'I'll have a word with the head honcho and see what I can find out,' he said, as he hauled himself from the car.

'Whatever you say, Pat.' Though she had serious doubts about his diplomacy skills as she watched him rumble across the road towards the main entrance. What in heaven's name would they make of him? she thought.

Pat asked to see the Director of the Cultural Centre and was shown to an office upstairs where Mahomed Sheriff greeted him warmly. A stout man dressed in a white kaftan, he had dark-brown eyes that danced above his grey speckled beard. Pat introduced himself and was invited to take a seat.

'Nice place you have here. My local parish priest would die for a packed congregation like that,' he said, referring to the prostrate worshippers he had seen in the central hall on his way to the director's office.

'How may I help you, Detective Sergeant?'

'I am investigating a murder and I need some information.'

Mohamed appeared startled. 'I am not a suspect, am I?'

Pat smiled and shook his head. 'No, don't worry.'

'Then I will help you all I can.'

Pat nodded in appreciation and cut quickly to the chase.

'Homosexuality.'

Mohamed looked more than puzzled. 'What about it?' he asked.

'What's the party line on it?'

'What do you mean by the *party line*?'

'Do you guys tolerate it or what?'

Mohamed placed his hands together, adopting a solemn posture.

'The practice of homosexuality is specifically prohibited in the holy Koran, which is the primary source for Sharia law by which all Muslims are governed,' he declared.

'OK, so it's not allowed, but is at least tolerated to some extent?'

Mohamed sat back and smiled.

'Sergeant, did you ever hear of the parable of the people of Lot?'

'It rings a bell,' Pat replied, rubbing his brow.

'They were the people of the prophet Lot's village, and it is sufficient to say they were greatly depraved and their greatest abomination of all was the practice of homosexuality.'

'So, there's no give then.'

Mohamed stroked his beard.

'It is said in the Hadith,' and he quoted: '"Whenever a male mounts another male the throne of God trembles and if you see two people act like the people of Lot, then kill the active and the passive ..." so to answer your question, Sergeant, the practice of homosexuality is not tolerated under any circumstances.'

'Well, that's pretty uncompromising. And the punishment?'

'The Koran says death.'

'And the method of execution?'

'The same as for adultery, stoning to death.'

'What about amputating limbs?'

Mohamed smiled. 'Sergeant O'Hara, all I can tell you is it is regarded as a grave infringement of God's law. The manner in which individual crimes are punished varies greatly from school to school.'

'What do you mean?' asked Pat.

'There are four different legal schools of interpretation, ranging from the liberal Hanafi School in Cairo, to the conservative Hanbali School in Saudi Arabia.'

'So?'

'Individual Islamic states vary in the degree to which Sharia law is applied. Turkey lies at one extreme, regarding Islam as a matter of private individual practice. At the other extreme lie the fundamentalist Islamic states of Iran, Saudi Arabia and Afghanistan.'

'So, in Saudi Arabia, traditional punishments, like the amputation of hands, are still carried out?'

'Yes, but often discouragement and repentance are considered more important to us than punishment.'

Pat nodded, and appeared deep in thought.

'Tell me, are there any individuals at the mosque who stand out as being hostile to homosexuals?'

'No, Sergeant, I'm not aware of any. But, as you know, every religion throws up extremists of one sort or another. However I can reassure you that if I hear anything, I will let you know.'

As he walked through the car-park, Pat noticed Barouche's motor bike parked near the entrance. He sat in beside Nicola.

'Well, Pat, how did you get on?'

'I am converted,' he quipped.

Just then Barouche appeared at the entrance on his BMW and took off towards town. Pat started the car and sped off after him. He followed him as far as O'Brien's Pub, then gave a blast of the siren and Barouche pulled in. Pat went to get out but Nicola placed her hand on his arm.

'Let me deal with this.'

She alighted from the car and walked towards Barouche who had dismounted his bike. He was tall and wore a black leather jacket. The first thing that struck Nicola when he removed his helmet was how handsome he was. Thick, dark, neatly cut hair, sallow skin, a strong chin and dark eyes.

'I am very sorry, Guard, was I travelling too fast?' he asked, in a soft and ingratiating tone.

'No,' replied Nicola, 'I am more concerned where you were last Saturday night.'

Barouche looked quizzically at Nicola, but didn't appear in any way concerned.

'We received a complaint from a taxi driver who claims a large motor cycle struck his wing mirror in Rathmines last Saturday night and didn't stop.'

Barouche appeared puzzled. 'What's that got to do with me?' he asked.

'The taxi driver didn't get the full registration number, 05 D 13 is all he got, but it's similar to yours and we have to check it out. Do you mind if I inspect your bike?'

'Not at all, Guard, please do.'

Nicola walked around the bike looking for damage. There was none. She took out her notebook.

'It doesn't appear to be damaged, but I'd better get a few details from you anyway. Your name and address please.'

'Dr Mohamed Barouche. 75 Milltown Heights.'

'How do you spell that?' she asked.

He spelt his name for her.

'And where were you last Saturday night?'

'What time?'

'Around midnight.'

'I went for a walk on Dun Loaghaire pier with my girlfriend, then we got some Indian take away and went back to my apartment around ten o'clock. We spent the night together.'

'What's your girlfriend's name and address?'

'Mary O'Toole; I am not sure of her exact address, but she works in St Vincent's hospital. Would you like me to ask her to contact you?'

She looked at him and gave him a smile.

'No, Doctor, I don't think that will be necessary, I am sure what you say is right and as I said before, the taxi driver didn't even get the full number of the bike, so we will probably leave it at that.'

'OK.'

'Sorry for troubling you, Doctor, and drive carefully, that's a big machine you have there.'

'I will, Guard, thank you.'

He put on his helmet and drove off. Nicola returned to the car and sat in beside Pat. She let out a sigh.

'Well?' he asked.

'He's a real charmer,' she replied, 'and I think we might be barking up the wrong tree.'

'Why do you say that?'

'Because he has an alibi for Saturday night.'

A look of amazement passed over Pat's face and then anger.

'For Christ's sake, Nicola, you didn't let him know we suspected him?' he asked.

'Of course not, I invented a story about a taxi driver reporting a hit and run and that his number was similar.'

Pat breathed a sigh of relief. Just then a white transit van pulled up behind their car and sounded the horn. They both looked around. The horn sounded again and Pat, fuming with rage, got out and stormed back to the van. The side door slid open and a young man in a sharp suit got out and gestured Pat into the van. Pat recognized a man sitting inside as Detective Sergeant Noel Mulhern from the National Surveillance team. He had worked with Pat in the murder squad and they knew each other well.

'Hello, Pat, I haven't seen you in some time. How are you keeping?'

'Not bad Noel, nice set up you have here,' Pat remarked, looking at the banks of high tech equipment.

'What's your interest in our doctor friend?' Mulhern asked.

'Just routine RTA,' Pat lied.

'So what were you doing in the mosque?' Mulhern countered.

Pat smiled and decided to come clean.

'He is a suspect for the murder last Saturday night.'

Mulhern raised an eyebrow. 'Why weren't we notified?'

Pat hesitated. 'It's not in the system yet.'

Mulhern let out a raucous laugh. 'One of your famous hunches, Pat?'

'You could say that. Why are you lot interested in him?'

'As you well know, security matters are divulged on a need to know basis, and I am not convinced you need to know,' Mulhern replied flatly.

'Come on, Noel, you've known me long enough and I need to know, it will go no further.'

Noel studied him closely, then took a file from under some tapes and handed it to Pat. It was headed CIA TOP SECRET. Pat took the file and began to flick through it. On the second page was a mug shot of Barouche.

Noel told Pat, Barouche lived and worked as a doctor in Montreal until two years ago. He was a close friend of Jahad Mactar, who was arrested along with two others at the border trying to enter the US with some bomb-making equipment.'

'Al-Qaeda?' Pat asked.

'No, the bloody boy scouts. Anyway, they are all serving life in the States. The Mounties had Mactar under surveillance since 9/11 and Barouche and he were good friends until Barouche was arrested in a drugs bust at a gay nightclub in downtown Montreal.'

'A gay bar, did you say?'

'Yes, and he had a small amount of hash on him. He was arrested and eventually let off with a caution. Mactar posted bail for him so he knew what Barouche was in for.'

'So?'

'So, drink or drugs are taboo for these guys, not to mention the gay stuff. The Mounties suspect that Barouche was actually a member of the cell but got thrown out when the others found out about the drugs bust.'

Pat leant forward and rubbed his brow.

'So, why are you guys still interested in him?'

'The CIA got a tip off that Mactar and his pals were moving the stuff across the border and our friend Barouche was the informant. After their arrest he came here. We know a few boys are operating out of Dublin and Barouche has been very friendly with them. He could be trying to get back in.'

'And the boys here have no idea that he ratted on Mactar?'

Mulhern shook his head. 'If they did, Barouche would be a dead man by now.'

'So what's your read on all this, Noel?"

'Personally, I think the guy is wired to the moon. He comes from a wealthy Saudi family, but hasn't been in contact with them for years. My guess is he is into the whole thing for kicks, and I wouldn't trust him as far as I could throw him. The lads seem weary of him, too.'

'Do they know he was arrested in Montreal in a gay bar?'

'We don't know that. Why?'

Pat shook his head. 'It doesn't matter.'

'Look, Pat, this is all off the record, right? You never saw that file and we never had this conversation.'

'OK, I understand.'

Pat returned to Nicola who was waiting patiently in the car. He drove off without speaking.

'Well?' she asked eventually.

'You don't want to know, but I think we are on the right track after all.'

Nicola appeared peeved at Pat's reluctance to divulge what he knew.

'Are you going to make this official?' she asked.

Pat turned to her. 'I am seeing Cummins tonight and I will tell him everything we have. I think we have enough for an arrest, but we had better leave it up to the brass.'

ten

Naguma sat alone on a bench in a strangely quiet Court 24. A prison officer stood at the back of the court reading a paper as two reporters sat in the vacant jury box, gossiping. The ancient oak-panelled walls and dim lighting created an austere and forbidding atmosphere. Gerry came in and took his seat, his junior behind him. Gerry nodded to the clerk and shortly afterwards Judge Maguire entered centre stage, a block of a man in his late sixties with the disgruntled face of a bulldog.

Prosecution counsel briefly outlined the facts of the case and called the officer in charge of the investigation. Gerry had already spoken to the officer outside and found him more than sympathetic to Naguma's plight. When he had finished giving his evidence, Gerry rose to his feet and cross-examined him and elicited that she was most co-operative with the police when arrested, had probably learned a salutary lesson from her experience before the courts and was unlikely to offend again. The sergeant left the witness box having done his best. Gerry then made an emotional and impassioned plea for leniency, stressing that she was a stranger in a strange land and was deprived of the companionship of friends and family. When he had finished, the judge looked down at Naguma.

'Stand up.' She pulled herself to her feet slowly. 'This is a very serious offence. Whilst I accept that you were merely a courier, a small cog in a much bigger machine, as your counsel put it, without you and your like the machine wouldn't work.'

Naguma's tearful eyes fell on Gerry, pleading for help, but he could do no more.

The judge continued, 'I am told you have no criminal record and that you co-operated to some extent with the Gardai. I will also take into account the fact that you pleaded guilty, even though I believe you hadn't much option in the circumstances. Your counsel has outlined many sad factors in your background that made you vulnerable to temptation. But I have a duty to the people of Ireland to send out a clear message to discourage people like you from agreeing to transport drugs in the future. I impose a sentence of ten years' imprisonment.'

Naguma slumped back on the bench as the judge hurried from the courtroom, having refused Gerry's application for leave to appeal against the sentence. Gerry approached Naguma to offer words of comfort, but she had already crumpled under the strain and had broken down completely.

eleven

Detective Superintendent Cummins was on the phone behind his desk when Pat knocked on the door.

'Come in.'

Pat entered the spacious office and Cummins gestured to him to sit down. He continued with his conversation and eventually put down the phone.

'That was the commissioner, wondering if there are any developments in the O'Shea case.'

'Are there?' asked Pat.

'What do you expect six days into the investigation?'

As Pat shrugged his shoulders, the superintendent detected the faint outline of a grin on his face. He sat back in his leather swivel chair and let out a heavy sigh.

'OK, O'Hara, what have you got for me?'

Pat leant forward clasping his hands together. 'A suspect.'

'Who is he?'

'A doctor working in St Vincent's Hospital.'

'And where did you get this nugget of information from?'

Pat outlined what he had discovered to date, excluding his conversation with Sergeant Mulhern. When he had finished he waited for Cummins's response.

'That's all very interesting. A doctor loses his watch, which happens to turn up near the crime scene. And he happens to drive a motor bike. And you want me to arrest this guy. Pat, are you mad or what?'

'It's a bit more detailed than that, I suggest you do a full profile on him,' Pat protested.

'What else are you talking about?'

'Let's say it's just a hunch. Carry out a full profile on our doctor friend, and you might be surprised what else turns up.'

'And in the meantime do a report on what you already have for the incident-room. We will add him to the other three hundred suspects presently on file.'

Pat got up to leave and, as he reached the door, he turned to Cummins. 'I suggest you place him at the top of your list.'

'I just might do that. And he wears a leather jacket, how interesting,' Cummins said, his voice laden with sarcasm.

twelve

Davey Byrnes Public House was thronged with the young trendy set, who worked in and around Grafton Street. It was half seven and, already on his fourth gin and tonic, Gerry was sitting alone at the marble-topped bar. There was no sign of the cronies he normally met up with after work, so he was left to his thoughts. And they were weighty. Naguma's case had troubled him all day. She was now locked in her cell, with her own thoughts, starting the first of her 3650-day sentence. She might get early release, but even the Department of Justice had clamped down on that in recent times. Regardless, it was unlikely she would ever see her daughter again.

And he was unemployed for the rest of the week, with nothing substantial on the horizon. The house would have to be sold. Little choice. It would break Emily's heart. He knocked back his gin and tonic and left. A recent shower had left the streets damp. He sauntered along Nassau Street, his hands thrust deep in his pockets. His steps were slow as commuters rushed by him on their way to the Dart station. He glanced to his left at the perimeter wall of Trinity College that ran the length of the street. A few golden autumnal leaves still clung to the large oaks in College Park, but the evening was grey and the air heavy.

As he stood at the pedestrian lights at the junction with Kildare Street, home to the Houses of the Oireachtas, his gaze was drawn to a tall, blonde-haired girl waiting to cross from the other side. Wearing blue jeans and a short leather jacket she cut an imposing figure. He thought he caught her sneaking a glance in his direction, but she turned and walked back towards Merrion Square. He followed her, mesmerized by her gracious walk, her endless legs floating over the granite pavement. Then she vanished into a small bookshop on Lincoln Lane. He peered in the window, spied her looking through the bookshelves and suddenly found himself doing likewise. He followed her through the maze of bookshelves and then lost her. Feeling uncomfortable in the surprising role of stalker, he made his way towards the exit. Then she reappeared, coming towards him. She threw her head back, and tossed her soft blonde hair from her sculptured face, as she glanced at him with cool green eyes. Then her lithe body touched his as she brushed by him in the confined space. He felt an enormous surge of excitement. Outside on the street, he felt strangely exhilarated as he lurked outside the bookshop. Then he took a grip of himself, and crossed the road where he sought refuge in the Lincoln Inn. The bar was quiet as he ordered a gin and tonic from the barman and sat at a table opposite the door. On the table lay a copy of the *Evening Herald* with a picture of Naguma under the banner headline, 10 YEARS FOR DRUG TRAFFICKER.

The door of the pub opened and the blonde-haired girl breezed in, looked around with an air of confidence, and sat at the table next to Gerry. Feeling strangely nervous, he opened the newspaper and hid behind it. She ordered a Jack Daniels from the barman, in a husky Eastern-European accent. She was young, maybe twenty-five, little more. He lowered his paper and glanced at her, hoping their eyes might meet, but she sat with her back to the wall staring vacantly into space and ignored him. His mobile phone rang. He took it from the breast pocket of his jacket, *home calling*, flashed on the small screen. He ignored the call. He wasn't sure how to engage the girl in conversation, and for once a suitable chat up line eluded him. His phone rang again, *home calling*, this time he answered it.

'I can't talk now, Emily,' he said abruptly, 'I'm at a consultation.'

The girl turned to him, and gave him a quizzical look. He was almost sure she winked at him.

'Are you a doctor?' she asked.

He put down the newspaper and turned to her.

'No, what makes you think that?'

'You just said you were at a consultation and I thought you might be a doctor,' she said, apparently unashamed at her eavesdropping.

Gerry laughed. 'No, I am a lawyer.'

'I see,' she replied, 'that must be interesting.'

'It's OK; what do you do yourself?'

She smiled at him and slid into a seat at his table bringing her drink with her. She then leant forward towards him and, as the smell of her perfume engulfed him, he swore he felt her full pale-pink lips kiss him gently on his cheek.

'I work in the industry,' she replied.

'What industry?' he asked naïvely.

She tossed her hair back with her hand, ignored his question, and this time definitely winked at him.

'I would like a Jack Daniels,' she said as she opened her leather jacket.

He called the barman and ordered them both a drink.

'My name is Gerry by the way,' he volunteered, but she seemed uninterested.

'And yours?'

'Carmen.'

'And where are you from Carmen?'

'I'm from Prague, but I live in an apartment beside the Herbert Park Hotel. It's only a short ride from here.'

He looked somewhat bemused, but nodded in approval at her knowledge of the geography of Dublin.

'Well, Gerry, do you want to have a good time with me?'

Gerry recoiled at the question as the penny eventually dropped.

'I am a happily married man,' he said defensively.

She laughed.

'What's so funny?'

'You are.'

'Why do you say that?'

'Because we both know that you followed me down the street and around the bookshop.'

'I didn't ...'

She placed her hand to his lips and took his hand in hers.

'Gerry, I think I know exactly what you need, and for a couple of hours you can be mine, I promise I will give you a good time.'

'Look, Carmen—'

Her eyes narrowed. 'Yes or no?'

'But ...'

'I said yes or no,' she pressed.

He had no idea who she was, but there was a confidence that surrounded her, a sexuality he found irresistible.

'Yes,' he whispered.

Carmen at once stood up and, without finishing her drink, left the bar with Gerry in tow. Next, he was seated beside her in a taxi. She held his hand, but didn't speak. What the hell was he doing? Next, she was standing beside him in a small lift, searching in her handbag for keys. Then in a small hallway from where she led him by the hand into a bedroom. A large double bed covered in a white sheet sat between two lockers, one with a bedside lamp. She stood in front of him, hands on her slender hips.

'It will be three hundred euros, upfront.'

He took out his wallet and handed her the money, which she counted in front of him. She smiled and then left the room. He took off his jacket, hung it on a hook behind the door and glanced around the sparsely furnished room. He whiffed the smell of talc as he sat on the end of the bed. Then heard the sound of muffled voices, followed by a long silence, which he found unbearable. He sat nervously with his hands clasped together as his son's face flashed before him, then Emily's. He should leave. Now.

Then the door opened and she was there – in thigh-high leather boots and a black leather bodice that hugged her tiny waist and pushed up her ample breasts. Her hands and arms were encased in long leather gloves and a pair of handcuffs hung from a studded belt that skirted her hips. He stood up nervously, but she grabbed his throat with her right hand and pushed him backwards against the wall. He raised a hand defensively but she grabbed it with the precision of a martial artist, spun him around and pushed his face against the wall. Then she pulled his free hand behind his back and he felt the cold steel of the cuffs cut into his wrists. His phone rang in the pocket of his jacket and he tensed up.

'Be a good little boy and I won't hurt you,' she said, as she thrust her knee into his groin. She threw back her head and laughed as he collapsed in a heap on the carpet.

Two hours later he sat at the pine counter in Crowe's public house in Ballsbridge, close to the American Embassy. Feeling guilty and humiliated. He downed three gin and tonics in short time and then was in the back of a taxi on the way home. He took a piece of paper from his wallet on which Carmen had scribbled her name and mobile number. He stared at it for a few moments and then angrily crumpled it in his fist. He wound down the window and was about to throw it into the night air to exorcise his guilt, but hesitated, wound up the window and carefully replaced the piece of paper in his wallet.

thirteen

It was 9 a.m. and Nicola and Pat sat in silence in a car-park off Sandymount Road. A heavy rain had settled on the city as they looked out across the bleak strand. The tide was out and the flat sea had left the shore. Pat seemed out of sorts.

'Pity Cummins didn't take the bait,' she said, breaking the silence.

'He will when he gets the profile on Barouche. And before you ask, yes, I filed a full written report and dropped it into the incident-room this morning.'

Nicola sighed heavily. 'Well, it's out of our hands then.'

Pat shrugged his shoulders. 'I suppose so.'

'Will I bother checking the guy's alibi?' Nicola asked.

'No, don't bother your arse, let the investigation team do it, that's what they are there for.'

There was a long pause. Pat eventually let out a heavy sigh.

'By the way, thanks for inviting me to the wedding. When is it?'

'Four weeks tomorrow.'

'Excited?'

'Of course I am.'

'And are you sure you're making the right decision?'

'Yes, I'm sure. Bill and myself have been engaged for six years now, so we're not exactly rushing into it.' She turned to him. 'Pat, can I ask you something personal?'

'Sure, fire away.'

'I asked you this before and you didn't give me a serious answer, why didn't you find someone else?'

'Too busy with the job.'

'That's rubbish, Pat, and you know it.'

'Yes I suppose it is,' he said as he turned to her. 'Truth is I never got

55

over my wife taking her own life. I still don't understand why she did it, but she took a lot of me with her when she went.'

Nicola saw Pat's eyes moisten and she looked away.

'And the job?'

'What about it?'

'I heard you were hung out to dry when the murder squad was disbanded.'

'You could say that,' he said, drily.

'Do I detect a sense of bitterness?'

'Bitterness? I don't know about that. All I know is that I am a guard for over thirty years. I broke my back night and day trying to make this a safer place to live. I was at the forefront of the fight against the Provos and the so-called crime lords of Dublin. I sacrificed everything I ever had, my wife, my friends, and in the end, because of the media, my job in the branch. Sure, I took a few short-cuts along the way, even broke a couple of rules now and again, but it's not a boxing match, Nicola, and those bastards don't play by the Queensbury rules.'

She hesitated before asking a question that she had wanted to ask since she first met him.

'Did you fit that guy up, as they say you did?'

Pat's face turned purple. 'No Nicola, I didn't fit him up. He was an evil whore who should never have been pardoned.'

Just then the radio crackled into life. 'Armed robbery Blackrock.'

They flew along the Rock road, siren wailing, flashing blue light on the roof. Nicola reached under the seat and checked the Uzi. Pat drove with one hand on the steering wheel as he reached inside his jacket and unclipped his holster. Within a minute the car screeched up the deserted main street of the small village, as shoppers and children huddled in doorways, screaming. A car was facing them outside the Ulster Bank at the top of the hill, the engine running, a lone hooded figure behind the wheel. Pat slammed on the brakes and the squad car skidded to a halt, blocking its path. Nicola left the car and rushed towards two hooded men carrying plastic bags and shotguns who had emerged from the bank. Pat struggled to undo his seatbelt as Nicola stood in the centre of the street, and raised her Uzi.

'Stop, armed Gardai,' she roared.

The words echoed around the empty street. The two men stopped and looked at her. The car revved. The men moved towards the car as Nicola took two steps closer, then lowered her Uzi.

'Stop or I will shoot,' she screamed, the nervous hysteria clearly audible in her voice.

The moment lasted an eternity as the two men hesitated. Nicola didn't see the motor cyclist outside the chemist across the road from the bank. Or him take an automatic pistol from the inside pocket of his leather jacket and lower it in her direction. She didn't hear Pat screaming to her to get down, as he aimed his Smith & Wesson at the gunman. But she heard a shot, quickly followed by a second louder one.

The gunman fell backwards through the window of the chemist as Pat raced towards Nicola. The two men in balaclavas jumped into the rear of the car and it screeched towards Pat, narrowly missing him. Pat knelt down beside Nicola who lay in a pool of warm blood. He screamed for help as he held her in his arms. But none came. He ripped off his jacket and stuffed it into the gaping hole at the back of Nicola's neck. And held her there, the two of them alone in the centre of the road until the ambulance arrived. The paramedics quickly took over, and bundled her into the ambulance where she lay, Pat by her side, holding her trembling hand. A respirator, clasped to her distraught face, muffled what she was trying to say.

'Stay with us Nicola. Stay with us,' Pat implored her.

At the Accident and Emergency unit in St Vincent's hospital, she was hauled on to a trolley and whisked through crowded corridors into the operating theatre. As the swing doors closed, Pat felt her hand slip from his, as he was pushed aside by frantic nurses. A doctor wearing a white coat and a surgical mask placed a hand on Pat's shoulder.

'Don't worry, we will do everything within our power to save her.'

It was Barouche. Pat staggered outside in a haze and sat anonymously amongst the hoards in the waiting area. The minutes slipped by, then an hour. He saw Brannigan arrive, then what he thought were Nicola's parents. Then, a tall, handsome young man he believed was her fiancé. He watched them pace up and down the corridor. And eventually they huddled around a consultant and Nicola's mother broke down as her daughter's death was announced. Brannigan and his side-kick Whelan hovered around the area for a while dealing with reporters. Pat eventually stood up, his white shirt saturated in blood and walked outside. He looked up at the grey afternoon sky and felt the rain wash away Nicola's blood from his face. Brannigan and Whelan approached him.

'What went wrong, O'Hara?' Brannigan barked.

Pat looked down at him, tears mixed with raindrops dripping from his forlorn face. He didn't answer Brannigan, removed his holster and the Smith & Wesson, and handed them to Whelan.

'You will need this for evidence.'

'I asked you a question, O'Hara,' Brannigan said, as he moved to block Pat's path.

Pat could feel his large fist clenching, almost involuntarily. He turned to walk away, but Brannigan grabbed his arm. Pat glared at him, his jaw strong and his teeth grating. He glanced down at Brannigan's hand, which still gripped his, and then looked Brannigan in the eye.

'Take your hands off me, you bastard.'

'Don't speak to me like that, Sergeant,' Brannigan replied shakily.

'I said, take your hands off me … Detective Inspector.'

Brannigan let go, and Pat walked off alone through the hoards of journalists and TV crews.

fourteen

As Emily pulled back the dark-blue curtains, Gerry heaved the quilt over his head to protect himself from the sudden burst of light. He felt her slight body on the bed beside him, as she sat down and placed a tray on a bedside table. He sat up slowly in the bed, bleary eyed with his head pounding.

'What time is it?' he asked, as he rubbed his eyes.

'Eleven, but I knew you didn't have anything on this morning, so I decided to let you have a lie in,' she said, as she poured him coffee from a silver pot.

'Thanks, this is a surprise,' he replied, looking at the fry Emily had prepared. 'Don't tell me I forgot our anniversary.'

She shook her head and smiled. 'It would be the frying pan and not the fry you would be getting if you did.'

He leant across for the cup of coffee.

'Where did you get the bruise on your arm? It looks nasty,' she asked, as she ran her slender fingers over the inside of his bicep.

'Got beaten up by a dissatisfied client,' he giggled, as he pulled the duvet up to his chest.

She leant forward and kissed him softly on his lips.

'Is everything OK, Gerry?' she asked, searching his eyes.

'Yes, why do you ask?'

'Because you were fairly pissed when you came in last night and it's only Monday.'

'I am sorry, Emily, that South African woman got ten years and I was seriously browned off. I went for a pint with a few of the guys.'

'It didn't have anything to do with what I found in your jacket pocket this morning then?'

A shiver ran down his spine, which he tried his best to disguise. 'What are you talking about?' he asked nervously.

There was a short silence as Emily gave him a frosty look.

'Gerry, you know exactly what I am talking about.'

'Honestly, I haven't a clue,' he said, his heart pounding.

'The letter from the sheriff.'

He breathed a heavy sigh.

'Why didn't you tell me about it?' she asked.

'I'm sorry, I didn't want to worry you.'

She placed her hands on his shoulders and massaged them gently.

'Look, Gerry, we are in this together. I know things aren't going great for you at the moment, but they will pick up, I know they will.'

He felt a sudden surge of guilt, of anger at himself.

'Thanks, Emily, I really appreciate your support. All I need is one good case and we will be flying again.'

'In the meantime, I will go back to work. And I don't care about your pride, I am going to cash in Daddy's bonds.'

'Oh no, you won't,' he said firmly.

She pulled away, stood up and walked to the window where she looked out across the heaving waters of Dalkey Sound.

'It's crazy; they've been lying there for years and will get us out of the mess we're in. My mind is made up and that's it.' She turned around. 'Only on one condition though.'

'What's the condition?'

'That we go skiing at Christmas.'

He smiled at her. 'It really means that much to you, doesn't it?'

She cocked her head, and brushed her long dark hair to one side with the graceful movement of her hand.

'Please,' she asked plaintively.

'OK, but I have a condition too.'

'What's that?'

'That you don't go snooping through my pockets again.'

She laughed as she left the room.

Gerry stood naked in the bathroom, his body bruised in five places that he could see and a scratch mark that was all too obvious on his right wrist. Looking in the mirror he smiled to himself. A smile he had never seen before. And it troubled him. He quickly splashed his face with cold water and returned to the bedroom. He donned a suit, shirt and tie and brought the tray downstairs to the kitchen, where Emily was listening intently to the RTE news.

'What's so interesting?' he asked, as he placed the plates in the dish-washer.

'A ban garda was shot dead in Blackrock this morning.'

'Christ, what happened?'

'It was during a bank robbery at the Ulster Bank.'

'Did they get the bastards?'

'One was shot dead at the scene. They chased the others out to Deansgrange, where the car crashed. Another was shot dead and the other two surrendered.'

'Wouldn't like to be in their shoes right now.'

She glared at him. 'Get your cute little ass into the Law Library, and try and drum up some work. Or do you want to be a kept man forever?'

He gave her a kiss on the cheek.

'Whatever you say, ma'am, you're the boss.'

fifteen

Mary O'Toole was from what they call a *respectable working-class background*. Reared in Drimnagh on the banks of the Grand Canal, her father a bus driver and her mother a cleaner in the Coombe Hospital. Mary was an only child and the apple of her parents' eyes. Plain, by any stretch of the imagination, she worked hard on her over-ripe pear-shaped figure. Of late, approaching thirty, she wore her hair short, dyed it blonde, and used a little too much foundation to disguise her rosy cheeks. But her large hazel eyes were full of laughter, and the male patients in St Bartholomew's Ward in St Vincent's Hospital, where she worked as a nurse, found them most engaging.

Mary had once fallen for the charms of a Greek boy she met in Crete while partying in Agios Nikolaos with some chums from college. The island romance had lasted only six days. But she wrote to him for the following three years, until he eventually announced that he was joining a monastery. She was unsure whether he was later ordained, as she never heard from him again.

She lived on the memories of that glorious summer for longer than was healthy and her mother thought her foolish for losing her heart so easily. Since then, friendships came easily to her, but love and even sex had eluded her.

She had bumped into Dr Barouche, on her way back from the radiology department, nine months earlier. She had, of course, known of him by reputation. Referred to by the nuns as the 'sheik', and by the other nurses as the 'cod', namely the catch of the day, she found him both handsome and charming, in an old-fashioned sort of way. She, and her ungracious colleagues, rated her chances at nil. But, much to her delight, he asked her for dinner. They soon became friends, then lovers and she had doted on him ever since.

Mary brought a tray with both their lunches from the self-service counter to a table where Barouche was waiting.

'What's wrong, Mo, you look as sick as a dead parrot?' she asked, as she placed his lunch before him and set the cutlery neatly in place.

'That poor police lady, we tried to save her but her time had come.'

'Ah don't be so sad, you did your best. Do you want some horse-radish with your beef?'

'No, thanks. Strange thing, she stopped me only yesterday on my bike.'

'Speeding again? I told you to be careful.'

'No, I wasn't speeding. She thought I had crashed into a taxi last Saturday night.'

'Why did she think that?'

'The driver wrote down a number and though it wasn't mine, it was very like it. Luckily I was able to tell her I was with you all night.'

'But we weren't together last Saturday night. I went to Jane's hen party, don't you remember?'

Barouche placed his hand to his forehead. 'You're right. I told her that we went for a walk on the pier, bought some Indian and stayed in my place.'

'Silly, that was Friday night. You have been working too hard.'

'But I was very definite to her. What will happen when they discover I told a lie?'

'And how are they going to find that out?'

'I gave them your name. They will check it with you, and then they will say I am a liar.'

She looked at him suspiciously. 'You didn't crash into the taxi driver, did you?'

'Of course not, Mary.'

'Then don't worry; if they ask me, I will say we were together. It will only be a white lie.'

He gave her a broad smile. 'I don't know what I would ever do without you.'

She felt a flutter inside. 'Let's not ever think of that. You remember our important date tonight, don't you?'

He rolled his eyes to heaven.

'It won't be too bad. Ma is dying to meet you and we can't put it off again.'

'I know. I will bring her flowers. Does your father smoke?'

'Like a trooper.'

'I will bring him some Cuban cigars.'

'I think that might work. But don't tell him you have a motor bike, he always told me to stay away from fellas on bikes.'

Barouche laughed. 'Maybe he was right.'

She took his hand and ran a finger over the back of it.

'No,' she said intently, 'for once my father was wrong.'

sixteen

The funeral was of state proportions with a guard of honour that stretched to the horizon. Surrounded by a sea of blue uniforms the President, Taoiseach and Minister for Justice performed their duties solemnly. Nicola's parents appeared blind to the protocol, as they were wrenched from Nicola's coffin when it was slowly lowered into the family plot in Shanganagh.

Cummins, in his blue uniform and gold braid, emerged from the crowds of mourners and approached Pat who was standing alone wearing a trench coat that had seen better days. He placed his hand on Pat's shoulder and offered him his sincere condolences. He then took him by the arm and led him along the gravelled pathway through the drizzling rain.

'I ran a check at Crime and Security on Barouche.'

Pat remained silent as Cummins continued, 'I don't know how you got your information and, to be honest, I don't particularly want to know either, but I think you might be on to something.'

'Are you going to arrest him?'

Cummins ignored the question. 'I am making a few more inquiries with the Royal Canadian Mounted Police, to see if there were any serious attacks on queers during Barouche's time there. There is a closed conference this afternoon to discuss where we stand, but I still have to persuade Brannigan.'

'You know we don't have enough evidence to charge him,' observed Pat.

'We have no evidence, full stop. But I think we have a reasonable suspicion and that's enough to bring him in.'

'Who will you get to interview him?'

'McAllister and Coyle, they are the best we have.'

'But they have no ammunition and this guy's pretty smart.'

'Pat, there's been a development.'

Pat stopped and looked quizzically at Cummins.

'The wino, what was his name?' asked Cummins,

'Pender.' Pat replied.

'He now claims he saw someone leaving the alley just before he entered it.'

'Does he describe the guy?'

'Not very well; tall and dark is all we can get out of him.'

'He won't be reliable, he was pissed out of his skull.'

'Sure I know that, but if he picks out Barouche at a parade and Barouche has denied he was there, the presence of Barouche's watch will support Pender and we might have enough to charge him.'

'But you'll never convict him on that.'

'Maybe not, but who knows we might turn up something in a search of Barouche's gaff?'

They walked on a short distance in silence. Cummins stopped and looked at Pat.

'You don't look so good, Pat.'

'It's been pretty rough. Nicola was a real gem, and I'm going to miss her a lot.'

'Sure. Look, I have spoken to your superintendent and it's agreed that you're to take some leave.'

'What!' Pat exclaimed as he became visibly agitated.

'Pat, take it easy, will you? If anything comes of all this I will give you the credit for it, but I want you offside for the moment, is that clear?'

Pat nodded reluctantly.

'I'll let you know how we get on.'

'OK, Superintendent,' Pat replied, as the two men parted company.

A conference of senior officers was held at Harcourt Square at 8 p.m. that evening. Detective Chief Superintendent Denis O'Malley, a canny Cork man with a ferret-like face, sat behind a large, tidy, leather-covered desk. Cummins was leaning forward in his chair and within the arc of the desk lamp his face appeared ridden with angst. Brannigan was sitting back in his chair, inspecting his nails, with a nonchalant air about him. O'Malley bore overall responsibility for the investigation and he asked Cummins to spell out his case. Cummins clasped his hands together and began enthusiastically.

'We have a whole lot of dirt on this guy. Al-Qaeda, and all that stuff about him being arrested in a gay bar in downtown Montreal.'

O'Malley waved his hand and then tapped a finger on the table.

'Jack, I don't want to hear all that nonsense. Just tell me what evidence you have.'

Cummins was slightly taken aback by O'Malley's abruptness. He sat back and spoke slowly.

'We have an expensive watch, covered in the victim's blood, which was found at the scene. It belongs to Barouche.'

O'Malley waited patiently for a few minutes. Then a look of bemusement crossed his face. He looked at Brannigan, who smiled at him, and then at Cummins.

'Is that it?' he asked, incredulously.

Cummins lowered his head and muttered, 'Yes, I'm afraid that's all we have at the moment.'

'Come on, Jack, you're not serious about this, are you?'

Cummins raised his head and looked O'Malley in the eye. 'I am deadly serious, Chief.'

'And has anyone asked Dr Barouche whether he might have mislaid his watch, or perhaps had it stolen?'

'No, we haven't gone near him; we didn't want to alert him that we're on to him. But he hasn't reported the watch stolen, and we checked with his insurers and no claim has been lodged yet.'

'For Christ's sake, it's been less than a week.'

'We also have a witness who saw the killer leave the alley after the killing.'

'Have you asked Dr Barouche to stand on a parade?' O'Malley asked.

'I told you already, we haven't gone near him.'

O'Malley stood up, and moved to a filing cabinet from which he took out a bottle of Middleton Rare Irish whiskey. He placed three glasses on the table and poured a generous measure into each and sat back down.

'So,' he said, looking at Cummins, 'why the hunch?'

Cummins took a sip of the whiskey, opened his hand and began counting fingers with the other.

'One, the killer amputated the victim's hands with skill, and Barouche is a surgeon.

'Two, the amputation of limbs is a ritualistic punishment recognized under Islamic Law, and Barouche is Muslim.

'Three, under Islamic Law homosexuality is a crime against God and punishable by death. The killer thought the victim was queer and therefore his death justified.

'Four. The killer wore a leather jacket and drove a large motor bike. Barouche wears a leather jacket and rides a BMW 600.

'Five. The killer was tall and dark. Barouche is tall and dark.'

He swapped hands and continued counting.

'Six, Barouche was expelled from an Al-Qaeda cell located in Montreal because he was suspected of being gay. Barouche is a fundamentalist who may be trying to prove himself to extremists residing here who are known to be weary of him.

'Seven, and this is my bet, he's a psycho.'

O'Malley stroked his chin and appeared deep in thought.

'What you're really telling me, Jack, is that the killer is going to attack again.'

Cummins nodded. 'That's my belief.'

'And if he does kill again, and we haven't acted on this information, weak though it is, the investigation will leave itself open to criticism.'

'Exactly. The media will be all over us like vultures.'

'So it's an arse-covering exercise, with only a very remote chance of yielding any results.'

Cummins nodded.

O'Malley turned to Brannigan. 'What's your view on all this, Noel?'

Brannigan sat back in his chair. 'My view, for what it's worth, is that we have very little to act on and that an arrest is premature. We are less than a week into the investigation and it's sheer madness to jump in with both feet.'

'And what if he kills again this weekend?' Cummins said, as he thumped the table angrily.

'Jack, take it easy, will you? I was asked to give my opinion and that's all I'm doing. Besides, if this guy is, as you seem to believe, psychotic, and the arrest leads to nothing, it will only encourage him further. We know that from experience.'

O'Malley stood up abruptly. 'OK, on balance I think we will go for it. Sure, if it comes to nothing, so be it, but in my view it's worth a try. When do we move?'

'First thing in the morning,' Cummins replied swiftly.

'Where?'

'We are going to do it very publicly outside the mosque; it will embarrass and unsettle him.'

'OK, get the briefing files prepared for the interviewers. And I don't want them briefed on the material from Crime and Security; it's classified and our American cousins wouldn't be too happy with us using it.'

'Are you definite on that? It's all we have to rattle his cage,' Cummins asked.

O'Malley placed his hands behind his back and shook his head defiantly.

'The information is classified and we can't use it without the CIA's approval. And I can tell you now, they won't agree.'

'Why?' Cummins asked.

'Because it would expose Barouche as an informant and we all know how valuable informants are. OK, gentlemen, get to work.'

seventeen

Early the following morning three units swooped on Barouche as he parked his motor bike in the car-park of the mosque. He didn't attempt to resist his arrest, but appeared shocked. He was brought to Pearse Street Garda Station where he was detained. He was asked if he wanted anyone notified of his arrest and he requested a solicitor. He was then taken to a room where he was photographed and finger-printed; when this was done he was taken to a cell and at 9 a.m. was taken to an interview-room.

The room was bright and airy, the only furniture a desk sitting in the middle with a chair on one side and two chairs opposite; in the corner, a video recorder and on the ceiling a wide-lens camera. One of the offi-cers placed a cassette in the recorder, turned it on and invited Barouche to sit down.

'As you can see this interview is being video taped.'

Barouche nodded.

'My name is Detective Sergeant McAllister and this is Detective Garda Coyle. I have to advise you are not obliged to say anything unless you wish to do so but anything you do say will be taken down in writing and maybe used in evidence. Do you understand that?'

'Does that mean I don't have to answer your questions?' Barouche asked.

'Yes, you have that right. Do you understand what you have been arrested for?'

'Yes, the murder of a young man. But I know nothing about it. I am doctor. I save lives. I don't take them.'

'Where were you last Saturday night at around midnight?'

Barouche looked at them and appeared hesitant. 'I was told I could see a solicitor and I haven't seen one yet. I don't want to refuse to answer your questions, but I think I should have legal advice first.'

'That's OK; we will break now and not ask you any more questions until you have had an opportunity of consulting your solicitor.'

Detective Garda Coyle escorted Barouche back to the cell area. Shortly afterwards he was brought to a small consultation room where a man in a shabby suit introduced himself as Dermot Kenny, solicitor. Dermot told him his rights and then continued, 'The first thing they will ask you is, do you have an alibi. Have you?'

Barouche shuffled nervously in his chair. 'I am afraid it's a little bit complicated.'

'A married woman?' Dermot enquired, with a grin on his face.

'No. I was stopped by the police six days ago and they asked where I was that night.'

'Why?'

'They said they were making enquiries into a hit and run accident.'

'Were they uniformed or plain clothes?'

'Plain clothes.'

Dermot raised an eyebrow. 'Unlikely, and it's too much of a coincidence anyway. They were probably testing the water.'

'I see.'

'Did you tell them where you were?'

'That's the problem, I told the lady policewoman that I was with my girlfriend.'

'So, what's the problem?'

'She was the policewoman who was shot the other day.'

'So?'

'So, I don't know if these policemen know about it or not.'

'They will know about it OK. If they ask you tell them the same story, but don't let on that you told the ban garda already.'

'OK, if you think that's best.'

'Have they asked for blood and hair samples?'

'No, not yet.'

'They will. Tell me, Doctor, have you anything to hide?'

Barouche placed his hands on the table and looked Dermot in the eye. 'Mr Kenny, I can assure you that I have absolutely nothing to hide. I didn't kill that boy.'

'Well, tell them that, and then volunteer to give them blood before they ask you for it. It's far better that you are seen to want to co-operate. Understand what I mean?'

'Yes, I understand.'

'They can get an order compelling you to provide samples anyhow.

But beyond that, refuse to answer any questions whatsoever. No matter what they ask you, simply say, on the advice of my solicitor I am declining to answer any further questions. Do you understand?'

Barouche frowned. 'Any questions at all?' he asked.

'Yes; if they ask you what you had for breakfast, don't tell them. Once they get you talking you might end up saying something innocuous that they will later use against you.'

'But I told you I have nothing to hide.'

Dermot slapped the desk with the palm of his hand. 'Tell me something, Dr Barouche, do you like gays?'

Barouche pulled back. 'Mr Kenny, homosexuality is against the law of God.'

Dermot grinned. 'See what I mean? The accused considers the practice of homosexuality to be an affront to the law of God himself. Before you know it they will have you down as homophobic.'

Barouche nodded, indicating that he understood.

'They say they have an eye-witness and want to hold an identification parade. Have you any objection?'

'I don't know. What do you think?'

'If you agree it will be done formally here at the station. I will be present to make sure the volunteers in the parade are of similar appearance to you and that everything is done by the book.'

'And if I don't agree?' Barouche asked.

Dermot shook his head. 'It looks bad. Anyway they will hold an informal identification later on, in court or wherever, and we won't know anything about it until it's over and done with.'

'So, it's better to agree to a formal parade?' Barouche asked.

'Yes, much better.'

'OK, will they talk to my girlfriend?'

'Yes, why?'

'It's just that I don't want her involved in all this. It will be most embarrassing for her and her family.'

'Have you contacted her since you came in?'

'No, she doesn't know I am here.'

'Will I arrange for her to come down to see you?'

'No, no, she'll go absolutely crazy,' Barouche protested.

'Do you want me to at least contact her and tell her that you're OK?'

'Yes, I suppose you should.'

'I'll also tell her not to talk to the police unless I am there.'

'Can you do that?'

'Yes, they can't force her to co-operate unless they arrest her and they aren't going to do that.'

Barouche again leant forward placing his hands on the desk. 'Mr Kenny, I don't care how much money this is going to cost, I want you to help me all you can, but I want you to protect my girlfriend above all else. Is that clear?'

'Very clear,' answered Dermot as he got up to leave. 'Don't worry, old boy, you will be out of here by eight o'clock tonight.'

Barouche was brought back to the interview-room where he told the detectives briefly what his alibi was, volunteered to give bodily samples and agreed to stand on an identity parade. He then refused to answer any questions, which was his constitutional right. The interview terminated after two hours.

That afternoon he was led into the parade room where he saw eleven other men of not entirely dissimilar appearance to himself. However Dermot objected to three of them on the basis that they had dust on their clothes and had clearly been recruited from a nearby building-site. The uniformed sergeant protested that he had done his best, bearing in mind that Barouche was a foreign national. Dermot stuck to his guns, pointing out that Dublin was teaming with foreigners, and the holding of the parade was adjourned for a further hour and a half, as guards were dispatched on to the streets of Dublin to find more volunteers. Barouche seemed impressed with Dermot's tenacity. Dermot knew though that his demands for fairness were eating up valuable time that would otherwise be used interviewing his client.

Eventually, eleven volunteers were assembled. Barouche was invited by the sergeant to take up any position he wished in the line-up. He stood between numbers four and five. After a few minutes, Pender was brought into the room. Remarkably, he appeared sober and reasonably groomed. Cummins was pacing up and down outside in the corridor, his fingers crossed behind his back. The sergeant then invited Pender to view the parade and he was instructed that if he saw anyone he recognized as being the man he observed leaving the alley on the night of the killing, to step forward and place his hand on the man's shoulder. Pender seemed all too familiar with the procedure, having been on many identification parades himself. He walked slowly along the line of men, inspecting each individual closely. One appeared more nervous than the next. He stopped at number four and looked at him with particular interest. He then moved swiftly to the end of the line-up, where he turned and walked slowly along the line again. This time he stopped in front of Barouche and looked him over. He then moved closer, theatrically studying every contour of Barouche's face. Pender stood staring into his eyes for what seemed, to those gathered, like an eternity. It appeared he was inviting Barouche to flinch under his gaze. Eventually Barouche lowered his eyes.

'That's like him,' Pender said, as he moved to the left and placed his hand on number four's shoulder, 'but it's not him. The fella I saw was older, with slicked back greasy hair.'

The sergeant led Pender from the room and thanked the volunteers for their public spiritedness. Cummins heard the news and was irate.

'The stupid eejit picked out the wrong man,' he declared to Brannigan, who was sipping coffee in the canteen.

'Looks as though your hunch was wrong,' he declared triumphantly.

Cummins snarled at him, 'The interviewers have one last interview with him, and it isn't over until the fat lady sings.'

'I bet you ten euros he doesn't confess.'

Cummins hesitated.

'Come on, Jack, put your money where your mouth is.'

Cummins smiled. 'OK, you're on,' he replied, less than confidently.

Brannigan let out a raucous laugh. 'Don't worry, I'll buy you a pint with my winnings.'

Pat appeared at the member-in-charge's desk in the cell area of the station, a place that was strictly out of bounds for detective branch.

'How are things, Pat? I'm really sorry about what happened to your partner,' Garda Frank Muldoon said as he shook Pat's hand.

'Thanks, Frank.'

'What brings you down here?'

'I want a word with the doctor.'

Muldoon laughed. 'Come on, Pat, you know the rules, no interviewing in the cells.'

'I don't want to interview him; I am not even part of the investigation team,' Pat protested.

'Then what are you at?' he asked, looking at Pat through squinted eyes.

'He tried to save Nicola's life. I never got the chance to thank him.'

Muldoon hesitated.

'Come on, Frank, it will only take five minutes.'

Muldoon picked up a large bunch of keys.

'OK, Pat, but just five minutes.'

Detective Sergeant McAllister and Detective Garda Coyle noticed the change in Barouche's demeanour as they commenced the last interview before his period of detention expired.

'When did you first notice that your watch was missing?'

Barouche remained silent.

'Why didn't you report it missing?'

Still no answer.

'Why, when the watch was so valuable, did you not make a claim to your insurance company?'

Barouche hung his head.

'If your girlfriend can back up your alibi, why won't she talk to us?'

Barouche raised his hand shielding himself from their questions. He looked up at his interrogators, his eyes moist with tears. The two experienced interrogators immediately stopped and there was silence in the interview-room, save for the whirring of the tape. Barouche eventually leant back, looked up at the ceiling, with his hands resting on the back of his head. He sighed, and then asked, 'How long will I get if I tell you what happened?'

The question took the detectives by surprise, but they knew they had him on the hook. Detective Sergeant McAllister spoke slowly. 'You will get life for murder, but with good behaviour you could be out in ten years.'

Barouche lowered his head, and wiped the tears from his eyes. 'OK, I did it,' he muttered.

'Will you make a statement telling us what happened?'

Barouche nodded in agreement.

McAllister reminded him he was still under caution, then quickly scribbled down the heading of the statement and waited for Barouche to start. Slowly and quite deliberately Barouche dictated his confession.

'I want to tell you what happened. I went into town last Saturday night. I wanted to kill a gay boy. I followed the boy from a bar on Georges Street and down an alley. I cut his throat and then cut off his hands. Then I went home, washed the blood from my clothes, and went to sleep.'

'What about the murder weapon? What did you use? And what happened to it?'

Barouche hesitated and appeared deep in thought.

'I used a surgical knife. I threw it into the river.'

McAllister wrote that down.

'Dr Barouche, are you going to tell us why you did it?'

Barouche remained silent.

'I asked, why did you do it?' the detective sergeant persisted.

Barouche shook his head. 'I don't want to answer any more questions,' he answered firmly.

McAllister read the short statement over to Barouche and asked him if it was correct. He agreed that it was and signed the statement. The detectives also signed it. He was then returned to his cell.

eighteen

Gerry was glued to the six o'clock news, as Emily was busy cooking dinner in the kitchen. At its conclusion, the newscaster announced that a doctor was to be charged at a special sitting of the District Court with the murder of Johnny O'Shea. The phone rang and Emily answered it.

It was Dermot Kenny, whom she loathed, but she feigned friendship for the sake of Gerry's career. After formal pleasantries were exchanged, she placed her hand over the mouthpiece and turned to Gerry.

'It's that cowboy Kenny, looking for you.'

Gerry rolled his eyes to heaven and gave her a gentle slap on the bottom as he took the phone from her.

'Hi, Dermot, please don't tell me that Naguma has topped herself.'

'No, but I have some good news for a change. The goose has eventually laid a golden egg.'

'What are you talking about?'

'I picked up the Georges Street murder.'

'Christ, well done.'

'And I am briefing you, if you will accept it of course.'

Gerry looked over to Emily and punched the air triumphantly.

'Thank you, Dermot, I would be more than happy to accept the brief.'

'And it gets even better,' Dermot added.

'In what way?'

'I just saw him in the Bridewell and I told him I would get him the best lawyer in the country.'

'And?'

'I told him it would cost him thirty thousand euros on the brief and three thousand a day. Is that OK?'

'Fantastic.'

'And even better, he is paying us up front, so I should be in funds early next week.'

'Jesus, Dermot, that's great.'

'I am lodging a bail application for next Monday, are you available?'

'Bloody sure I am.'

'OK. I'll ring you tomorrow with more news.'

'Thanks, Dermot.'

He replaced the receiver and immediately did an exaggerated Irish jig around the room, hollering at the same time. Patrick stood in the doorway clinging to his mother's arm. Had daddy gone mad? Gerry danced over to Emily, grabbed her by the waist and twirled her around.

'What's going on, you madman?'

'I have my breakthrough, and what a case. The media will be all over it.'

'Not the gay murder,' she exclaimed.

'Yes, and it's not the usual legal-aid rubbish either,' he roared, as he lifted a bemused Patrick above his head.

'Pack the ski boots, honey, we are off to Austria for Christmas.'

Emily stood watching Gerry with tears in her eyes. She hadn't seen him this happy in years. She disappeared into the kitchen and emerged with a bottle of Moët and two glasses, which she placed on the table.

'Here's to my clever husband,' she said, as she popped the champagne, 'I love you, Mr Hickey.'

'And I love you, Mrs Hickey,' he said, as he wrapped his arms around her. 'And you, too,' he said, holding Patrick's hand. 'And even bloody Dermot Kenny.'

After dinner, when the air of excitement settled, Gerry suggested that they both go to Finnegan's Pub in Dalkey village for a few drinks. Emily said she couldn't get a babysitter at such short notice, but insisted that Gerry go alone and meet up with some of his pals who were permanent fixtures in the trendy pub. Gerry agreed, then sped out the door and into the night air. As he strode along Coliemore Road, seemingly impervious to the rain that cascaded from above, he took out his mobile phone, dialled Carmen and within twenty minutes was in her apartment in Ballsbridge.

nineteen

Barouche's bail application was successful despite strenuous objections from the State. However he was temporarily suspended from his post in St Vincent's Hospital pending the outcome of the trial. His face, emblazoned across every tabloid, was known the length and breadth of the country, and he seldom left his apartment. Mary arrived one evening to cook a special dinner to celebrate their first anniversary as a couple. His apartment was modern and expensively furnished. The living room was decorated in taupe, with a couple of cream leather sofas flanking a large mirrored coffee table. Mary sat curled up beside Barouche with her head resting on his chest as he stroked her hair. She had never asked him if he killed Johnny O'Shea, as the thought that the man she knew and loved was capable of such madness was beyond her wildest nightmares. But the trial was only a fortnight away and she needed to know what was likely to happen.

'When are you seeing the lawyers?' she asked.

'Tomorrow afternoon.'

'And what are you going to tell them?'

'The truth, of course.'

There was a long silence.

'Which is?' she asked gingerly.

He gently raised her head with his hands and searched her eyes.

'That I am innocent.'

She gave him a warm smile.

'I know that, Mo, I meant about the alibi.'

'Mary, I think I should tell them the truth. We both know I got mixed up about the date and it's better to be honest about it now.'

'But I already made a statement to your solicitor saying we were together,' she protested.

'Yes I know that, but I don't want you going into court and telling lies on my behalf.'

'But they have that stupid statement they forced you to sign, if you don't have an alibi the jury will convict you.'

'That's not nearly as bad as you perjuring yourself before God.'

'God has nothing to do with this. It's about survival.'

He kissed her gently on her forehead. 'Will you wait for me, if I am convicted?'

'Of course I will wait for you. But don't change the subject. If the jury know you told the police you were with me on the night of the murder and I am not called as a witness on your behalf, they will put two and two together.'

'That's my decision and it's final,' he said firmly.

She stood up and looked down at him with burning eyes.

'No, Mo, that's where your wrong, it's our decision. We are in this together. This all started with a stupid taxi driver reporting a Mickey Mouse hit and run accident. You made a stupid mistake that anyone could make and now it looks as though the alibi is a set up. I won't allow that to happen. I am going to give evidence that we were together that night whether you like it or not.'

He pulled back from her rage, then reached forward and gently took her hand.

'You know something, I don't deserve you, Mary,' he said lovingly.

She smiled. 'Of course you don't, but you are stuck with me now. So are we agreed on the alibi?'

'OK, whatever you say, but only if you promise to wait for me if it all goes wrong.'

'It won't go wrong, but I promise anyway.'

'OK, we have a deal,' he said as he took her into his arms.

'Can I come to the consultation tomorrow?' she asked.

'No,' he said firmly. 'It will look bad if you are seen to be too close to my case.'

twenty

Eamon Dempsey SC was a large portly man with a booming voice. In his early fifties, he was a vastly experienced prosecutor. He also enjoyed a reputation, amongst his colleagues, of being scrupulously fair. His office in the Distillery Building on Church Street adjacent to the Four Courts was a plush affair, with the *Irish Reports* and other weighty legal tomes lining the walls. His secretary showed Cummins and Geraldine McNamara, a principal solicitor from the Chief State Solicitors office, into Dempsey's office. He politely asked them if they would like tea or coffee, but they declined. A pile of documents was sprawled out on the desk in front of him.

'So, where do we start?' asked Cummins.

'I would say it's all rather straightforward; let's start with the confession.'

Cummins nodded,

'It's rather terse to put it mildly,' observed Dempsey, 'not much detail.'

'But it's a confession. He signed it and it's all on tape, so the officers are protected against any accusations of impropriety,' Cummins responded defensively.

'Yes, I know that. But the jury will still examine it very closely and I am a bit concerned that it doesn't offer any real insight into the crime.'

'What do you mean by that?'

'The statement doesn't contain any facts that weren't already known to the Gardai. In fact, the dogs in the streets know that the poor unfortunate chap had his throat slit and his hands amputated.'

Cummins leant forward towards Dempsey.

'Mr Dempsey, exactly what are you suggesting?' Cummins said, somewhat aggressively.

Dempsey raised a hand to ward off the superintendent's anger. 'Steady on, I am not suggesting any impropriety. But confessions have become notoriously unreliable in recent years. We all know about tribunals of enquiries set up to examine disputed confessions. It's not that the Gardai have concocted them; it's merely that there is a lot psychological evidence available nowadays suggesting that people who are under pressure can confess to crimes that they didn't actually commit.'

'Like the Lyons case,' observed Cummins.

'Exactly. And the confession we have here is so bereft of detail that someone who actually hadn't committed the crime could easily have made it up.'

'Yes that's true, but what about the watch?'

'Well now, in my view that evidence is vital, because it is independent evidence that supports the proposition that the accused was at the scene, which in turn corroborates the confession. By the way, I note that the witness is a vagrant; I trust he will be available to give evidence at the trial?'

Cummins frowned. 'We are having a bit of difficulty serving a summons on him, but we are pretty sure we will find him before the trial.'

'It doesn't help that he picked out an innocent volunteer at the identification parade, but I suggest you put all your efforts into ensuring he is available, because without him we can't place the watch at the scene.'

Cummins nodded.

'Have you uncovered a possible motive yet?'

Cummins shook his head. 'Nothing we could throw out to a jury anyhow.'

'I see. Has the Notice of Alibi served on behalf of the accused been fully investigated?'

'Yes. His girlfriend is sticking by him.'

Dempsey smiled. 'What else did you expect? But it won't wash with the jury. Is there anything else I should know?'

'Well,' Cummins hesitated, 'our boys in Crime and Security have a file on Barouche.'

'Really? Is it in any way relevant to this case?'

'No, not really.'

'Then I don't want to know about it. Is that all?' Dempsey said, looking at both of them.

'Yes,' said Ms McNamara, 'thank you very much for your time.'

Upstairs in the same building Barouche and Dermot were sitting across the desk from Gerry and his junior counsel, Patricia Quinn. Ms Quinn was blonde and pretty. She wore a dark-blue trouser suit and designer spectacles, which helped disguise her youth. Dermot had brought her into the case because he played golf with her father and it was her first jury trial. Gerry cut quickly to the chase.

'Doctor, the confession alone will convict you unless you can give me some strong basis on which to challenge it.'

'What do you mean by challenge?' enquired Barouche.

'The prosecution have to prove the statement was made voluntarily before the jury get to see it.'

Barouche looked bemused. 'What do you mean by voluntary, Mr Hickey?'

'It means that the statement must have been made freely without any hint of a threat or an inducement.'

'I see, and if there was a threat made to me?' enquired Barouche.

'Then the statement would be inadmissible in evidence. But I should point out to you that I have read the interview notes and Ms Quinn has viewed all the tapes and it doesn't appear that any threats were made against you. In fact quite the contrary, the police appear to have treated you very well.'

Barouche shook his head defiantly.

'You disagree?'

The doctor shuffled nervously in his chair.

'Is there something you're not telling us?'

Barouche didn't answer.

'If you want us to mount an effective defence on your behalf, you must tell us everything.'

'I can't, my life is in danger.'

Gerry looked surprised. 'What do you mean?'

'I can't tell you that, Mr Hickey.'

'Look, everything you say to us is absolutely confidential and won't go beyond these four walls. I can assure you of that.'

'Absolutely confidential?' Barouche appeared interested.

'Anything said by a client to his lawyer in the preparation of his defence is absolutely privileged and no one, and I mean no one, can compel us to divulge the contents of this conversation. Does that put your mind at rest?'

He appeared more comfortable. 'I was an informant for the CIA,' he told them in a hushed tone.

Dermot couldn't control himself. 'Jesus, what has that got to do with this?'

'It has everything to do with it,' Barouche responded angrily.

Gerry gestured to both men to calm down.

'Doctor, you had better spell out clearly what relevance this has.'

Barouche took a deep breath and then began, 'I was an Islamic fundamentalist when I lived in Canada. Extremist is more like it. I met a man called Moctar and some other young men in a mosque in Montreal and we became very friendly. We met frequently in the mosque and I eventually learnt that they planned to bomb the subway in New York. They asked me to help them. I don't know what I was thinking of at the time, but I was very angry with the Americans for invading Iraq, so I agreed. When I look back on it now it was a crazy thing to do. I had completely lost my judgement at the time.'

Barouche hesitated.

'Go on', Gerry urged.

'Three weeks before the planned attack I was arrested in a bar in Montreal. I had some cannabis on me and the police were going to charge me. It would have ruined my career so I did a deal with them and they dropped the case against me in exchange for information. That's when the CIA became involved.'

'So what happened next?'

'My friends were arrested with bomb-making equipment when they crossed the border into the US. They are all serving life imprisonment now.'

'And do they know you betrayed them?'

'No, I would be dead if they did.'

'So what did you do then?'

'The CIA put pressure on me for more information on the activities of Al-Qaeda, but I didn't have any to give. I knew I had made a big mistake in getting involved with all this so I decided to move away and start a new life. That's why I came to Ireland.'

Gerry sat back and slowly tapping his pen on the desk he surveyed Barouche.

'So, Doctor, what has all this got to do with you signing a confession to murder?'

'When I was in the cells in the police station this crazy man came in.'

'Do you know his name?'

'No, but he was a huge guy. I saw him in the hospital when I was treating the poor lady policewoman who was shot—'

Dermot interrupted, 'This is all crazy stuff; what has it got to do with the case?'

Gerry glared at him. 'Please continue, Doctor.'

'He took out a gun.'

'What type of gun?'

'A Smith & Wesson revolver.'

'What did he do with it?'

'He put it on the bunk between us. He was very angry. His eyes were like those of a madman. He told me that he had broken the news of the young man's death to his mother. He said he had made a promise to her that he would get the killer. He really believed I killed the guy.'

'And then?'

'Then he told me he knew I was an informant.'

'How did he know that?'

'He said he had seen a CIA file on me. He threatened to spread the news that I was an informant around the mosque unless I confessed to killing the boy.'

'So?'

'Mr Hickey, the vast majority of my fellow Muslims are decent, law-abiding people, but I know there are a few extremists in the mosque. If they heard I was an informant I would be executed.'

'So, you told him you did it?'

'No, he said he didn't want me to confess to him. He told me to make a statement at my next interview, or he would carry out his threat. I believed him and I was terrified. Anyway I knew about what happened to the victim from the questions they had asked me at the earlier interviews and I decided to make up a story.'

Gerry sat back and appeared deep in thought.

'And that's why there is so little detail in your statement,' he observed.

'Yes. I knew nothing about what really happened.'

Gerry stood up and left the room. He returned a few minutes later and sat down.

'Detective Sergeant Pat O'Hara, he's the guard who broke the news to the mother and he was also the ban garda's partner. I remember that guy; he was in the murder squad, wasn't he, Dermot?'

'Yes, he took the infamous confession that led to the squad being disbanded.'

Gerry couldn't disguise his enthusiasm. 'It gets better by the minute,' he said.

Barouche became distressed and interrupted, 'But you can't use any of this,' he said frantically.

'Why not?'

'Because it will be in the newspapers and I will be a dead man.'

'Don't worry, Doctor, we will apply to the judge to hear the evidence *in camera* and none of it will be made public.'

'Can you do that?'

'Only in exceptional circumstances, but I have no doubt that the judge will decide that this is one of those rare circumstances.'

A faint smile crossed Barouche's face but quickly faded as he leant forward and addressed Gerry. 'Before I go, I need to talk to you about my alibi.'

Gerry shook his head. 'If we get the statement ruled inadmissible, that will be the end of the case and you won't need an alibi.'

'And if you don't get it ruled inadmissible, what then?'

'Put bluntly, you're in serious trouble.'

'Why do you say that?'

'Because, then it all goes public and we won't be able to rely on what you just told us, will we?'

Barouche nodded in agreement.

'And if the jury hear the confession, coupled with the fact that your watch was found at the scene, I rate your chances at nil.'

'Is the finding of the watch that important?'

'Yes, because it supports the confession.'

'OK, I understand. You will do everything you can to help me, won't you, Mr Hickey?'

'That's my job.'

Gerry stood up and shook hands with Barouche as he showed him into the atrium. Dermot remained behind in the office.

'That's all fairly off-the-wall stuff,' he observed, when Gerry returned to the office.

'But it makes sense.'

'Do you really think so?'

'Yes I do, and if we discover that the guards have a CIA file on Barouche, our case will be stronger.'

'Will I write and ask them to have O'Hara in court?'

'No, I want it to come as a surprise. Who's the judge?'

'Mrs Justice Elizabeth O'Hanlon.'

'Can't get a fairer judge than that. You know, Dermot, we just might be on to a winner.'

'The media will go crazy.'

'To hell with the media.'

twenty-one

Shortly before midnight Detective Garda O'Malley and another detective were sitting in an unmarked car in an alley off Dawson Street. Detective Superintendent Cummins had given clear instructions that Dan Pender was to be tracked down on the eve of the trial, kept under observation until the following morning, when he was to be lifted and escorted to the court. O'Malley's mobile phone rang.

'Any sign of him?' Brannigan asked.

'Yes, he is in an alleyway running between Dawson Street and South Frederick Street,' the detective replied.

'Is he there for the night?'

'Looks like it, he's well tanked up.'

'OK, you guys can leave him be.'

'But our instructions are to bring him to court in the morning.'

'I know that, but if he is bedded down for the night you may as well go off and do something useful. Pick him up at six o'clock, give him some breakfast and then bring him down to the Four Courts.'

'Whatever you say, Detective Inspector.'

An hour later, long legs in high heels picked their way through cardboard boxes and discarded beer cans that lay about the ground in a poorly lit alleyway opposite Renards Night Club, on South Frederick Street. Darren, half asleep beneath one of the boxes, stirred and watched as the girls descended the steps into the fashionable nightclub across the road. It was a bitterly cold night and his unsteady hand lit the butt of a cigarette. He needed a drink badly. He turned to a neighbouring box, home to his companion for the night and kicked it angrily.

'Come on, Pender, give me some of your wine, you miserable whore.'

A bottle rolled out from beneath his neighbour's blanket and Darren picked it up. Placing his lips around the top of the bottle he held his head back and gulped until the bottle was dry. He then wiped his mouth with the sleeve of his hoodie, and cast the bottle against the brick wall. It smashed into several pieces. Lying back, he pulled a damp blanket up to his chin and roared in anger the first two verses of one of his poems.

'Run, run the race of tiny men home to your dwellings and the
    warmth of fire
For the Lord is coming as the wind to sweep away the leaves of
    life.'

'Mmmm ... ah to hell with it, I can't even remember the words of me own bleedin' poems.'

He turned to Pender. 'I was once in love you know.'

Pender didn't answer him.

'What would you know about love anyway, you old bollocks?' He rolled over and rested his head on the ground, closed his eyes and felt himself drifting off. Suddenly he felt his hand covered in what he thought was oil. He sat up and groped in the darkness. The oil had saturated the cardboard box beneath him.

'What the hell?' he exclaimed, as he jumped up. 'Pender, get up someone's after pouring oil over us.'

But Pender didn't stir. Darren pulled back Pender's blanket and gasped when he saw a knife protruding from Pender's back.

twenty-two

The neat front gardens on Whitworth Road glistened in the bright morning sun as a sharp frost stubbornly refused to thaw. Mrs O'Shea emerged from the front door wearing a dark-brown, full-length coat, brown leather gloves and a pillar-box hat perched on her head. As she slid awkwardly along the icy pathway in her high-heeled shoes, Pat went to her assistance and linked her arm.

'Mind yourself there, it's like an ice rink.'

She looked up at him and smiled. 'Thank you, Sergeant.'

'Mrs O'Shea, it's Pat, for God's sake.'

'OK, but only if I'm Eleanor.'

He held the door open for her and she slid into the front passenger seat. As they drove down Constitution Hill, past the shimmering granite of Kings Inns standing imperiously in its own parkland, Pat asked the obvious question.

'Eleanor, where's your husband this morning.'

She lowered her head and opened her handbag, which was sitting on her lap. She took out a white linen handkerchief and softly brushed the tip of her nose.

'He has no interest,' she said, her voice heavy with sadness.

Pat raised an eyebrow. 'No interest?'

'None; he is in Spain at the moment. All he seems interested in these days is his bloody golf.'

'I thought he might be here to support you.'

She let out a half laugh. 'Support. He hasn't supported me for years.'

'I see,' Pat replied solemnly.

'To be honest with you we should have gone our separate ways years ago, but stupidly hung on for Johnny's sake.'

'I'm sorry.' He turned to her and smiled. 'By the way you look great this morning.'

'Why thank you, it's a long time since I got a compliment from a gentleman.'

'I don't believe that for a moment.'

She looked away to hide her blushes.

'Is it going to become clear at the trial that Johnny wasn't homo-sexual?'

Pat turned to her. 'Is it really that important to you?'

'Not to me, but Johnny wouldn't have liked it.'

'I'm sure the full truth will emerge,' Pat said reassuringly.

He swung the car around on to the Quays and the full majesty of the Four Courts came into view, looking resplendent in the bright morning sunlight. Beneath its huge columns a large group of protesters were walking up and down carrying placards and chanting 'Equal rights for gays, stop gay bashing.' Pat parked the car and they fought their way through the thronging crowd. As they stood in the vast Round Hall outside Court No. 2, beneath a sky-blue dome that floated high above, wigged and gowned barristers rushed back and forth plying their trade. Barouche, wearing a dark-grey suit, crisp white shirt and a black tie, was standing across the hall holding Mary's hand in full view of the jury panel. Immediately Eleanor's eyes were upon him, and they burned with hatred. She tapped her shoe on the stone floor to distract herself as she fought to control her anger. Unable to retain her dignity, she left Pat's side and strode purposely towards Barouche, at the same time reaching inside her handbag. She thrust a photograph of Johnny into Barouche's face, looked up at him and through tight lips growled.

'You bastard.'

Barouche looked at her as Mary quickly stepped between them, facing Eleanor. Pat appeared at Eleanor's shoulder and she felt his large hand gently wrap around hers. Barouche looked sympathetically into Eleanor's glazed eyes and said softly, 'Mrs O'Shea, I didn't kill your son.'

Pat put his arm around Eleanor and ushered her away.

'I'm sorry, Pat, I couldn't stop myself,' she said, trying to fight back the tears.

'I understand how you feel. Come on, we'll go for a coffee. The case won't be starting for a while.'

Inside the oak-panelled courtroom, Dempsey was seated in the front bench flicking through his opening speech, which was roughly scrib-bled in his barrister's notebook. Gerry battled through the crowds, Patricia in tow, weighed down with law books. He slid across the front bench and whispered to Dempsey, 'I need to see you outside.'

The two lawyers stood together in a quiet corridor that led to the judge's chambers. Gerry told Dempsey the nature of his application. Dempsey then left, spoke to Cummins and returned after a few minutes. The two men approached the judge's tipstaff and indicated that they wanted to see the judge in chambers. The tipstaff vanished into the judge's room and returned shortly afterwards and escorted them into the inner sanctum.

Heavy mahogany furniture lent an air of antiquity to the large musty room. In a corner, the judge's black silk gown hung from a coat stand, on top of which her wig was perched precariously. Mrs Justice O'Hanlon was seated behind a large desk, a lamp illuminating the papers in the case, which she had been in the process of reading. She lifted her eyes over her half-moon glasses and smiled.

'Good morning, gentlemen,' she said, as she gestured them both to sit in the two green leather chairs opposite her. 'What can I do for you?'

She was a tall, erect woman who, even when seated, had a commanding presence. Close to retirement, her grey hair swept back from a once beautiful face, she had a genteel manner that disguised her uncompromising approach.

Gerry addressed her in a respectful, almost ingratiating, tone.

'I have a preliminary application to make to you, Judge.'

'Shouldn't that be done in open court?' she said sharply.

Gerry leant forward in his chair. 'I am challenging the admissibility of a statement made by my client and I need to do it *in camera*.'

'A confession,' she corrected him.

'Yes, a confession,' he conceded.

'And what is the basis of your challenge?'

'That the statement, sorry, confession, was secured from my client by means of a threat.'

'What kind of threat?'

'That he would be exposed as an informant.'

She sat back in her chair, tapping her long nails on the desk.

'That's interesting,' she observed. 'And your client doesn't want this to come out in open court.'

'No, he doesn't. He fears for his life.'

'And what was the nature of the information, you say he was passing to the police?'

'It relates to terrorist activity.'

'IRA?' she enquired.

'No, Al-Qaeda.'

She smiled. 'Well, that's a first for me. Who was he passing the information to?'

'The CIA.'

She turned to Eamon. 'Is there any truth in all this?'

'Yes, Judge, I have just made some enquiries from the officer in charge of the case and he tells me that the accused gave information to the CIA.'

'So what's your attitude to the defence application that this aspect of the case be heard in private?'

'This is a very high profile case, Judge.'

A look of anger crossed her face and she interjected at once. 'Don't give me that argument. Is there a special rule of law that applies to cases that attract the interest of the media?'

'No, Judge, I am sorry.'

'So you should be. The day judges start deciding cases based on what the mob demands will be a sad day for the administration of justice. Now what's your argument?'

'I am objecting because it's a fundamental rule of law that justice must be administered in public, save in exceptional circumstances. I submit it would not be in the interests of justice to exclude the public from hearing the evidence on which you must eventually decide whether to admit the statement.'

'But isn't the protection of the identity of informants of paramount importance?' the judge asked.

'Yes, that's true,' Dempsey replied.

'And it matters little whether the informant passed the information to the Gardai or another law-enforcement agency.'

'That's also true.'

'Then how can you say that you object to the evidence being heard in private?'

'Because we will be claiming privilege over the information in any event.'

She became visibly impatient.

'I don't understand your argument. This man says he was an informant, and that is agreed. He says the Gardai threatened to make this fact known publicly, thereby placing his life at risk, and as a result of this threat, he confessed.'

She turned to Gerry. 'That's right isn't it?'

'Yes, Judge, that's our case in a nutshell,' he replied.

'So the only questions I have to concern myself with are, firstly was the threat made and secondly, if it was made, did the fear thereby induced render his confession involuntary?'

Both men nodded in agreement.

She turned to Eamon. 'And if I hear this evidence in public, then the world and his mother will know that the accused is an informant and that will place his life at risk.'

'But, Judge,' Eamon interrupted, 'it is the accused who will have been responsible for bringing this into the public domain.'

She threw her hands in the air. 'But I am told he has no choice, it goes to the heart of his defence.'

Gerry cut in. 'And if it is heard in public my client will be unable to raise it as an issue and will thereby be denied a legitimate defence. It is akin to the *innocence at stake rule*.'

The judge sat back, surveying the lawyers, her expression closed to further argument. She sat forward and delivered her ruling.

'Gentlemen, it is a fundamental rule under the constitution that justice shall be administered in public. There are, however, limited exceptions to that rule, and I believe this is one of them. To refuse this application would, in my view, be tantamount to denying the accused in this case the right to rely on a defence to the charge. So I propose to accede to the application and to hear that aspect of the case *in camera*.'

'Will this take long?' she asked Gerry.

'There will only be two relevant witnesses.'

'Eamon, have you any evidence of guilt other than the confession?' He shook his head.

'Then, gentlemen, it appears to me that the sensible thing to do is to deal with this as a preliminary issue. I will empanel a jury now and send them away until tomorrow morning. Any objections to that?'

Eamon and Gerry shook their heads and left.

The judge made her way to the courtroom. The only persons present were the court registrar, the stenographer, Barouche and his lawyers, the prosecution team and Superintendent Cummins and Inspector Brannigan, who were seated at the back of the court. Gerry rose to his feet.

'May it please the court, I am objecting to the admissibility of my client's alleged confession on the basis that it was secured as a result of a most grave threat made against him whilst he was detained in Pearse Street Garda Station. The actual terms of the threat I prefer to reserve until my cross-examination of Detective Sergeant O'Hara, who, it is alleged by my client, made the threat. I do not require evidence from the detectives who actually took the disputed confession since there is no allegation of impropriety being levelled against them. For the purposes of determining the issue the only witnesses that I require are the detective sergeant and the member in charge of the station, Garda Frank Muldoon. In the event of a denial of the accusations, I will be asking for discovery of certain documents held at Crime and Security Branch at Garda headquarters, but perhaps I will deal with that, if and when it arises.'

He then sat down. Brannigan turned to Cummins with a look of astonishment on his face. He leant sideways and whispered, 'I don't believe it. Bloody Pat O'Hara.'

Pat was called from the hallway outside and he walked into the hushed court with a look of bemusement on his face. He glanced across at Cummins as he made his way to the witness box, but Cummins looked away. He took the Bible in his right hand and took the oath. Dempsey raised himself to his feet and addressed the judge.

'I have no knowledge of the allegations being made against this witness and since he is not part of the prosecution case I will merely tender him for cross-examination.'

He sat down and Gerry rose slowly to his feet.

'Detective Sergeant, my client will say in evidence that you visited him in the cells at around 5.45 p.m. on the day of his arrest, is that true?'

Pat at first appeared surprised by the question but his eyes betrayed the swiftness of his thought.

'Yes, I did visit your client.'

'How many years are you in the Gardai?'

'Thirty years.'

'And you served some of that time in the murder squad, isn't that right?'

'Yes I did.'

'So you know all about the Treatment of Persons in Custody Regulations?'

'Yes, of course I do.'

'And you know that interviews are now recorded?'

'Yes, I am aware of that.'

'And that questioning of suspects is prohibited, except in the formal surroundings of the interview room where everything that transpires is videotaped?'

'Yes.'

'And it naturally follows that questioning of a suspect in the cell is not permitted.'

'I would agree, but I didn't question the suspect.'

'No, and he agrees with you in that regard. What then was the purpose of your visit?'

Pat turned to the judge. 'If I may explain, Judge. Three days earlier my partner, Detective Garda Nicola Murphy was shot and critically wounded when we tried to thwart a bank robbery.'

Gerry interjected. 'What has that got to do with anything, Sergeant?'

The judge rounded on Gerry. 'Let the witness finish,' she growled.

'Thank you very much, Judge. Garda Murphy was taken by ambulance to the accident and emergency department of St Vincent's Hospital. I actually met and spoke to Dr Barouche in the hospital and he assured me that he would do everything in his power to save her life. And I believe he did. Anyway, I greatly appreciated the efforts that he made and the kindness he showed me. That's why, when I heard he was in custody, I visited him in the cells and thanked him for what he had done.'

'Come now, Detective Sergeant, do you honestly expect the court to accept that?'

'It's the truth.'

'Had you taken any steps prior to his arrest to express your gratitude?'

'No I hadn't.'

'Called to the Accident and Emergency department perhaps?'

'No.'

'Or even sent the doctor a card?'

'No, this was the first opportunity I had.'

'Why do you say that? Sure you had four days.'

'Naturally I was devastated by the loss of my partner. But I had also killed a man and even though I had no choice in the circumstances, I was greatly troubled by what I had done, to such an extent that I visited my parish priest and discussed the matter with him.'

'I can well appreciate that. So, were you in the Garda station by chance?'

'No. My superintendent was concerned about my welfare and he told me to take some time off.'

'So you weren't actually on duty then.'

'No, I wasn't.'

'What were you doing there?'

'When I heard of the doctor's arrest I decided to go and see him.'

'Did you tell your superiors?'

Pat glanced down at Cummins and lowered his eyes. 'No I didn't. I honestly didn't think there was anything wrong with what I was doing.'

'But I still don't understand why you thought this was an appropriate opportunity to express your gratitude to Dr Barouche.'

'He was on my turf, so to speak. Yes, I knew he was a suspect, but he had shown me kindness and the least I could do was to return the compliment.'

'I see; you thought your visit might have a twofold effect. Firstly, it would allow you to express your sincere gratitude and secondly, seeing a familiar and friendly face might offer him some comfort.'

'Perhaps.'

'You were the first guard to arrive at the scene of the murder, were you not?'

'Yes, that's right.'

'A gruesome scene.'

'Yes, it was.'

'And you took a statement from a Mr Pender.'

'Yes, that's right.'

'So, to some extent you were involved in the investigation, weren't you?'

'To a very limited extent.'

'I wonder whether that is entirely correct, Detective Sergeant. Did you not suspect that my client was the killer?'

'He couldn't be excluded from our enquiries.'

'Come now, please answer the question.'

'Yes, I did suspect him.'

'Were you present when my client was stopped by your deceased colleague?'

'I was.'

'And what was all that about?'

Pat hesitated before answering. 'It was a subterfuge; we pretended that we were investigating a hit and run accident and Detective Garda Murphy asked him where he was on the Saturday night, the night of the murder.'

'So, even at that early stage, he was a suspect in your mind at least.'

'Yes, he was.'

'At that time had he been officially nominated as a suspect by your superiors?'

'No, I don't believe he had.'

'So, this was a frolic of your own.'

'I wouldn't call it a frolic; it was a hunch and Detective Garda Murphy and I investigated it.'

'Did you share your hunch with anyone else other than Detective Garda Murphy?'

'At that time, no. I advised my superiors of my suspicions in the following days.'

'Did you have any input into the decision to arrest Dr Barouche?'

'I was consulted, but I don't believe that my views ultimately influenced that decision.'

'And when you were consulted, what view did you express on the matter?'

'I expressed the view that there were reasonable grounds for an arrest.'

'Please, Detective Sergeant, let's not hide behind legalese. You believed my client was guilty, didn't you?'

'I don't agree with that proposition. I am a professional police officer. Yes, I agree that I pursued a hunch that your client might be the culprit, and yes, I tried to gather evidence against him, but had I turned up anything to indicate his innocence, I would have developed that also, so he could be eliminated from the list of suspects.'

'How many suspects were on your list?'

'I think there were over three hundred.'

'No, Detective Sergeant, on your own personal list.'

'Just your client. But other detectives were working around the clock dealing with the other suspects.'

'Did you attend any conferences?'

'No, I didn't.'

'Did you discuss the case with any of the other detectives to see what they might have turned up?'

'No.'

'It might appear to an observer that you were pursuing your own agenda.'

'I don't believe that is right.'

A sardonic grin crossed Gerry's face. 'Of course not; you already told us that if anything came to light that tended to exclude my client as a suspect, you would have pursued that.'

'Yes, that's my duty.'

'So, of course, when he was confronted with this non-existent hit and run accident and gave an alibi, and identified his alibi witness, you immediately visited her and took a statement from her.'

'No, we didn't.'

'But why not?'

Pat didn't answer the question immediately and appeared deep in thought. Eventually he answered. 'I don't know why we didn't do it. My colleague handed a report into the incident room and we assumed someone else would take care of it.'

'Forgive me for saying this, but it appears that you were only interested in establishing my client's guilt.'

'I don't agree with that.'

'Were you under some pressure?'

'What sort of pressure are you talking about?'

'You had broken the news to Mrs O'Shea, had you not?'

'Yes, I had.'

'And promised her that you would bring her son's killer to justice?'

'Yes.'

Gerry placed his finger to his lips and then stroked his chin.

'Tell me, Detective Sergeant, how do you think I became aware of that?'

'I presume it's somewhere in the statements.'

'No, that's the strange thing. Detective Sergeant, it's not. Nowhere in any of the statements is it disclosed that you made her that promise.'

'I'll take your word on that.'

'But my client's instructions are that you told him that when you saw him in the cells.'

'So?'

'How could he have known that you made Mrs O'Shea that promise unless you told him?'

'I don't know, but I can't remember saying it to him.'

'You are a member of the Emergency Response Unit, are you not?'

'Yes, that's right.'

'My client will say in evidence that you placed a Smith & Wesson revolver on the bunk when you came to the cell.'

'That's a lie.'

'Do you carry a Smith & Wesson revolver?'

'Yes, it's official issue.'

'So, how did my client know that unless you produced it?'

'I don't know, but I think it's common knowledge.'

'Did you know that my client had been an informant for the CIA?'

Pat was startled by the content and directness of the question. And he wasn't given much time to reflect on an answer.

'Please answer the question, it's either yes or no.'

'Yes, I did.'

'Did you have sight of a CIA file on him?'

Pat remained silent.

'Answer the question, yes or no,' Gerry pressed.

'Yes,' Pat replied hesitantly.

'Such files are held in the Security Branch at Garda Headquarters, isn't that right?'

'I believe so.'

'And are only shown to members on *a need to know basis?*'

'Yes, that's right.'

'My client's instructions are that you told him that you knew he was an informant.'

'That's not true,' Pat protested.

'And that you had seen a CIA file on him.'

'No, I absolutely deny that I said that to him.'

'And that unless he confessed to murdering Johnny O'Shea, you were personally going to let it be known around the mosque that he was a traitor and, as a result, he would be killed by extremists.'

Pat shook his head defiantly. 'That's complete and utter nonsense.'

'How does he know that you were aware he was an informant?'

'I don't know.'

'How does he know that there is a CIA file on him?'

'I have no idea.'

'How does he know that you saw a copy of that top secret file?'

'I don't know that either.'

The judge appeared deeply troubled and intervened.

'Detective Sergeant, that's a fair question and I would like your comment on it. You see, this man is going to give evidence about all this and apparently he is going to say that you told him you knew he was an informant because you had read a top secret file; do you understand that?'

'Yes, I understand.'

'And you are telling me that you didn't say that to him?'

'Yes, that's right.'

'But how could he have known that you had actually viewed that file unless you told him?'

'I don't recall telling him.'

'No, don't change your answer now. You said, and I have made a note of it, that the suggestion was complete and utter nonsense. And it would be a strange thing indeed if you went to see him merely to offer your gratitude for trying to save your colleague and then told him you had read in a CIA file that he was an informant.'

'Yes, I agree, but it didn't happen, Judge.'

'Well now, address the question: how does he know that you saw the file?'

'I honestly can't answer that question; perhaps it was an educated guess.'

The judge sat back and rubbed her brow.

'I see, thank you Detective Sergeant. I am sorry for interrupting. Please carry on with your questioning, Mr Hickey.'

'That's a lot of guesswork on his part, isn't it, Sergeant?'

'Perhaps, I only advance it as a possible explanation.'

'Like knowing you made a promise to Mrs O'Shea.'

'Yes.'

'And that you carried a Smith & Wesson revolver.'

'Yes.'

'And that you appeared convinced of his guilt and really believed it was him.'

'Yes, I see what you're driving at.'

'He is going to say that after your visit to the cell he was absolutely terrified and did as you told him and invented a short statement to prevent you from carrying out your threat.'

'I never told him to invent a statement.'

'No, because you were convinced he did it, you told him to confess to the detectives who were interviewing him.'

'That's not true,' Pat protested.

'I have no further questions,' Gerry declared and resumed his seat.

The judge glanced at the clock. 'It's nearly one o'clock, I will rise now until a quarter past two.'

Cummins and Brannigan sat together having lunch at a small circular table in the crowded Chancery Inn close to the Four Courts when Pat entered the bar. He glanced over towards them, but they looked away. He sat on a stool at the bar and felt like ordering a pint. The barman approached him.

'What can I get you?'

Pat hesitated. 'An Irish stew and a cup of black coffee please.'

He felt like he had done for years, isolated and alone. And his evidence hadn't gone down well and he knew it. In the far corner of the pub Gerry and Dermot were debating the morning's work.

'I think we have them over a barrel,' Dermot declared as he slurped his vegetable soup.

'For once I tend to agree with you, Dermot, the judge didn't seem convinced of O'Hara's account.'

'You can say that again, did you see the look on her face when O'Hara couldn't answer her questions? Game, set and match, me thinks.'

'Let's hope so. Barouche's girlfriend seems a pleasant young lady.'

'Yes, I feel sorry for her.'

'What do you mean?'

'Come on, Gerry, we both know the bastard did it.'

'Why do you say that?'

'Call it a gut feeling, but I never liked him one little bit. Shifty eyes.'

Gerry laughed. 'So everyone with shifty eyes is guilty of murder. I hope they never appoint you to the Bench.'

'That's not likely; I am in the wrong party anyway. But in all seriousness, Gerry, do you think that she knows her partner was going to bomb New York?'

'Somehow I doubt that.'

'Then I rest my case. And my bet is he would have gone ahead with it if he hadn't been arrested.'

'Perhaps.'

'So human life means nothing to him.'

'But that was different, it was political.'

Dermot frowned. 'Murdering the innocent is never political. Sure don't we know that from our own experience in this Godforsaken country?'

'Let's not get into that debate again,' Gerry said firmly.

'And to make matters worse he ratted on his mates. I tell you, I don't like him one little bit.'

'Is that so, Dermot? You don't seem to mind the colour of his money.'

'Work is work. Who's going to win the game on Sunday?'

twenty-three

That afternoon Mohamed Barouche was called to give evidence. He swore on the Koran, and testified in accordance with the instructions he had given his lawyers. He was clear, concise and confident in his answers as Gerry brought him through his evidence. When Gerry finished, Dempsey heaved his considerable bulk to his feet and began his cross-examination.

'Doctor, you are a highly intelligent man, are you not?'

'I don't know. I consider myself well educated, if that's what you mean.'

'No, Doctor, I mean intelligent.'

'Well, I can't really answer that question.'

'Perhaps even cunning.'

Barouche shook his head. 'Mr Dempsey, I am a practising Muslim, honesty and integrity are very important values that we strive to attain.'

Dempsey allowed himself a sardonic smile as he moved closer to the witness box.

'So that's why you decided to become involved in a conspiracy to slaughter innocent civilians in New York.'

Barouche appeared unhinged and hesitated.

'Please answer the question, Doctor,' Dempsey pressed Barouche.

'Yes, I had agreed to retaliate against the American administration for its policy in the Middle East and its unjustified attack on Islam.'

Dempsey waved his hand dismissively. 'Doctor, I am not interested in political speeches, or the rights or wrongs of American foreign policy. All I am interested in is establishing that you conspired with like minded people to bomb New York and slaughter innocent civilians.'

'Yes, it's true that I conspired with them, but I don't believe I had it in me to actually go through with it. I was younger then, and influenced by a lot of extremist talk.'

'But you didn't pull out of the operation because of moral pangs, you were effectively told to get lost by your fellow conspirators.'

'Yes, this is true.'

'Because you had betrayed the religious values so dearly held by your comrades.'

'I suppose you could say that.'

'And you resented them for it, did you not?'

'Yes, I suppose to some extent I did. I was confused.'

'To such an extent, that you betrayed them to the authorities.'

'Yes, this is true.'

'So, helping the CIA was really about revenge,' Dempsey said flatly.

'That is a very harsh word, sir.'

'Can you think of another word that reflects your motive at the time?'

Barouche thought for a moment. 'No, I can't.'

'And you didn't give information to the CIA to save innocent lives, but to extract revenge.'

'Yes, to some extent.'

'And to save your own skin.'

'I don't understand what you are getting at.'

'You were arrested in a gay nightclub, is that not correct?'

Gerry looked quizzically across at Dermot and frowned. Barouche hadn't mentioned this at the consultation.

'I didn't know it was a gay club. I was with some friends, other doctors from the hospital. We were relaxing after a hard day's work.'

Dempsey raised an eyebrow. 'And you had drugs in your possession.'

'Yes, I had a small amount of cannabis for my own use.'

'And if you were prosecuted, it would have caused you acute embarrassment in your community.'

'Yes, I suppose it would.'

'Because you would have been seen as a homosexual who also took drugs.'

'It's possible that some people might have taken that view, but it wasn't true.'

'So, after you were arrested, you struck a deal with the CIA whereby you would pass on information and in exchange you would avoid prosecution.'

'Yes, that's correct, sir.'

'And avoid embarrassment.'

'Yes, but I still don't see what you're driving at.'

'You see, Doctor, from that day on you deceived your brothers in arms, didn't you?'

'Of course. I hardly told them I had become an informant.'

'You lied to them and led them into a trap, like lambs to the slaughter.'

'Mmm.'

'And the lies came easily to you, didn't they?'

'Maybe they did.'

'Because they served your best interests at the time.'

'You could say that. I was in a very difficult position.'

'And you abandoned your cause, your beliefs, and even your friends merely to save your own skin.'

'I don't think it's as simple as that. I had my career as a doctor to consider.'

Dempsey smiled. 'I see, all right, Doctor, to save your skin and your job.'

Barouche lowered his head and didn't answer.

'So, you are a man capable of betraying everything that is dear to you, including the truth, to salvage your own selfish interests when it suits you.'

Barouche remained silent.

'Is that what you are doing here, Dr Barouche?'

'I don't understand.'

'Are you lying now in order to save your own skin and your career because you confessed to murder?'

'No, sir, I am not lying,' Barouche replied defiantly.

'You knew that the CIA had a file on you, isn't that right?'

'I didn't know that.'

'Do you honestly expect us to believe that a well-educated man like yourself wouldn't have known that a professional intelligence agency such as the CIA was bound to have a file on a prominent informant?'

'When you put it like that, I suppose they would.'

'There is no supposing about it, you knew they did.'

'Possibly I did, I didn't really think about it.'

'And you knew when you came to this country that they would have contacted our intelligence service and advised them of your activities.'

'I didn't know that for sure.'

'But common sense would have convinced you that they did.'

'Yes, possibly, but there again I had no difficulty in getting a work permit.'

'And when you became a suspect for this murder, was it not likely that the police would look into your background?'

'That's reasonable to conclude, yes.'

'So, Doctor, it is indeed a logical conclusion that Detective Sergeant O'Hara, being involved in that investigation, would have been aware of your background as an informant, is it not?'

'He told me he saw the file.'

'No, you guessed that, because common sense dictates that a thorough investigation would lead an experienced detective to investigate your past.'

'I knew it because he told me.'

'I suggest you knew it because it couldn't have been otherwise.'

'I understand what you are saying, sir.'

'In the same way you knew he carried a Smith & Wesson because it is a firearm that is known to be standard issue to members of the force.'

'I saw the gun, I saw it.'

'No, Doctor, you say you saw the gun. Sure, all you had to do was to look it up on the Internet and you would have discovered that Smith & Wesson are official issue.'

'I didn't check the Internet; I didn't need to.'

'You also knew from reading the Book of Evidence that Detective Sergeant O'Hara brought Mrs O'Shea to the morgue to identify her son's corpse, didn't you?'

'Yes, I saw that in his statement.'

'Would it be such a strange thing in those circumstances that he would promise a distraught mother that her son's murderer would be tracked down?'

'I suppose not.'

'And assure her that the police would do all in their power to solve the case?'

'Yes.'

'You see, Doctor, I have to suggest to you that you have cunningly invented a web of deceit based on educated guesswork dressed up as fact.'

Barouche leant forward and placed his hands on the brass rail of the witness stand.

'I have told the truth. The sergeant threatened me in the cell.'

'You must have been astonished that a police officer would behave in that way.'

'I certainly was.'

'That he would produce a firearm to you.'

'I was shocked.'

'And breach your anonymity as an informant.'

'Yes, I had been told my secret was safe.'

'Force you into making a false confession.'

'Yes.'

'By threatening to expose you as a traitor.'

'He put the fear of God into me.'

'To such an extent that you were prepared to admit to a murder you didn't commit, Doctor?'

Barouche pondered for a few minutes. 'I saw it as the lesser of two evils.'

'And when you were leaving the police station you must have been outraged by your treatment.'

'That's putting it mildly, sir.'

'Just look at that document for a moment.' Dempsey handed Barouche a copy of the custody record.

'Look at the end of the document and read the last entry.'

Barouche inspected it closely and then read from it: 'I asked the prisoner had he any complaints to make about the manner in which he was treated whilst he was in custody and he replied he hadn't.'

'Is there a signature immediately after that entry?'

'Yes, there is.'

'Whose signature is it, Doctor?'

'It's mine.'

'Can you explain how it is that you came to sign that, if you were treated as badly as you claim?'

'I just wanted to get out of the police station.'

'So, yet another lie, to get you out of the pickle you were in.'

'No, I felt that it was a waste of time telling them what happened, they were all in it together as far as I could tell.'

'And then you were brought to the Bridewell station.'

'Yes.'

'And you had a consultation with Mr Kenny your solicitor.'

'Yes, but it was brief and to the point.'

'You had seen him twice that day, had you not?'

'Yes, I believe so.'

'Once for twenty minutes before you were questioned.'

'Yes.'

'No doubt he advised you fully of your rights.'

'Yes, he did; he told me not to answer any questions.'

'Was he present later in the day at the identity parade?'

'Yes, he was.'

'And there is little or no doubt that he was acting in your best interests.'

'I felt I could trust him, if that's what you mean.'

'Indeed. So, naturally you told him that you had falsely confessed to a murder you hadn't committed because you had been threatened in the manner you now suggest.'

Barouche fidgeted nervously in the witness box without answering the question.

'Well, Doctor, did you tell him your story?'

'No, I didn't tell him at that time.'

'When did you first tell him the story?'

'A few weeks ago.'

'I see. Have you a reasonable explanation for hiding what you say is the truth from your own solicitor for so long?'

'I couldn't tell him I was an informant, and that was a crucial part of the story.'

'Story indeed. But you told us you trusted him.'

'It's much more complicated than that, sir.'

'Really, Doctor, or perhaps it's very simple. Perhaps it took you a little time to invent the lies that would save your skin and your career.'

'That's not right. I am telling the truth,' Barouche protested, as Dempsey sat down.

The judge listened intently to legal argument from both lawyers and reserved her decision on the admissibility of the statement until the following morning. Pat wandered across the deserted Round Hall towards the exit. Outside, Cummins was leaning against one of the granite columns drawing heavily on a cigarette. Pat stopped and looked at the dark evening sky as the heavy snow that had been forecast began to fall.

'Fancy a pint?' asked Cummins.

Pat turned to him and smiled. 'I thought you were mad at me.'

'I was bulling, but on reflection I suppose your heart was in the right place.'

'In that case I could murder a pint.'

They sat at the counter of the Chancery Inn waiting for their pints of Guinness to settle.

'Strange coincidence that,' Pat remarked.

'What?'

'Pender being murdered on the very day he was due to give evidence against Barouche.'

'Do you think it's more than a coincidence?'

'Well, it was very convenient for our doctor friend.'

'That fact hadn't escaped me, Pat, but the investigation team believe it was no more than an argument between two winos. Darren Walshe is about to be arrested for it, his prints are all over the knife.'

'I am sure they know what their doing.'

Cummins turned to Pat.

'You know that Brannigan is like a madman and he's going to put you on a disciplinary charge if the judge criticizes you in her judgment.'

'What's wrong with that bastard anyhow?' Pat asked.

'I don't know. He was always a bit of a loner and never really one of the lads,' Cummins replied.

'Do you reckon he's bent, or what?'

Cummins laughed. 'I don't know what he likes or dislikes, but rumour has it he was abused by a Christian Brother when he was in school, and that's what has him so bitter.'

'Is he married?'

'No, he lives alone in a Portobello.'

'Jack, I know you work with the guy, but he's as odd as two left feet and I can't stand his guts.'

Cummins sighed. 'I don't care what you say about him, he's a bloody good investigator and that's all that counts.'

Pat rubbed his eyes. 'Maybe it's time I quit anyway. I think I have had enough.'

Cummins took a gulp of his pint and savoured it for a few moments. He wiped the froth from his lips and turned to Pat.

'We had some fun in the old days though, didn't we?'

A broad grin crossed Pat's face. 'Do you remember that eejit who confessed to the Dollymount murder and claimed to the jury the only reason he confessed was because we slipped some truth serum into his tea?'

Cummins let out a raucous laugh. 'And your man with the stammer who handed a note to the cashier in the Bank of Ireland on Baggot Street, demanding that she hand over the takings. He had written it on the back of his dole card and left it after him.'

Pat laughed. 'I will never forget the look on his face when he arrived home and found us drinking his beer in the living room waiting on him.'

The two men fell into laughter and spent the rest of the evening swilling pints and recounting endless stories of their time in the force.

Mary and Barouche were huddled together on the cream leather settee in his apartment. Barouche pulled away as Mary kissed his earlobe.

'What's the matter with you, Mo?'

'What do you think?' he answered.

'There's no need for the sarcastic tone. I know you're worried about the case, but it's out of your hands now.'

'I can't stand all this waiting around.'

'Well, you have no choice. By the way, why were we not allowed into the courtroom today?'

'The lawyers said it was normal legal procedure.'

'And did you tell the judge that they forced you to sign that stupid statement?'

'Yes, of course I told her that.'

'And did she believe you?'

'How do I know?' he said angrily, as he sat forward and rested his head in his hands. Mary took hold of his shoulders and gently massaged his neck.

'Everything will be OK. Don't work yourself into a state.'

He pulled away and stood up. 'I am not getting into a state. You don't seem to understand the prejudice out there against people like me. I get it every day, in the supermarket, on the street, even at work.'

'Come on, Mo, aren't you exaggerating a little?'

'No, I am not,' he snapped. 'Why else do you think the police are out to get me?'

'I don't know, I never understood that.'

'Because of my religion, that's why. And the judge will be the same, I know she will.'

'I don't believe that for one minute. Look, let me make you a cup of herbal tea,' she said, as she stood up and took his hand in hers.

He pulled away. 'I don't want a cup of tea, or anything else from you,' he said harshly.

She wrapped her arms around his waist and held him tightly.

'Mo, don't be like this with me. I love you so much.'

She felt his body shake and then he placed his hands on her shoulders and held her at arm's length.

'That's the problem, Mary,' he snapped, as he looked down at her with tears in his eyes.

'I don't understand,' she pleaded with him.

He took her hand and sat her down on the settee. Somehow he seemed more relaxed and his anger had subsided.

'Mary, I'm really sorry. I love you with all my heart, but when I was sitting in court today a dreadful reality dawned on me.'

'What was that?'

'That I could be found guilty of something I didn't do.'

'That won't happen, Mo.'

'But it might happen, and if it does I will go to prison for a very long time.'

Mary looked down at his trembling hands. She looked into his eyes and saw sadness.

'I told you before I would wait for you, and I meant it.'

He slowly shook his head. 'I don't want you to do that for me. It's bad enough that my life will be ruined without dragging you down with me.'

'That's nonsense. I am nothing without you, and I will never leave you, no matter what happens.'

Barouche took her in his arms.

'I love you, Mary, and I don't ever want to leave you, but let's see what happens in the morning,' he whispered softly.

twenty-four

The following morning an air of anticipation hung in the air outside Court Two. The protesters could be heard chanting outside and the reporters had returned in numbers to hear the opening speech for the prosecution. Mrs O'Shea sat on a wooden bench with Pat by her side. Very little passed between them. She watched as Gerry walked through the crowds and strode confidently into the courtroom. A short time later Dempsey, shoulders hunched, followed him in. A garda then closed the doors and hung a sign. *No entry, hearing in camera.*

Barouche was already inside, sitting dispassionately in the dock. Cummins and Brannigan sat together at the back of the court, Cummins with his fingers crossed. An eerie silence prevailed as the judge delayed her entrance. After what seemed an eternity, her tipstaff emerged and commanded those present to rise as Judge Elisabeth O'Hanlon entered centre stage.

She put on her reading glasses, poured a glass of water and began reading from her written judgment. Her tone was so grave, that those present were gripped with a sense of foreboding.

'The case at hearing before me is one of the most horrific murder cases to be tried in this historic courtroom. A young man was murdered in a savage and depraved way. However, I cannot allow my natural revulsion for the killer, or my horror at what he did, influence me in my decision. As far as this issue is concerned, the onus is on the prosecution to satisfy me beyond reasonable doubt that the alleged confession was voluntary. I have heard the evidence of Dr Barouche and Detective Sergeant O'Hara. Their accounts conflict dramatically. On the one hand the accused gives a plausible account of his encounter with Detective Sergeant O'Hara. In particular I found it difficult to understand how the accused was aware that a CIA file was available to the investigating gardai and was actually viewed by the detective sergeant, unless, of course, this fact had been communicated to the doctor in the manner suggested by him. On the other hand, I find it inexplicable that the accused failed to disclose his considerable grievances to his solicitor when he saw him shortly after he signed the confession. There may well be an explanation for this glaring omission but none has been advanced to me. The accused has a dubious past, showing himself on occasions to be capable of calculated deceptions. However, I have to decide whether on this occasion he has raised a doubt in my mind concerning the prosecution case. If this were a civil case, where the standard of proof is on the balance of probabilities, I would have little hesitation in preferring the evidence of Detective Sergeant O'Hara. But the standard of proof we are dealing with here is much higher and I am left with a nagging doubt as to whether or not this confession was voluntary. In those circumstances I am left with no choice but to rule in favour of the defence, and exclude it from evidence.'

Barouche glanced anxiously at Dermot who gave him the thumbs up. Dempsey then addressed the judge.

'In the light of Your Lordship's considered judgment, the prosecution is unable to call any evidence to support its case against the accused. In those circumstances I reluctantly ask Your Lordship to direct the jury to find the accused not guilty.'

As the judge left the courtroom, Barouche walked over to Gerry and vigorously shook his hand. Outside, Mary stood alone and spotted him at the top of the steps. His smiling face said it all and she ran to him and the two embraced like long lost lovers.

On the far side of the hall Pat looked on in disgust. He quickly ushered Mrs O'Shea from the building, past the protesters who had yet to hear the news.

'What's going on, Pat?' she asked, with a bemused look on her face.

'I'm really sorry, Eleanor, but he got off on a technicality.'

She staggered, as her knees buckled beneath her. Pat took her firmly by the arm.

'Come on. I will explain everything to you over lunch.'

She looked into his eyes and froze. For a moment she felt anger welling up inside, and then a strange sense of relief. She was not alone; Pat was there to share her nightmare with her. She stood on her tiptoes and kissed him gently on the cheek.

'Thank you so much, Pat.'

He looked uncomfortable and blushed in a way she found attractive.

'For what?' he asked.

'For being you, Pat.'

Gerry joined Dermot and Patricia for a celebratory lunch at the Clarence Hotel. After lunch he phoned Emily with the news.

'Hi, I have some good news.'

'Don't bother, I already heard it on the lunchtime news,' she said angrily.

'I'm sorry, Emily, I should have phoned you, but Dermot brought us out for lunch.'

'You and who else?'

'Patricia.'

'I see,' she said frostily. 'Why are you ringing me?'

'I thought the two of us might go for dinner tonight.'

'I don't know, Gerry, I am really pissed off with you at the moment.'

'Don't be like that, we can go somewhere special.'

Emily hesitated. 'Oh, all right, will you book it, or will I?'

'I will, I'll be home at around eight.'

'Why so late, isn't the case finished?'

'I have some paperwork to tidy up in the office.'

'OK, see you later.'

Gerry strolled up Grafton Street, the fine buildings glowing in the late afternoon sunlight. Hoards of shoppers heaved their way past countless buskers and street performers. He rounded the corner into Johnston's Court, a narrow alley, and home to a number of exclusive jewellery stores. There he ran the gauntlet of ragged Romanian beggars sprawled in his path. Mothers held aloft their screaming babies, daring Gerry to ignore their plight. He walked through imposing iron gates and found himself in the sanctuary of Clarendon Street Church. Inside, a small number of elderly women prayed in silence. Gerry sat in a pew, bowed his head and clasped his hands tightly. As the smell of scented candles engulfed him, he closed his eyes and found himself sitting at a dining-room table, his kid sister kicking him on the shins under the table. His father chuckled to himself as he recounted yet again a joke, the one about the Negro who walked into the bar with a pig under his arm. And they all laughed, not at the joke, but because his father's chuckles were contagious. And, as he watched his mother's laughter lines dance around her sparkling blue eyes, he felt warm and secure. And under the canopy of his parents' love, he and his sister sheltered from the many vagaries of adolescence.

But life at home in Dalkey wasn't like that. He had been faithful to Emily from the very beginning, leaving aside a drunken one-night stand with a girl he picked up in a nightclub in Leeson Street. Patrick was a fantastic kid, but Gerry, immersed in his career, never seemed to have time to make those special moments for him.

And what the hell was going on with him now? He knew all about obsession from his work, as his clients were normally consumed by it. And with the lies they told, first to strangers, and eventually to themselves, reality inevitably became blurred and gave way to a carefully constructed fantasy world. Could this be happening to him? He would have to get help.

He left the church and found himself listening to a taxi driver yapping on about the gridlock and the leaking port tunnel. The taxi stopped at a pedestrian crossing as a statuesque girl wearing black boots, a short denim skirt and denim jacket strode confidently across the road. The taxi driver passed some obscene comment, and Gerry looked away.

And then he felt light-headed. Maybe the wine at lunch had gone to his head. He had the breakthrough he longed for and the briefs would soon be piling up on his desk. From now on it was a clear run to the winning post. And everything would be fine at home and he would be a good husband and father. His head became lighter as he was engulfed by a sense of euphoria. Then he felt the leather belt tighten around his neck.

'Go easy, Carmen, that really hurts.'

Lying face down with his hands tied behind his back, he felt her nylon-encased knee thrust down into the nape of his neck forcing his head deeper into the satin pillow.

twenty-five

The following morning Gerry stood back and admired his handiwork with more than a little satisfaction. The Harley Davidson motor bike stood proudly on the gravel driveway, gleaming in the afternoon sun. He went inside, donned his leathers, and told Emily that he was taking his pride and joy for a spin.

'Take care of yourself on that damn thing,' she cautioned, as the engine rumbled into life.

The road wound its way from Rathfarnham towards Ticknock, as the concrete maze of suburbia gave way to pine forests and babbling streams. Gerry pulled the bike into a lay-by, and surveyed the view. Far below, the City of Dublin hugged the coastline. The white sand of the crescent shaped Dollymount Strand glistened in the bright sunlight and, beyond, the cliffs of Howth Head rose steeply from the deep waters of Dublin Bay. On he went, following a narrow road that snaked higher and higher. He left the forests far below and crossed the peat bogs that carpeted the rolling hills. As the afternoon sun settled over the Blessington Lakes and the moorland grasses turned from green to burnt ochre, he couldn't but feel he was riding through some vast African veldt. At Sallygap, where four roads converged, he turned south-east into a verdant valley and let out the throttle. His bike tore across the tarmac, hugging sharp bends and leaping over humpback bridges. Then the road rose sharply again. Eventually he pulled his bike into a small lay-by cut into the craggy rock. He turned off the engine, removed his helmet and climbed a low stone wall. On the far side, the mountain fell away steeply. To his right, a waterfall cascaded over giant boulders and tumbled into an eerily dark loch hundreds of feet below.

The evening sky took on a pinkish hue as Gerry lay down on the grass, and surveyed the beauty that lay all around him. How life could change so quickly. The Sunday newspapers had covered the Barouche trial extensively and his name was everywhere. He had pulled off a major coup, and his was now a household name. Gerry Hickey, senior counsel *extraordinaire*. The rumble of an approaching motor bike interrupted his thoughts. A Yamaha, he guessed. The motor bike cut its engine just above where he lay. He glanced up and saw a tall man wearing leathers and a helmet. As the man approached, he took off his headgear and greeted Gerry.

'Good evening, Mr Hickey, lovely evening isn't it?'

'Hello, Detective Inspector, fancy meeting you up here,' Gerry said in a friendly tone to Brannigan.

'Nice bike you have there,' Brannigan commented, as he sat down on the grass next to Gerry.

'Thank you. It's my only vice. Is that a Yamaha you have?' Gerry asked.

Brannigan nodded. 'You know your bikes, Mr Hickey.'

Gerry gave a contented smile.

'Wallowing in all the glory, are we?' Brannigan quipped.

Gerry sensed hostility in Brannigan's tone. He looked at him intensely.

'I have a job to do and I don't take any pleasure in having a cut at you guys,' he replied.

Brannigan raised his hands defensively.

'I am sorry, Mr Hickey, I didn't mean it like that. That bastard O'Hara got what was coming to him. It's guys like you who keep us on the straight and narrow. I take my hat off to you.'

'That's very magnanimous of you, Detective Inspector.'

Brannigan shrugged his shoulders. 'It's really just a game, isn't it? And all's fair in love and war, that's what I say. As soon as the battle's done, it's better to bury the hatchet and move on.'

'Does O'Hara feel the same way?'

Brannigan sniffed the evening air. 'O'Hara is a strange fish; you'd never know what's going on in that head of his. He's obsessed with the job, breathes it night and day. I guess the poor bastard has nothing else to think about.'

Gerry glanced at the sky, eyes narrowed in thought.

'But we have our bikes, right?' he said.

'Right, and is there anything more thrilling than coming to a deserted place like this, opening the throttle and letting her rip?'

With that Brannigan stood up and brushed the grass from his trousers.

'No doubt we'll be doing battle again sometime soon,' Brannigan said.

Gerry smiled sardonically. 'No doubt we will, Detective Inspector.'

'I'll look forward to that, you're a challenging opponent,' Brannigan said, as he climbed the wall. 'And regardless who comes out on top, we'll have a pint afterwards.'

twenty-six

A shaft of morning light lay across the large oval table in the opulent boardroom of St Vincent's Hospital. Dr Alan Stanley, a suave consultant in his early fifties, impatiently tapped his Mont Blanc pen on the table. Several other members of the assembled board chatted enthusiastically about social trivia. The door burst open and Dr Rosemary O'Neill, a petite and graceful woman who looked younger than her forty-six years, apologized for her tardiness and sat opposite Dr Stanley. He called the meeting to order.

'Good morning, ladies and gentlemen, we have just one matter on the agenda and that's the future, if any, of Dr Barouche in this hospital. Has anybody any views?'

Professor Barry raised his hand. 'A point of order, is this not a matter for the Medical Council?'

Dr Stanley responded swiftly. 'They are only concerned with matters of malpractice. No malpractice is alleged here.'

'I see,' Professor Barry said apologetically. 'I just wanted to be sure we had jurisdiction to deal with the issue.'

'Well, has anyone any views on the matter?' Dr Stanley repeated.

The first to speak was Mr Martin Hannifan, a heart surgeon. He was a gruff man in his sixties renowned for his poor bedside manner and for possessing the hands of an artist.

'It seems to me that the man has to go,' he said tersely. 'The staff won't tolerate him in the hospital.'

Dr Stanley nodded approvingly and added, 'Whatever about the staff, Barouche's position dealing with the public in the Accident and Emergency Department is simply untenable.'

'It might solve the problem of the waiting lists.' Mr Hannifan's remark was greeted with laughter.

'So, we have to get rid of him then,' Dr Stanley declared.

There seemed to be general agreement until Dr O'Neill, her tone soft and measured, said, 'Barouche is an excellent doctor.'

'Yes, we all agree on that, but the man's been tried for murder,' Mr Hannifan said firmly.

'And acquitted,' Dr O'Neill responded quickly.

'On some technicality,' Dr Stanley countered.

'Do we know the basis of the judge's decision?' asked another consultant.

'Hold on here a minute, gentlemen. Are we here to re-try Dr Barouche?' Dr O'Neill asked.

'Of course not, Rosemary,' Dr Stanley replied patronizingly.

She glared at him, but remained calm.

'I must confess to having a limited knowledge of our criminal justice system, gentlemen, but I believe I am right in saying that every citizen enjoys the presumption of innocence,' she said flatly.

Mr Hannifan let out a sigh of exasperation. 'Let's get real here,' he said, aggressively.

Dr O'Neill carried on undeterred. 'Dr Barouche has been tried in the courts, found not guilty, and regardless what the media or anyone else thinks, he is entitled to take up his life where he left off.'

Mr Hannifan responded swiftly, 'A verdict of not guilty is not a positive finding of innocence. It merely means that the prosecution were unable to prove their case beyond reasonable doubt.'

'So he reverts to the position he was in before he was arrested, just like any one of us sitting around this table, presumed innocent of any wrongdoing.'

Hannifan shook his head defiantly. 'I understand your argument, Rosemary, but I don't think it's quite that simple,' he replied.

'Why not?'

'Dr Barouche has brought a great deal of adverse publicity on the hospital and the public simply won't tolerate his continued employment here.'

'So, Martin, why are we meeting at all? You have already made up your mind that Dr Barouche be exiled, simply because the mob demands it.'

There was silence around the table. Dr Stanley intervened and spoke in a conciliatory tone. 'Come on, Rosemary, we have a duty to our patients. How are they going to react to being treated by a killer?'

'And who says he's a killer?' she said, her voiced raised in exasperation.

'There is a perception—'

She cut across him. 'And if the media ran a story that you had AIDS, when there was absolutely no evidence that you had, would we be meeting here in your absence to destroy your career?'

'That's a different situation entirely. A simple blood test would determine whether I had AIDS or not,' he countered.

'But Dr Barouche doesn't have that luxury. How can he possibly prove his innocence?' Dr O'Neill replied.

'I don't know the answer to that question.'

'The answer is simple. He doesn't have to establish his innocence because he is entitled to the presumption of innocence. The state brought its case and lost. He remains entitled to that presumption and I'm certainly not going to take it away from him to satisfy some other agenda.'

Professor Barry intervened in an effort to take the heat out of the debate. 'What do our solicitors advise?'

Mr Hannifan flicked through a file in front of him.

'There's a lot of mumbo jumbo but the bottom line is he will have a cast iron case against us if we sack him. They suggest we buy him off.'

'That makes sense,' Dr Stanley replied.

Dr O'Neill began to shake with rage. She leant forward, placing her hands on the table and glared at her colleagues.

'Each and every one of us at this table have devoted our lives to curing the sick. It was my vocation in life, a childhood dream. I have absolutely no doubt, having worked with Dr Barouche, that it's a dream he shares. I have seen him holding the hand of the dying and watched him toil night and day trying to ease people's suffering. Whether I believe, or even suspect, that he is capable of murder is irrelevant. He was tried by due process, and each of us is bound by the verdict. He will not be bought off, he will fight us through the courts and, mark my words, gentlemen, he will win hands down.'

She sat back and folded her arms, her expression closed to further argument. After a long silence, Dr Stanley glanced around the table.

'Anyone else any strong views one way or the other?'

There was no response.

'Very well, we'll put it to a vote and get on with the real work. Can I have a show of hands?'

twenty-seven

Gerry sat nervously in the waiting room of the Andersen Clinic. Situated in the basement of a fine Georgian house on Fitzwilliam Square, the clinic was a small unit, and specialized in sexual problems. Gerry had, with some reluctance, discussed his problem with Father Malachy, a drinking companion in Davey Byrnes. Father Malachy had listened with interest to Gerry's dilemma and referred him to the clinic, which was used by clergymen who had been discovered to be sexually deviant. Gerry wasn't entirely sure what to expect. A receptionist opened the door and invited him to follow her down a dark corridor at the end of which was Dr Sarah Belton's office. Dr Belton was seated behind a tidy desk. She was unquestionably a beautiful woman. Her long dark hair was swept off her face and cascaded over her slender shoulders. Her eyes, as dark as black pearls, smouldered beneath her thick, but perfectly groomed eyebrows. She remained seated and gestured to Gerry to take the comfortable chair opposite her.

'I thought there might be a couch,' Gerry said, jokingly.

She gave him a half smile, then took a pen in her hand and began to scribble on a pad. She wore a grey tweed trouser suit and a white blouse. Gerry thought that she was no older than thirty-five, at a stretch, forty.

'Well, Mr Hickey, I am Dr Belton, but I prefer you to call me Sarah. And I will call you Gerry, if that's OK with you?'

Gerry nodded in agreement.

'Before we begin, I would like to get some background information on you.'

Gerry settled into his chair.

'Firstly, how old are you?' she asked.

'Forty,' Gerry replied.

'Are you married?'

'Yes.'

'For long?'

'Fifteen years.'

'Did you marry for love?'

Gerry was slightly taken aback by her directness. She cocked her head and raised an eyebrow, as she awaited his reply.

'Yes, very much so.'

'And are you still in love with your wife?'

'Yes, I am. She's the reason I'm here.'

Sarah nodded and smiled. 'Have you children?'

'Yes, a ten-year-old son.'

'Are you close to him?'

'I would like to think so. But with work I never seem to have enough time for him.'

'And your parents, are they alive?'

'No, my mother died eleven years ago after a long illness. My father died of a heart attack last year.'

'Did you love your mother?'

Gerry's eyes moistened. 'More than she ever knew.'

'Do you regret that?'

Gerry looked at her quizzically. She continued, 'That you never told her just how much you loved her.'

'I never really thought about that, but I suppose I do regret it.'

'And what about your father?'

Gerry sat back.

'I admired him a great deal. He was a respected GP and well-known rugby player in his day.'

She looked at him, and again cocked her head.

'No, I didn't love him,' he replied. 'We weren't close.'

'Siblings?'

'A younger sister, and before you ask, we are very close.'

She smiled. 'You learn quickly, Gerry.'

Gerry felt strange. He was used to asking the questions, not answering them, and he felt no resistance to Sarah's intrusive questions.

'And what is your work?'

'I am a senior counsel. I specialize in criminal law. It's pretty high pressure stuff.'

'Do you enjoy it?'

'I find it worthwhile and rewarding, but I wouldn't go as far as saying I enjoy it.'

'What do you not like about it?'

Gerry rubbed his brow and thought for a moment.

'The pressure, there is a lot of pressure.'

'What sort of pressure?'

'Clients place themselves in my hands; I am their only hope, their only protection against injustice, and that creates a burden of responsibility that occasionally I find overwhelming.'

'In what way?'

'I lose a lot of sleep thinking about my cases.'

Her eyes narrowed as she studied him closely.

'Is there more?'

'There are times I feel totally swamped by the whole thing, want to walk away and do something less demanding.'

'I see. Have you any financial problems?'

Gerry laughed. 'They never seem to leave me, but money or the lack of it never really bothers me.'

She stopped writing and placed her pen on the table.

'Would you like some tea or coffee?'

'Coffee please,' Gerry replied.

Sarah stood up and walked towards the door. Her trouser suit was unflattering, but he couldn't but follow her nubile body with his eyes as she left the room.

'So, Gerry,' she said, as she resumed her seat. 'What brings you here to see me?'

He hesitated as he felt her eyes upon him. He lowered his head and muttered, 'I think I have a serious sexual problem.'

She smiled. 'I kinda guessed that,' she said whimsically.

Gerry appeared startled. Was it that obvious? he thought.

Sarah continued, 'As you know, it's my area of expertise; therefore, it is reasonable to conclude that's why you came to see me.'

A look of relief crossed his face. 'Of course,' he remarked.

There was a moment's silence, and then Sarah threw her head back and ran her hands through her hair.

'Well, are you going to tell me what your problem is, or do I have to start guessing?' she asked.

'Sorry, I was distracted for a moment. I am spending a lot of time with an escort.'

'I see,' she replied. 'You're an attractive man, why do you feel the need to see a prostitute?'

Gerry hesitated and she leant forward and fixed him with a stare. 'We'll move along much quicker if you shed your embarrassment and answer my questions,' she said sternly.

He looked at her and took a deep breath. 'I like to be dominated by her.'

'In what way?'

'Physically.'

'And what about mentally?'

'Yes, I suppose I like that too.'

'Does she inflict pain on you?'

'Not so much pain, she just controls me, wears leather gear and ties me up, that sort of thing.' He was beginning to regret that he had come to the consultation.

'And is she good at it?'

Gerry appeared surprised by the question. 'Yes, she knows what she's doing, if that is what you mean.'

'Does she turn you on sexually?'

Gerry shook his head. 'Not really. We never have sex. She just roughs me up a bit and I feel light-headed, almost drunk.'

'And how long does that feeling last?'

'Only while I'm with her.'

'And after it's over, how do you feel?'

'Initially, when I first started seeing her, I felt embarrassed and ashamed. But now I look forward to seeing her again.'

'How often do you see … can we give her a name?'

'Carmen.'

'How often do you see Carmen, the prostitute?'

'Once, sometimes twice a week.'

'And how long have you been doing that?'

'A few weeks now.'

'And before you started seeing her, did you fantasize about leather-clad women beating you up?'

Gerry laughed. 'No, I didn't,' he replied indignantly.

'Are you sure about that?' she pressed.

'Yes I am sure. I enjoyed a perfectly normal sex life with my wife, nothing kinky at all,' he replied firmly.

'So how did you find yourself suddenly exploring your darker submissive side with Carmen?'

'It was purely by chance.'

She looked at him and stroked her chin with her fingers.

'Somehow I doubt that, Gerry.'

'No, it's the truth. I met her by pure chance on the street. When I first saw her I thought she was a beautiful woman, and that's why I went with her; she introduced the domination stuff.'

'Is it Carmen, or what she does to you?'

Gerry sat back. 'I like her a lot and after our sessions we often sit around drinking coffee and chatting about all sorts of things. She has had a very difficult life, but I'm sure you don't want to hear about that.'

Sarah shook her head.

'To answer your question, I see her because of the way she makes me feel during our sessions.'

'So, do you fantasize about other women controlling you in the same way?'

'Yes, I do.'

'Often?'

'Too frequently. It's beginning to get a grip of me, and that's why I decided to get help.'

'Do you feel addicted to it?'

Gerry nodded.

'Because when you are with this powerful woman you are no longer in control of your own destiny and all your responsibilities and worries are banished for a few hours,' Sarah declared.

'Exactly,' he said enthusiastically, as a small carriage clock on the cabinet chimed.

'And the more you allow your imagination to run wild, the less you feel you are in control of your own life.'

'Yes, that's exactly how I feel.'

She sat back in her chair and placed her pen on the desk.

'Well I think that's enough for today. Can you come and see me next week?'

Gerry nodded. As she stood up to show him to the door, he appeared reluctant to leave.'

'Have you a diagnosis yet?' he asked tentatively.

She gave him a broad grin. 'We'll discuss it further next week. Make an appointment with my secretary on your way out, and don't worry, I'm sure we will be able to sort you out.'

After he left, Sarah's receptionist came into her office.

'He was kind of cute. What's his problem?'

'Never mind, Karen,' Sarah replied sternly.

'But he is cute, isn't he?' Karen persisted.

Sarah seemed to ponder the question, then smiled. 'I suppose he is, in a boyish sort of way,' she replied.

twenty-eight

It was a fresh morning as Pat sauntered amongst the shoppers on Henry Street. In the distance, the Spire, a lofty, needle-shaped monument, glistened in the sunlight. The cityscape had changed dramatically over the previous few years. Cafés and bars encroached on to the streets where the young and the beautiful drank and ate alfresco. The faces had changed, too. The Eastern Europeans had arrived *en masse* to seek their fortune in the new land of milk and honey. And how they loved to work. The Chinese too, were everywhere. And the Africans, mainly Nigerians, idly hung around street corners, waiting patiently for their asylum applications to be rejected.

Pat loved the strange faces, the languages he didn't understand and the criminals he didn't recognize. He turned on to Moore Street, once the stomping ground of the city's Molly Malones, unlicensed street traders, selling anything from bananas to lighters, two for a pound. But they had vanished and the street had become a market-place for immigrants, where they could buy anything from stolen mobile phones to Afro haircuts. Amongst the hordes, Pat found a flower seller and bought two bunches of fresh daffodils, one for Nicola's grave and one for Mrs O'Shea, on whom he intended to call that afternoon. As he walked along Parnell Street an unmarked garda car pulled up beside him and the passenger window rolled down.

'Pat O'Hara, how are ye keeping, you old bollocks?'

Pat leant on the roof of the car. 'Mind your language, sonny, or I'll report you to the Garda Complaints Board,' he bellowed into the car.

'You bollocks, I love you, O'Hara.'

Pat laughed. 'What are you up to these days, Danny?'

'Still working vice. I heard the Barouche trial didn't go too well.'

'You could say that; we got ambushed by a smart ass bigwig.'

'Hickey.'

'Yes, do you know him?'

The detective looked at his colleague who was in the driver's seat. 'Do we know him?' he laughed. 'Sure, isn't he a regular customer of a Czech whore working out of a fancy apartment in Ballsbridge.'

'Is that a fact,' observed Pat.

'Want us to bust him?'

O'Hara shook his head. 'No thanks, Danny, not on my account anyhow. He was only doing his job.'

The detective laughed. 'We just might do it anyway for the craic, scare the living daylights out of him.'

Pat banged on the roof of the car. 'Get out of here before I bust you for parking on a double yellow line.'

After visiting Nicola's grave, Pat drove to Whitworth Road where he arrived unannounced. Mrs O'Shea seemed pleased to see him and surprised, if slightly embarrassed, when he produced the bunch of flowers. They sat in the front parlour sipping tea and chatting.

'Pat, what went wrong at the trial?' she asked eventually.

Pat shrugged his shoulders. 'He got off on a technicality; it wasn't the first time and unfortunately won't be the last time a killer walks free on some point of law dreamt up by his counsel.'

'So, is Mr Hickey to blame?'

'Eleanor, blame might be putting it a bit strongly.'

'What else can you call it?'

'I suppose he is responsible in so far as he raised the point. But he had to do it, that's his job.'

'But he's responsible for my son's killer walking free.'

Pat sighed heavily. 'Eleanor, you have to put it behind you, what's done is done.'

She shook her head defiantly. 'No, Pat, I can't let go that easy. I owe it to Johnny and I won't rest until someone pays for what happened to him.'

Pat studied her face closely. 'And exactly what do you mean by that?'

She looked away.

'Eleanor, I asked you what you meant.'

'Nothing, I just think someone should pay for it, that's all.'

'I have explained to you that Barouche has been acquitted; he can't be tried again.'

'I know that, Pat.'

'And officially the investigation has been re-opened and the Gardai are looking at other suspects.'

She became agitated. 'That's nonsense and you know it. He was the right man, you told me that yourself.'

'Yes I did, and I still believe it. And that's why you have to let go, and accept that you will never get justice.'

She glared at him and he saw a look that troubled him cross her face.

'I will get my own justice,' she said firmly.

'Eleanor, please don't consider doing anything stupid. You have suffered enough. If you don't let go, this whole thing will eat away at you forever.'

She looked at him through tearful eyes. 'Pat, I wish I could let go, but I can't.'

He leant forward. 'But you wouldn't do anything stupid, would you?'

'Like what?'

'I don't know, but I don't like the way you're talking about people paying for what happened.'

She lowered her head.

'Listen to me, Eleanor, I have been around a long time, investigated hundreds of cases, and I have never seen a victim's grief being cured by revenge. Revenge is for the mob, and believe me, it won't soften your tears.'

'Then what will?' she snapped.

'Preserving all the good memories you have of Johnny when he was alive, and getting on with your own life.'

'But what's left for me, Pat?'

Pat stood up and walked to the window and stared out at the neatly kept garden. He turned to her and decided to bare his soul.

'My wife took her own life ten years ago.'

A look of astonishment crossed her face. 'I'm sorry, I didn't know.'

'That's OK; I normally don't like to talk about it, but I want to now.' He sat back down opposite her and clasped his hands together.

'Her name was Mary, and I loved her from the day we met in the small pub in Ballybunnion. She was warm like a summer breeze, giddy like a child and full of joy. We married after a year and I was transferred to Dublin. She never liked the big smoke, hated the hours I worked. I was so caught up in the job I took my eye off the ball. And then she was gone. Consumed by a depression that crept up so quietly we never saw it till it was too late. We got help, the counsellors did their best, but it had eaten away her soul. Then one day I came home from work to find she had ended her nightmare. I blamed myself, for not loving her the way she deserved. For not being there when she needed me. Then I went off the rails. Drank day and night. I wanted to destroy myself and nearly did. Everything went wrong in the job and I felt the world was against me. I resented everything and everyone. And then one day I woke up and realized that life didn't have to be like that. I knew the last thing Mary would have wanted was for me to go the way she had gone.'

Pat wiped a tear from his eye, leant across and took Eleanor by the hand.

'Eleanor, would Johnny have wanted you to hide away for the rest of your life grieving over him?'

She looked at him warmly. 'I suppose not.'

He smiled. 'Well then, let's go out tonight, go to one of those fancy restaurants in town and wash away our demons with some fine wine. What do you say?'

She looked at him and hesitated. Then a slight glint entered her eyes.

'OK, Pat, but only on one condition.'

'And what's that?'

'We go Dutch.'

He laughed. 'No way, I thought we might go to an Italian.'

She laughed and slapped him on the chest. 'You big oaf,' she said.

He shrugged his shoulders. 'What did I do now?' he asked.

twenty-nine

Gerry sat in the back of a taxi on his way to see Darren Walshe at Cloverhill Prison. He opened the pale-pink envelope with trepidation. Emily and he had rowed the night before, and the letter was sitting on the kitchen table in the morning. It read.

Dear Gerry,

I am writing this letter because you never seem to have time for me these days and I simply don't know how else to express my feelings. I thought everything was OK between us over Christmas and I really enjoyed our skiing holiday. For once we were together as a family and it was lovely to see yourself and Patrick messing about in the snow. However, since we got back everything has gone so badly. I know you are under pressure at work, I know that financially things aren't great and you're doing your best to get us into the black, but there are more important things than your career. I don't know what's going on, whether you have met someone else or what, but you never seem to be at home and always have an excuse. You haven't come near me in our bed for weeks and, call it intuition, I know that something or someone else occupies your mind right now. I don't know what place you have gone to, but I know that Patrick and myself aren't welcome there. I have felt miserable over the last couple of months, unloved and unwanted. I don't know what has happened to you, but I want my old Gerry back, the Gerry who held me in his arms and told me that he would love me forever. Come back to me Gerry, wherever you are.

Love
Emily

Gerry placed the letter in the breast pocket of his jacket and stared vacantly out the window at the torrential rain. He met Dermot Kenny in the waiting area of the modern soulless prison. Plastic chairs screwed down to a linoleum floor, heavily barred windows and penetrating neon lights. Dermot thought Gerry appeared distracted, distant. After a short time a prison warder showed them into the consultation room where a wide vinyl-covered table separated them from Darren.

Darren had been granted bail on condition that he came up with an independent surety of €10,000. There was little hope of the likes of him finding a bails person to pledge that sort of money against him turning up for his trial, so he had remained in custody. Gerry thought he looked well for it, and marginally more presentable to a jury.

'Hello, Mr Hickey, I wish I could say it's nice to see you again, but it isn't,' Darren said drily.

Gerry gave him a half smile, and opened his barrister's notebook in a businesslike way. He looked at the papers on the table for a few moments and then sighed heavily.

'You're in a lot of trouble this time, Darren,' he said sombrely.

Darren's eyes flashed to Dermot and then settled on Gerry.

'I didn't do it, Mr Hickey,' he protested.

Gerry sat back and raised an eyebrow. 'Well, let's look at the evidence, shall we?' he responded coldly.

Darren shook his head violently. 'Did you hear me, or what? I said I didn't kill the guy, I don't want to hear the evidence.'

Dermot intervened. 'Calm down, Darren, we have to go through it with you, that's our job. You can tell us what your case is when Mr Hickey has finished.'

Darren leant back in his chair and folded his arms.

'Go on then, tell me the lies the pigs have come up with.'

'Well, the prosecution case is fairly straightforward,' Gerry began. 'Garda John Geraghty says that when he entered the alleyway he saw you standing over Pender's body with a knife in your right hand.'

'Lies,' Darren declared.

'What part of it is a lie?' Gerry asked.

'I was kneeling down, I was.'

'Standing or kneeling, were you holding a knife in your hand?'

'Yes I was, but it was my left hand.'

'He says he called on you to drop the knife, and you immediately ran out the far end of the alleyway.'

133

PATRICK MARRINAN

'That's fair enough; go on,' Darren replied.

'Why did you run?'

'Wouldn't you?' Darren snapped.

'Just tell me why you ran,' Gerry asked impatiently.

'I ran because I knew those pigs wouldn't believe a word I had to say, that's why.'

'Garda Geraghty states he chased you along Molesworth Street, and eventually caught up with you on Kildare Street, where he arrested you.'

'Yeah. Does he say I resisted arrest?'

'No, he doesn't.'

'That's fair enough. Go on.'

'The knife was forensically examined. It was covered in blood. The blood was DNA profiled and matches Pender's blood. What's more, your fingerprints were found on the handle of the knife.'

Darren became agitated. 'Sure, I just told you I dropped the knife.'

'Settle down, Darren,' Dermot intervened again. 'Mr Hickey is merely telling you what the prosecution case is.'

Darren nodded and Gerry continued, 'The knife was single-edged, seven inches in length and two inches at its widest point. The pathologist examined it, and in her view the knife is similar to the weapon used to inflict the fatal injury.'

'Of course it's the knife, didn't I take it from his back? But I didn't kill him.'

Gerry looked at Darren. 'Then who did?' he asked.

'How do I know, Mr Hickey?'

Darren pointed to the Book of Evidence, which was sitting on the desk between them.

'Did you read the statement I made to the pigs?'

Gerry shook his head. 'I didn't see any statement.'

'I made a statement to Brannigan, told him exactly what happened.'

'Are you sure about that, Darren? The guards say you were too drunk to be interviewed.'

'I told you I made a statement to that grease ball, signed it and everything, I did.'

'But it's not referred to in the Book of Evidence,' Gerry said with a puzzled look on his face.

'I told him I woke up and found Pender with a knife sticking out of his back, I pulled it out and then the pigs arrived. I told him I didn't kill him and he seemed to believe me.'

'That's all very interesting, but the jury will want to know why you ran away if you had nothing to hide,' Gerry remarked.

'Come on, Mr Hickey, give us a break here, will ya? You sound as though you already have me convicted. Why would I kill him, he was me mate?'

'And what about the evidence of the porter from the Salvation Army hostel?'

'What about it?'

'He says you and the deceased were put out of the hostel the night before for fighting, and when you were evicted he heard you roaring at Pender, "*I will kill you, you bastard, I will rip your guts out*".'

Darren rubbed his brow. 'I don't remember that, I was pissed out of me head. I never hurt anyone in my life. That's not my style, Mr Hickey, you know that.'

'But you don't deny saying it?'

'I can't deny it, but if I said it, I sure as hell didn't mean it.'

'And then there is the evidence of the ranger in St Stephen's Green. He says on the following afternoon he had to have strong words with both of you for fighting. He claims you were aggressive and abusive towards him and, more importantly, towards Pender.'

Darren laughed. 'That grumpy old bollocks was always giving us hassle. We were both pissed, that's the way we carry on everyday. It was just a bit of fun.'

'And around the time of the killing a passer-by claims to have heard someone shout *you miserable whore* and heard the sound of breaking glass.'

'I don't remember that, either.'

'And broken glass was found in the alleyway by the Gardai.'

Darren leant forward and buried his head in his hands. He then peered up at Gerry.

'What are you trying to tell me, Mr Hickey?'

'I am telling you that the case against you is very strong.'

'And my word counts for nothing? Is that it, Mr Hickey?'

'It's not what I think that counts; it's whether a jury will buy your story.'

'And a jury is hardly going to believe the word of a low-life scumbag like me, that's what you're telling me, isn't it?'

'We have to live in the real world, Darren. Can you think of anyone else who had a reason to kill Pender?'

Darren shook his head defiantly. 'Mr Hickey, I'm not going to plead guilty to something I didn't do. I want to fight this case all the way,' he said firmly.

'That's your entitlement and we will do the best we can for you in the circumstances.'

Darren looked Gerry in the eye. 'Do you believe me, Mr Hickey?'

Gerry averted his gaze, gathered his papers and stood up. 'It doesn't matter what I think, Darren, and it's not for me to judge you. I will see you at the trial next Monday – wear something smart in court.'

Dermot shook hands with Darren. 'Don't worry, we will do everything we can to help you,' he said reassuringly.

Darren looked at him and then glanced at Gerry who was already standing outside the consultation room.

'Sure, Mr Kenny,' Darren muttered, as he was led away by a prison warder.

As Gerry and Dermot walked through the car-park, Dermot turned to Gerry.

'You were a bit hard on him in there.'

'He hasn't a chance, you know that, Dermot.'

'Perhaps not, but he's not the worst. You could have been a little bit more sympathetic towards him.'

'I am his lawyer, not his nanny.' Gerry paused. 'You think Barouche killed Pender, don't you, Dermot?'

'It's a strong possibility, but I can't prove it.'

'How would he have known where to find him?'

'I don't know.'

'Did the guards even question him about it?'

'Nope. Detective Inspector Brannigan is in charge of the case and Darren was his only suspect.'

'Can you give me a lift to Fitzwilliam Square?' asked Gerry.

'No problem,' replied Dermot.

thirty

The Unicorn was a fashionable Italian restaurant close to St Stephens Green. Barouche's dark eyes glistened in the candlelight as Mary gazed across the table at her lover. He had received a letter from the hospital that morning, informing him that he was back on duty the following Monday, and the good news called for a celebration. Mary was conscious of the other patrons' eyes upon them, but shrugged off the unwanted interest. Barouche however appeared distracted as his eyes wandered around the restaurant.

After missing her period Mary had taken a pregnancy test which confirmed her suspicions. She had kept the good news from Barouche, as he appeared worried about his future in the hospital and the time didn't seem right. Tonight, however, she would break the news and felt confident that he would share her enthusiasm.

Then a waitress appeared at their table. She was young, not yet twenty-five, with olive skin and dark eyes that promised something forbidden. She held a notepad lightly in her slender fingers and smiled warmly at Mary as she took their order. When she had finished she repeated the order in a Polish accent, so soft and sexy that Mary at once despised her. She extended a slender bare arm and gathered the menus and the wine list, then took her perfectly formed body away. And Mary couldn't but notice Barouche's eyes follow her as she went, until Mary, consumed by jealousy, was forced to intervene.

'Here's to your return to work,' she said, as she clinked his glass.

'Thanks, Mary.'

'For what?'

'For the support you gave me throughout the trial.'

She smiled. 'You're more than welcome.'

Barouche had begun drinking heavily after the trial, which surprised Mary since alcohol was very much taboo for Muslims. He had also stopped attending the mosque. Mary didn't really understand the ins and outs of the Koran, but had always admired Barouche's devotion to his faith and his conservatism when it came to moral issues. It gave him solidity that she thought was sadly lacking in Irishmen of her generation. As he knocked back the glass of red wine and quickly replenished it, she felt slightly uncomfortable with this new departure.

'Are you looking forward to returning to work?' she asked.

Just then the waitress returned with the starters and Barouche's eyes were upon her.

'Sorry, what did you say?' he said, when the waitress had gone.

'I just wanted to know how you felt about going back to work.'

'I am a bit nervous. I don't really know what to expect.'

She reached across and placed her hand on his. 'Don't worry, Mo, I am sure everyone will be thrilled to see you back. You're a really popular guy.'

'Thanks, but my popularity might have dropped since the whole murder thing.'

'I don't think so. The other nurses have been very supportive of me throughout.'

'That's you,' he replied. 'It might be a different story with me.'

'You're wrong; everyone I spoke to believes you're innocent.'

He lowered his head. 'But there will be others who have doubts.'

'Well, you can't do anything about that, so stop worrying.'

He looked at her and smiled. 'You have some leave due to you, don't you?' he asked.

'Yes, what have you in mind?' There was a tone of anticipation in her voice.

'I think you should take a break, go on a holiday with your friends. You've gone through hell.'

'I wouldn't want to go anywhere without you,' she protested.

'I will be working flat out for the next few months, so we won't be seeing so much of each other. It's a good time to catch up with your friends.'

The waitress returned and, as Barouche handed her his plate, Mary thought she saw him give her a wink. She immediately stood up, dropping her napkin to the ground as she headed to the ladies. When she returned Barouche asked her was she OK. She nodded, but conversation was strained for the rest of the evening. Barouche seemed preoccupied with the lovely waitress and Mary began to feel plainer and frumpier as the evening wore on. She didn't deserve this, she thought. After all, she had stood by him in his darkest hour, at times nursed him like a child. And this was the thanks she got, ignored all night, told to take a holiday. Thoughts of telling him about the pregnancy evaporated as her face became flushed with anger and her narrow lips tightened. Eventually she declared herself unwell and suggested they leave. Barouche, giddy with the wine, seemed insensitive to her darkening mood. Outside the restaurant he held her close and tried to kiss her. He asked her what was wrong as she pulled away. She shrugged her shoulders, said it was that time of the month and that she was out of sorts. He asked her back to his apartment, no doubt to satisfy his inflamed libido, fuelled by fantasies of his Polish goddess. She politely declined; she wasn't going to be used in that way. On Merrion Row she hailed a taxi, wished him well on his return to work the following Monday. He appeared mystified and said he would ring her the next day. As the taxi pulled away she noticed him stagger off towards the clubs on Leeson Street.

At home she tossed and turned in her bed as a cold sweat ran down her back and a sense of panic engulfed her. She had dreamt the night before of Barouche holding her tightly when she broke the news. Of tears of joy flowing down his cheeks, then a proposal of marriage and the security of having him by her side forever. But the Polish goddess had put paid to that.

Perhaps she had overreacted, she thought. Perhaps it hadn't been the waitress at all; most men would have been mesmerized by her. More likely it was his heavy drinking and the easy abandonment of his faith. Mary's thoughts returned to the Round Hall in the Four Courts, as they often did since the trial. When she had sat alone on the wooden bench looking at the glass doors with the sign *in camera* posted outside. And how Barouche had refused to discuss what had happened in court in her absence. She thought of how she was prepared to give him a false alibi and how conveniently that had fallen into place for him. Her thoughts were swamped with doubts, about Barouche, about her own future and the future of the child she was carrying.

thirty-one

Gerry sat staring out the iron-barred window of the waiting room in the Andersen Clinic. Sarah popped her head around the door and gave him a warm smile. She looked different, her long hair caught up in a tight bun. As he followed her down to her consulting room he noticed her knee-length, black leather boots, tight black velvet skirt and white fitted blouse. She sat opposite him, legs crossed, her full red lips flirting with a gold pen she held in her slender fingers.

'If I ask you a question, will you be entirely honest with me in your reply?' Sarah asked eventually.

'Of course,' he replied, without blinking an eyelid.

'Have you seen Carmen since we last met?'

He couldn't disguise the smile, and it answered her question.

'More than once?' she continued.

'No, just the once. Is it against the rules?'

'Absolutely not. I want you to continue to see her for as long as you feel the need.'

Gerry looked somewhat bemused. 'Do you think that I *need* to see her?'

'Yes, I think you do. It's probable that Carmen is your mechanism of escape from what you perceive to be the undue burdens you carry in your daily life.'

'I see.'

'But in my view there is also a latent fetish streak within you that arouses you sexually. This is much more deep-rooted. Probably a throwback to childhood when you found comfort, even early arousal, in certain items of clothing that you have now become obsessed with.'

'I don't understand.'

'Say, as a teenager, the sight of a stiletto heel gave you your first erection, your subconscious mind will continue to associate a stiletto heel with sexual gratification. The more deep-rooted this becomes, the more likely it is that sex without the object becomes difficult.'

'Really.'

'In your case the fetish appears to be for leather, probably rooted in some early sexual experience.'

'OK, so what do I do about it?'

She sat back and regarded him closely. Then she leant forward placing her hands on the desktop.

'Let's cut to the chase, Gerry, is she boyish-looking?'

Gerry drew back in his chair. 'What are you getting at?'

'Never mind what I'm getting at, just answer my question,' Sarah snapped.

'Well, she's very tall, and fit. Androgynous is how I would describe her.'

'Have you ever fantasized that she was a man?'

Gerry shuffled nervously in his chair. 'Come on, Sarah, are you suggesting I am gay or something?'

'And would there be something wrong with that?'

Gerry thought for a moment. 'I suppose not, but I'm not gay. I can assure you of that.'

'Have you ever been with another man?'

'Absolutely not,' he said firmly.

'Or fantasized about being with another man?'

He shook his head. 'No, never.'

'Or been mildly attracted to another man?'

'No.'

She leant back in her chair and studied him closely.

'I don't believe you,' she said bluntly.

'Why not?'

'I ask the questions. Tell me, are you always this open and frank?'

'I thought it's what you wanted; absolute candour you said.'

'Yes, but I rarely find my patients so forthcoming.'

Gerry looked at her quizzically.

She continued, 'Most of my clients live in a world of deceit that they are very reluctant to divulge. With you it flows like wine from a bottle. You told me the last time that you loved your wife and you were here out of desperation to preserve your marriage.'

'Yes, that's right.'

'Have you ever told your wife about your fantasies?'

'No, I haven't.'

'Why not?'

'I'm terrified she will be repulsed.'

Sarah raised an eyebrow.

'What's wrong?' Gerry asked.

'Is what you have divulged to me in our sessions all that repulsive?'

'I don't know, you tell me.'

'It seems like a bit of innocent fun. Domination is now part of mainstream entertainment. There is hardly a movie out there without a tough heroine kicking male ass. It's natural for close partners to try to satisfy their partner's sexual fantasies.'

'Really?' he said with interest.

'Yes, unless, of course, there is something you're not telling me.'

'I have told you the truth.'

Sarah sat back in the chair tapping her pen on the desk.

'Gerry, I'm going to be very frank with you, and I don't want you to be offended.'

'OK, fire away.'

'I think your marriage is over and you know it.'

Gerry pondered what she said. 'Then why I am I here?' he asked.

'I'm not sure yet. Perhaps you're acting out some other fantasy.'

'What do you mean by that?'

She put down her pen and closed the file lying on the desk in front of her.

'We'll explore that the next time.'

Gerry leant forward and rested his hand on the desk.

'Sarah, have I done something to offend you?'

She appeared surprised by the question.

'Why do you say that?'

'You seem to have gone a bit frosty on me. Do you think I'm some sort of weirdo?'

She tossed her head back and let out a laugh. 'Not at all.'

'Are you sure about that?'

She smiled. 'Yes, I haven't diagnosed you as a weirdo, not yet anyhow.'

Gerry went to Donaghy and Nesbitts for a pint of the 'black stuff'. He soon found the company of some young barristers and regaled them with stories of stunning legal battles, most of which he claimed to have won. At midnight, half cut, he got a taxi home.

thirty-two

The light of a full moon cast cobwebs of shadows across the stone floor in Darren's tiny cell. He lay on his back gazing through iron bars at the blackness. Life had been one long nightmare for him, a trundle through grey city streets in an unending quest for drugs. He had met many people along the way, whom he had never really known. In and out of prison, it had been a continuous cycle.

Though the sea lay all around where he lived, he had rarely set eyes on it. Never lay on his back on the white sand of Dollymount Strand on a warm summer's day, or walked the Dublin mountains and listened to the music of its waterfalls. The fecking gear, that's all he had ever known.

But along the way he had found a soulmate and occasionally jumped with joy. His cheeks glistened with tears as Suzanne's angelic face ghosted into his imagination. She seemed to be beckoning him, then faded as quickly as she had appeared. Despair was second nature to him, instinctive. As he reached for the blade he had concealed in his shoe, he felt at ease, at peace with himself. And as he ran the blade across the vein on his wrist, he was engulfed by a sense of relief. It would soon be all over. As the blood left him, he began to feel light-headed, and recited a poem quietly to himself, about the lovers on some Greek pot he had learned in school. For once the words came easily to him, and were like music to his ears. Then he closed his eyes, and allowed himself a smile. This was his last trip, and no coming back.

The following Monday in a strangely quiet Court No 2 in the Round Hall, the case of the Director of Public Prosecutions v Darren Walshe was called with great ceremony by the registrar. Gerry announced to Mr Justice McBride that his client had passed away. Mr Kenneth McGovern SC appearing on behalf of the prosecution entered a *Nolle prosequi*. The judge passed no comment, but thanked the jurors for attending. Since there was no business for them, they were free to leave. As Gerry left the front bench, he stopped and looked at the empty dock. He glanced at Dermot and then hurried away.

thirty-three

Saturday night in the Accident and Emergency Department of St Vincent's hospital was the busiest night of the week and the bedlam and mayhem resembled that of a field hospital in some war-torn country. Barouche had been on duty since the night before and was due to knock off at six. However that afternoon there had been a serious road accident on the Stillorgan dual carriageway. Six people seriously injured, two of them critically. So Barouche had volunteered to stay on, and he spent most of the evening trying to resuscitate the elderly lady driver of one the vehicles. At nine he was slumped on a chair at the nurses' station. Denise Coughlan, a senior nurse, approached and placed a sympathetic hand on his shoulder.

'Doctor, you did great in there. I think you saved her life.'

Barouche looked up at her. 'She's still critical,' he replied, his face taut with stress.

'I think she's over the worst, she should pull through,' replied Denise.

'You think so?'

'Yes. Listen, you look wrecked, why don't you go home and get some rest?'

'I'm OK,' he said, shrugging off her concern.

'No, go on home,' she persisted. 'You're not supposed to be on duty tonight anyhow.'

Barouche shook his head defiantly. 'I want to stay; that lady could relapse at any moment.'

'If you won't go home, why don't you go over to the doctors' quarters and get some sleep? Bring your bleep with you, and we can page you if there is any deterioration in her condition.'

Barouche stretched out his arms and then stood up. 'OK, I'll go up to Radiology first; I want to have a word with Dr Williams about the X-rays.'

'OK, I know where you are if we need you.'

'Thanks, Denise.'

Mary rang Barouche's mobile phone, but there was no reply. She rang again, to no avail. She then phoned her friend who was working in A & E.

'Fidelma, I'm trying to contact Mo, is he there?'

'He was around earlier, but I haven't seen him for a couple of hours. I thought you two were going to *Riverdance* tonight.'

'Yes, we were, he was to collect me at eight, but he never showed up.'

'Mary, it's been crazy here all day; I know he's been working flat out.'

'Maybe, but he normally calls me if he's going to be late. He's never left me sitting twiddling my thumbs like this before.'

'Did you try the doctors' quarters?'

'Yes, but he's not there.'

'He's probably at home in bed; he looked exhausted when I last saw him.'

'Maybe. Look, if you see him tell him I am on the war path.'

thirty-four

On Sunday morning Jacinta Doyle was walking her black Labrador along the West Pier in Dun Loaghaire. The low sun was glaringly bright, as she squinted to watch the ferry slice through the still waters of Dublin Bay. When she approached the Victorian cast-iron bandstand, her dog became agitated and started barking. She pulled tightly on the leash, but he pulled against her and she was forced to release him. He bounded off, leash trailing behind him, and vanished into an opening in the granite wall that led to the rocky, seaward side of the pier. She called the dog several times, but he didn't respond. She followed and slid through the gap in the wall. On the far side she froze and then let out a loud scream that echoed eerily around Scotsman bay.

The naked body of a fair-haired young man entangled in seaweed was spread-eagled across a huge rock, a gaping wound across his neck, his head almost severed. His clothes and shoes were laid out neatly beside him.

An hour later, Cummins and Brannigan stood together outside a white tent that had been erected over the body, as the state pathologist conducted a preliminary examination of the corpse. The *locus delicti* was within fifty metres of a small public bathing area, which was also a well-known haunt for homosexuals. Here those too ashamed to leave their closets, sought the company of fellow gays who paraded around the area as soon as night fell. Cummins was overcome with a sense of foreboding.

The pathologist, wearing her white overalls, finished her examination and emerged from the tent.

'It's fairly straightforward, gentlemen,' she observed, in a businesslike way. 'A young male with his throat slashed from ear to ear. And cleanly if that's of any use to you.'

Cummins let out a heavy sigh. 'Any other injuries?' he asked tentatively. The pathologist shook her head. Cummins sighed with relief.

'But there is this,' she said, beckoning the two men to the entrance to the tent. 'Please stay there, gentlemen, we don't want any contamination, do we?'

Cummins and Brannigan remained outside as the pathologist gently turned the young man's head to one side.

'Oh Christ,' responded Cummins, as he observed a small bald patch behind the young man's right ear, from which hair had obviously been removed. He looked at Brannigan.

'It's the same one who did O'Shea.'

'Maybe not, Jack,' Brannigan said. 'It might be a copycat.'

Cummins shook his head wearily. 'We never released the details about the hair in the O'Shea case. Anyway, the only other similarity is the slit throat, a copycat would have severed a limb or two.'

Brannigan nodded in apparent agreement.

'What's the time of death, Doctor?' Cummins asked.

'Approximately one a.m., certainly not before midnight or later than two.'

'Thanks, Doctor, I'll talk to you later if I may.'

'Certainly, Superintendent. I should have finished the post-mortem by late afternoon.'

Cummins turned to Brannigan. 'Cordon off the pier, and get the scenes of crime boys to fine comb the entire area, the killer must have left something behind.'

The forensic examiners spent the morning looking for clues but unearthed nothing of obvious significance. Samples of rock, soil and gravel were carefully packaged in evidence bags and removed to the forensic science laboratory in Phoenix Park. As the morning wore on the search was extended to cover a greater area. Empty beer cans and bottles were collected, rubbish bins emptied. Anything that might throw up a clue closely examined.

What did become clear, from an examination of the pattern of blood splatters on the pier wall, was that the young man had been attacked close to where his body was found. And his clothes, which were not bloodstained, had been removed before the fatal injury was inflicted.

Cummins remained at the scene all morning, pacing up and down the pier praying for something, anything, to be unearthed.

*

Pat O'Hara rose from a disturbed sleep and sat bleary-eyed at a small kitchen table in his apartment. He reached for the empty whiskey bottle and chucked it in the bin. After three cups of black coffee he turned on the radio and set about cleaning up the untidy kitchen. Then he went to the bathroom, splashed his face with cold water and stared at himself in the mirror. He looked a mess. As he shaved, his ears pricked when he heard a newsflash on the radio. He walked into the kitchen and slumped on to a chair as the newscaster reported the chilly news.

Pat turned off the radio and sat at the table with tears in his eyes. Barouche had killed again, as he knew he would. He clenched his fist and thrust it down on to the centre of the table with such force that splinters flew in all directions. Had he not messed up the prosecution, Barouche would be in prison and the young man would still be alive.

Having downed a couple of whiskies he rang Cummins.

'Jack, it's Pat.'

'Hang on a second,' Cummins replied.

After a few minutes, Cummins continued, 'Sorry for keeping you. Brannigan was on my shoulder and there would be holy war if he thought I was talking to you.'

'To hell with Brannigan, is it our man?'

'Looks like it, Pat.'

'Was the body mutilated?'

'No, but he took the same souvenir, just as you said he would.'

'Can I come out there?'

Cummins responded quickly. 'Are you joking or what? Brannigan would have a seizure.'

'You're in charge, Jack, I want in on this one.'

'Can't be done, Pat, and you know that. Look, I'll ring you later and let you know if we turn up anything.'

'Are you going to take Barouche in?'

'Pat, you know we can't touch him unless we have something solid, especially after the last cock up.'

'He'll kill again, Jack, and you know it,' Pat protested.

'Maybe, but I can't do anything about it. I'll ring you later.'

Early that afternoon Cummins chaired a conference at Dun Loaghaire Garda Station. Brannigan, the local superintendent Tom Shortt, and a large number of detectives attended. The first task was to establish the last known whereabouts of the deceased, who had been identified as

149

Colin Hegarty. His mobile phone had been recovered and his call register showed he had phoned several friends on the Saturday night. All of them would have to be tracked down and interviewed. One of the numbers found in his phonebook was a gay help line, which confirmed Cummins's suspicions. Individuals known to the gardai who frequented the bathing area late at night would also have to be interviewed, in the hope that they may have seen something significant. After the conference Cummins and Brannigan strolled back down to the scene.

The day had remained dry, but a strong easterly wind was blowing off the Irish Sea. As they approached the pier, Cummins was sickened by the sight of hoards of onlookers, some taking photographs, gathered outside the taped off area.

'Noel, it never ceases to amaze me the morbid curiosity people have for murders.'

Brannigan shrugged his shoulders. 'I think if they saw it close up and personal the mystique might vanish,' he said drily.

Cummins took a deep breath of sea air and sighed heavily. 'This one is tricky, Noel.'

'Why do you say that?'

'Because you and I know that it's the same guy who murdered Johnny O'Shea.'

'Perhaps.'

Cummins stopped and turned to Brannigan. 'What do you mean *perhaps*? Sure isn't it another gay killing with a similar *modus operandi*? And hasn't he left his calling card?'

'It appears that way,' Brannigan said coolly, as they walked on.

'Jesus, Noel, you're a cautious bastard. But assuming for the moment I am right, we already have a prime suspect.'

'Jack, he was acquitted, or has that small detail escaped you?'

'He signed a confession, for heaven's sake.'

'And we all know how that came about. Your old friend O'Hara at his dirty tricks again.'

'You don't know that for sure. Anyway, even if Pat did lean on him a little, I can't see a suspect confessing to a murder he didn't commit.'

Brannigan stopped and looked at Cummins.

'That's nonsense, Jack. Look at the Birmingham Six and the Guildford Four. And we have had a few dodgy confessions in this jurisdiction too. I'm telling you, if we get bogged down with Barouche again, this investigation will go nowhere.'

'Maybe.'

'And I don't care what O'Hara or anyone else says, we keep an open mind on this one for the moment.'

'Come on, we have to check him out at least.'

Brannigan shook his head in disagreement. 'If we go snooping around Barouche his lawyers will be all over us like a plague of locusts.'

'Perhaps, but do me one favour.'

'What's that?'

'At least keep him at the back of your mind.'

'Sure, Jack, as long as you do too.'

Cummins nodded in agreement.

'I hope we get lucky on this one,' Cummins said, as they approached the scene. 'This bastard hasn't finished yet.'

Cummins strolled down the pier and cast his eye over the elegant yachts bobbing gently on their moorings. He stopped and admired the cast-iron Victorian bandstand, where once brass bands played to young families and couples, dressed in their best Sunday garb. Softer times, he thought. As the sun settled over the Dublin mountains and dusk fell, Detective Garda Kieran Doherty summoned Cummins and Brannigan to a grassy area just off the road and approximately a hundred meters from the *locus delicti*. The detective pointed to a short tyre track plainly left by a motor cycle. He knelt down and, using a pencil, pointed out certain features.

'As you can see this is a good imprint, and left here recently. The tyre has the unique thread of a Pirelli Diablo, which is relatively common to large touring bikes.'

'Any particular makes?' asked Brannigan.

'I'll check that out, but off the top of my head I would say BMW and Yamahas.'

'Anything else?' asked Cummins.

'Yes, the tyre has been damaged.'

Cummins knelt down and was guided by the detective's pencil. 'In this area you can see indentations that are inconsistent with the tyre pattern and probably caused by a nail or some other sharp object,' the detective said.

'If we get a match, can you tie it down?'

'Same as a fingerprint, Superintendent,' the detective replied enthusiastically. 'I'll get a cast done of it which should throw up some more unique characteristics.'

'Good man,' said Cummins, as he led Brannigan away by the arm. 'Come on, we're going to the morgue.'

At the morgue, the pathologist had finished her post-mortem and had already left. The clothes of the deceased had been carefully bagged and were on their way to the laboratory to be microscopically examined for any foreign fibres that may have been shed by the perpetrator's clothes.

Detective Garda Masterson, a fresh-faced detective with flaming red hair, had assisted the pathologist and bagged samples during the post-mortem. He was busy labelling the exhibits when Brannigan and Cummins approached.

'Anything of interest there?' enquired Brannigan.

'Unfortunately the nail scrapings didn't show anything even resembling blood or human tissue,' the detective replied.

'What about hair?' Cummins asked.

The detective shook his head. 'Just some natural material which I think is probably hide. We'll look more closely at it later.'

'That's not much use to us,' remarked Brannigan. 'Anything else?'

The detective smiled. 'We have this.'

The detective held aloft a small, see-through plastic evidence bag.

Cummins took it in his hand and examined it closely. 'Looks like an eyelash,' he observed.

'Got it in one,' the detective replied.

'How do you know it's foreign to the body?' Brannigan asked.

'Because the deceased is fair, this eyelash is dark.'

'Where was it found?' Cummins asked enthusiastically.

'Lying in blood inside the neck wound.'

'Probably fell from one of the examiners,' Brannigan cut in.

'Well, only two people went near the body before it was bagged, myself and the pathologist.'

'So?' Brannigan responded.

'It's not coated in mascara, so we can rule her out, and it sure as hell isn't mine,' he said, eyes raised towards his own hair.

Cummins rubbed his hands together gleefully. 'Good work, Masterson. Can you get a DNA done as soon as possible?'

'We'll have that done by the morning, Superintendent.'

At eight that evening a conference was held at Dun Loaghaire Garda Station and Cummins announced the possible breakthrough. After the conference he phoned Pat.

'Any news, Jack?' Pat asked, with an air of anticipation.

'We may have struck gold, an eyelash was found on the corpse and it's possibly the killer's.'

'Can you match the DNA against Barouche's?'

'That could be a problem,' Cummins said flatly.

'Why?'

'Because the blood samples taken from him during his first arrest have been destroyed.'

'What do you mean, destroyed?' Pat asked incredulously.

'That's the law, Pat. His solicitors wrote to us after the trial and asked us to confirm it was done.'

'Well, bring him in again, and get another sample.'

'We have no grounds to arrest him.'

'What do you mean, no grounds?' Pat said angrily. 'We know it's Barouche.'

'Look, Pat, we have been through this before. This time everything is going to be done by the book. Do I make myself clear?'

'OK, OK. Did they find anything else?'

'Tyre tracks in an area where we think the deceased may have been hanging around shortly before his death.'

'What type of vehicle?'

'A large motor cycle.'

'Do we know the make of the tyres?'

'Pirelli Diablo.'

'BMWs use them, don't they?'

'So I am told; we are having it checked out.'

'It's Barouche, Jack, you know it is.'

'You might be right, but at the moment we have very little to go on. You know we need a reasonable suspicion before we can bring him in.'

There was a long pause.

'OK, Jack, and thanks for keeping me up to date. Let me know if there are any more developments.'

thirty-five

'Mo, where the hell were you last night?' Mary roared into the phone.

Barouche sat up in the bed and rubbed his bleary eyes.

'What time is it, Mary?'

'It's past eleven. I want to know where you were last night,' she persisted.

'I was working.'

'No you weren't,' she snapped. 'I checked up on you.'

'What do you mean *you checked up on me*?'

'Let's just say I made some enquiries and you're lying to me.'

There was silence.

'Well, where were you? And don't lie to me.'

'I told you I was at work,' Barouche protested. 'And to be honest I don't particularly like your tone.'

'I don't give a shit whether you like it or not, tell me where you were. I have a right to know.'

'Look, Mary, I'm not going to be cross-examined like this by you or anyone else. You don't own me, and I don't have to explain myself to you.'

She hung up and Barouche angrily threw his mobile on to a chair beside the bed. He got up and went into the kitchen where he made himself a mug of coffee. He returned to the bedroom and lazily climbed back into bed. He leant across and glanced at his mobile phone. Fifteen missed calls. He checked his call register and they were all from Mary, the first at nine the previous night, and the last at five that morning. Just then his phone rang, *Mary calling* flashed on the screen. He pushed the reject button and turned off his mobile.

Mary looked across the table at her father who was reading the *Mail on Sunday*, or more likely studying the pictures of the scantly clad models. Though he had never shown any real interest in her life he had provided her with a good education, offered her encouragement when she needed it, and never once criticized her. Mary had a gut feeling that her father didn't approve of Mo, though he had said nothing negative to her about their relationship. Outwardly, he always welcomed Mo to the house. Her mother, on the other hand, thought it wonderful that her plain daughter had snared a doctor.

'Dad, can I talk to you?' Mary said, without thinking.

He laid his newspaper on the table, took off his reading glasses and glanced across at her. 'Is it important?' he asked.

She looked at him, hesitated, and her eyes moistened.

Without speaking he stood up, took his tweed jacket from the back of his chair and called to his wife, who was upstairs in bed.

'Anna, Mary and myself are going for a walk. We won't be long.' He glanced down at Mary. 'Come on, hurry up then.'

As they strolled along the banks of the Grand Canal her father threw crumbs of bread to the ducks. His pace was unhurried, almost idle.

'What's up with you?' he asked softly.

She had never really spoken to him about anything of importance, but his demeanour was sympathetic, almost encouraging.

'Dad, I don't know how to tell you this,' she said nervously.

And then she felt his warm hand holding hers, which he hadn't done since she was a child.

'Is it about you being pregnant and all that?' he asked casually.

She stopped in her tracks and looked up at him. 'How did you know?'

He gave a half laugh. 'Ah sure, don't I remember well your mother and her mood swings when she was carrying you? And the same flushed cheeks.'

A look of astonishment crossed Mary's face. 'But I don't understand, why didn't you say anything?'

'Well now, I didn't know for certain until you asked me if you could talk to me. I knew then all right.'

'And you don't mind?'

He shrugged his shoulders and smiled. 'Why would I mind? I don't have to rear the little devil.'

Mary's body shook as she laughed. Then she cried as she hugged her father. And his arms, wrapped around her trembling body, were strong and comforting.

'Have you told the Arab?' he asked.

'No.'

'And why not?'

She lowered her head and hesitated. He placed his hand gently under her chin, lifted her head and searched her eyes.

'You're not sure of him, are you?' he asked.

She shook her head.

'Is it because of the murder trial?'

She nodded.

'Do you think he killed those boys?'

A look of bewilderment crossed her face. 'What do you mean *boys*?'

'Mary, did you not hear, another one of those gay boys was found murdered this morning. They reckon it's the same guy who killed the O'Shea kid.'

Mary's knees buckled. Her father took her by the arm and guided her to a wooden bench overlooking the canal lock.

'Mary, are you all right? You look as if you're after seeing a ghost.'

She placed her head in her hands and began to sob. He held her and waited until she was ready to bare her soul. After some time she composed herself.

'Dad, last night Mo and I were supposed to go to *Riverdance* at the Point, but he never turned up. I rang him all night, but he wouldn't take my calls. I thought he might be with another woman; there's a gorgeous young doctor in the hospital and I saw them going into the Merrion Inn the other night. Anyway, I rang him this morning and he lied to me about where he was last night.'

'Where did he say he was?'

'At the hospital, but I know for certain he wasn't there.'

'That doesn't mean he was out killing someone, now does it?'

'I suppose not, but why did he lie to me then? He's changed since the trial. What's more, he stubbornly refuses to tell me what happened in court. I don't know what to do.'

'How has he changed?'

'He's drinking a lot and has stopped going to the mosque.'

'What else is troubling you?'

She hesitated. 'I think he used me to set up a false alibi for his trial, and did it very cleverly, like pretending he didn't want me to give evidence at all. I have this terrible feeling that he manipulated me. I can't put it into words, but I simply don't trust him any more.'

Her father stood up and walked to the canal bank where he threw the last of his crumbs to a swan that was brooding nearby. He then returned and sat beside Mary.

'Before I give you my opinion, I want you to know I am proud of you, Mary, always have been. And if you don't go off and leave us, it will be great having you and the baby around the house.'

A tear ran down her cheek as she squeezed his hand. 'Thanks, Dad.'

'As for the Arab, I don't believe he killed anyone. He seems a nice young man, looking after the sick and doing all that work for charity. And he's good to you; I noticed that, always considerate and gentlemanly. Call me old-fashioned, but that impressed me a lot. I know he's Muslim, but to be honest I don't really know much about those people. But I firmly believe it's better to have some religion, whatever it is, than none at all.'

Mary looked at him and smiled. He wasn't quite the bigot that she had presumed.

'Now, if I'm right and he didn't kill anyone, then he's been to hell and back. I can't even begin to imagine what it must be like to be tried for a crime I didn't commit, my picture splashed all over the papers. It's no wonder the poor man has turned to drink. And if he's not used to the gargle, it may explain why he's gone off the rails a wee bit.'

'But why did he lie to me?' Mary asked.

'Maybe he's covering up his drink problem. If I were you, I would sit him down and talk it through with him. Ask him out straight what went on in court and don't take no for an answer. My gut feeling tells me that if he had anything to hide he would have legged it after the trial.'

'But why do I feel this way, Dad?'

'Maybe it's the whole pregnancy business, you might not be thinking straight at the moment.'

'Maybe you have a point. Should I tell Mo I'm pregnant?'

'I think the man has a right to know, but tell him after you have spoken to him about the other stuff.'

Mary looked at her father and gave him a warm smile. 'Dad, thanks for all the help and support.'

'That's no problem, but can we leave your mother out of this for the moment? I'll handle her when all this settles down.'

Mary laughed, and gave him a huge hug.

thirty-six

Pat stood in the porch of Eleanor O'Shea's home as Mr O'Shea opened the door.

'What do you want?' O'Shea snapped.

Pat was taken aback by his rudeness. 'Is Eleanor there?' he asked.

'No, she's not. And even if she was, you're the last person she wants to see. Now clear off out of here.'

As he went to close the door, Pat heard the sound of sobbing coming from the kitchen. He placed his large foot between the door and the frame.

'I want to see her,' Pat demanded.

As O'Shea tried to block his path, Pat swatted him aside with the brush of an arm. Eleanor was sitting at the kitchen table, her head buried in her hands, her body trembling. Pat glanced around the room and spotted the broken Delft scattered across the floor.

'Eleanor, what's wrong?' he said softly.

There was no response.

'She is fine, now just get out of here and leave us alone,' O'Shea said firmly.

Pat looked around and glared down at him.

'I wasn't talking to you,' he growled.

As Pat approached Eleanor, she turned away. He knelt down beside her, and gently brushed the hair from her face. Her eyes were blood-shot and her left cheekbone was swollen. She held a bloodstained paper tissue to her nostrils.

'Pat, you had better go,' she whispered, her voice quivering.

Pat stroked her hair.

'Do as she says and get out of here, or I will call the gardai,' O'Shea shouted from the doorway.

Pat felt a sudden surge of rage and clenched his fists. He stood up and rumbled towards O'Shea, who retreated quickly. Pat stood over him as he cowered in the corner of the hall, arms raised defensively across his face. Pat opened the hall door, grabbed O'Shea by the collar of his shirt, and threw him into the front garden.

'If you so much as touch her again, I'll break your neck,' Pat roared.

He took a step towards Pat, whose response was swift as he rushed towards O'Shea like a charging rhino. O'Shea turned on his heels, scampered over the low hedge, and fled up Whitworth Road.

Pat returned to the kitchen and made some tea. He placed a cup on the table in front of Eleanor and sat down beside her.

'Are you OK?' he said, patting her cheek with a damp towel.

She winced, and then nodded. 'You get used to it,' she said softly.

'How long has it been going on?'

'A long time now.'

'Why didn't you tell me?'

She lowered her head. 'Pat, I'm terrified of him.'

'Not any more you're not, we will get a barring order against him in the morning.'

'He'll go crazy; he'll kill me.'

'Over my dead body. Where has he gone now?'

'Probably up to his brother's in Inchicore, why?'

'Give me the address, I'll go and have a quiet word with him.'

She looked at Pat and he smiled.

'Don't worry, I won't hurt the little bastard, but you'll find I have remarkable powers of persuasion.'

'OK, Pat. I don't know what I would do without you.'

He smiled. 'Are you feeling any better?'

'Not really. When I heard about the murder on the news it brought it all back. I know what that boy's parents must be going through. Is it Dr Barouche again? Did he do it?'

'That's what we think, but we have no evidence.'

Eleanor placed her hand on Pat's shoulder and looked him in the eye.

'Will you get him this time?'

Pat hesitated. 'Yes, this time I am going to nail the bastard to the cross.'

She smiled. 'Can you stay with me for a while? I can make you some dinner, you look tired.'

'I would like that very much.'

thirty-seven

On a sodden Tuesday morning Mary was sheltering under her umbrella at a bus stop close to her family home. When the car pulled up beside her and the driver leant across and opened the door, she recognized Detective Sergeant Pat O'Hara. She wasn't quite sure why she got into the car, or why she agreed to listen to him, but she did. He told her that Mo was a killer, and that she was in danger. When he told her about Mo's past and his activities in Montreal, she began to think it was all a terrible nightmare. The detective insisted that Mo would kill again, that he took souvenirs from his victims, locks of hair or something. She couldn't understand why she listened to his ramblings, or why she took his card with his mobile number and agreed to ring him if she discovered anything suspicious. She felt, when she left the car that she had in some way betrayed Mo.

Barouche phoned Mary that afternoon, told her he had something important to tell her and asked her to call around to his apartment that evening. She stood in the elevator, full of trepidation, not knowing what to expect. Was she to receive her marching orders? Of late Mo had turned into an inconsiderate drunk, who had treated her like dirt. Gone were the respect and the warmth he had heaped on her when they first met. But for reasons she found hard to fathom she still hoped he would revert to the old Mo.

The door opened and Barouche gave her a warm smile. He looked a mess, unshaven and gaunt. She followed him into the living room, where the lights were dimmed, and heavily scented candles sat around the fireplace. The music of Leonard Cohen added to her sense of foreboding. He gestured her to sit on the cream leather sofa, which she did. Old family photographs and what appeared to be personal letters were strewn across the glass coffee table in front of her. On the floor, a couple of cardboard boxes contained trinkets, and what appeared to be mementos of one sort or another. He offered her coffee, which she accepted, and then vanished into the kitchen. She leant forward and glanced through the photographs. Some were of his family: brothers and sisters, but most were of his mother, who had passed away three years previously. And there were some of Barouche and other young Arab men at a table in what appeared to be a restaurant. When she heard his approaching footsteps, she sat back on the sofa.

He glanced down at the photographs, then at Mary. He brushed them aside and placed a mug of coffee in their place. He then slumped into an armchair opposite her. There was nothing said and she felt his dark-brown eyes upon her, studying her closely. After what seemed an eternity, he sat back and wearily rubbed his eyes. Then he took a deep breath, sat forward, elbows resting on his knees. He looked at her with an intensity she had never seen before. For a moment she felt threatened, even frightened.

'Mary, I want to tell you the truth,' he said, in a sombre voice that sent a shiver down her spine.

She was unsure of what to say, so she merely nodded.

'I want to tell you everything about myself, absolutely everything.' He hesitated and then continued, 'This isn't easy for me, and when I am finished you will probably walk out of that door and I will never see you again.'

Mary's hands began to tremble, so she clasped them together tightly, in an effort to disguise her unease. He then told her about what had happened in Montreal and the full circumstances of the trial. She sat and listened patiently, but was unable to disguise her horror at what was unfolding. When he finished she looked deep into his eyes,

'Why didn't you tell me all this before now?'

'I was scared of losing you.'

She leant across the table and took his hands in hers.

'I'm glad you have eventually decided to tell me the truth. But why have you been acting so strangely recently?'

'It's the pressure, Mary. I wasn't sure how to tell you and needed time to work it all out in my head. When you kept asking me questions, it drove me further into my shell, and made telling you even more difficult.'

'Mo, we have been through so much together, and then suddenly you went all cold on me. I thought you were going to dump me.'

Mo held her hands firmly. 'Dump you? What gave you that idea?'

Mary lowered her head. 'Mo, I saw you.'

'What do you mean, *saw me*?'

'With Karen.'

'What are you talking about?'

'I saw you going into the Merrion Inn with her. What's going on between you two?'

Mary looked closely into his eyes, but he averted his gaze and shrugged off her question with a laugh.

'Don't be silly, there is nothing going on between us. I needed to talk to her about something and we went for a drink, that's all.'

'And last Saturday night.'

'What about it?'

'Were you with her?'

'I told you I was working. Ask Denise Coughlan. She will tell you I was in the hospital all night.'

Mo got up, walked to the window and stared out at the darkness. After a few minutes he turned and looked down at her with tears in his eyes.

'You still think I had something to do with the murders, don't you?'

She hesitated. 'No, Mo, I don't. I am more worried about Karen.'

He sat down beside her and put an arm around her. 'Do you mean that?'

She cocked her head to one side and smiled at him.

'I know you could never harm anyone, why do you think I stuck by you through all this? I love you, Mo.'

He let out a heavy sigh and smiled. 'Mary, you have no idea how much that means to me.'

'So what about Karen? You haven't answered my question.'

He turned away again and laughed. 'I need to know,' she persisted.

As he pulled away and vanished into the bedroom her suspicions deepened. He returned and sat back down beside her.

'I needed her advice about something.'

'About what?'

'About this,' he said, taking a tiny, black-leather box from his pocket. 'I wasn't sure if it was right.'

He handed her the box. She looked at him, his dark eyes sparkling in the candlelight.

'What is it?' she asked, her heart thumping.

'Open it and see.'

Her hands trembling, she opened the box, then gasped and placed a hand to her mouth. A two-carat diamond solitaire shone so brightly it dazzled her. He took her hand from her mouth and held it with both of his.

'Mary, will you marry me?'

She momentarily lost her breath, and tears flooded down her cheeks. She wrapped her arms tightly around his neck, and held on to him as though she never wanted to release him.

'Well, do you need time to think about it, or what?'

She laughed. 'Of course I will marry you.'

She placed the ring on her finger and watched the light dance as she moved her hand from side to side. Mo stood up and took his jacket from a chair.

'I have to go to the off licence to get some champagne, I'll be back in a few minutes,' he said, as he rushed out the door.

Mary sat back on the sofa, and kicked her legs in the air. She got up and walked into the hall where she posed in front of the mirror, inspecting the ring from every possible angle. When Mo returned, she would tell him of the pregnancy. She went back to the living room and sat down on the sofa, giggling to herself.

She wasn't sure why she noticed the small silver box sitting on the bookshelf, or why she was drawn to it. Neither was she sure why she opened it with such trepidation. But when she did, and saw the two locks of hair neatly tied in two bundles, she fainted and fell backwards on to the sofa.

The next thing she knew, was Mo kneeling beside her with a glass of water in his hand. He gently prised the box from her grasp.

'It came this morning,' he said calmly. 'I don't know what to do with it.'

She fought hard to find her breath. 'What do you mean, it came this morning?'

Mo stood up and retrieved an envelope from the bookshelf.

'It arrived in this morning's post. I don't know what it is, or what it's supposed to mean, there was no note with it.'

'But you must know what it is?' she asked incredulously.

He shook his head. 'I have absolutely no idea.'

She began to tremble and struggled for words. What the hell was going on?

'Are you OK?' he asked.

She took a deep breath. 'I'm fine,' she answered.

'Why did you pass out?'

'I don't know.'

He went to the kitchen, where he popped the champagne and returned with two glasses. Mary's mind was racing. She hadn't known about the locks of hair before Pat O'Hara told her. Was it just a coincidence that he told her that very day? Had he sent the box to Mo? Or was Mo the killer? She looked at him closely. He appeared unconcerned that she had found it. What was she going to say? As her mind raced in all directions she was again consumed by doubt.

'Mo, do you think that it might have something to do with the murder case?' she asked tentatively.

He shook his head. 'What could it possibly have to do with that?' he asked, with a bemused look on his face.

'I don't know,' she said. 'But maybe you should ring the solicitor and tell him about it, just in case.'

'OK, I'll ring him in the morning.'

'No, Mo, I think you should ring him right now,' she said firmly.

'At this hour?'

'Yes,' she insisted.

He regarded her closely. 'Mary, why are you so worried about this?'

'I'm not worried, but it's a very strange thing to get in the post, and in the circumstances I think you should tell your solicitor immediately.'

'It can wait until the morning,' he said dismissively.

'No, ring him now,' she snapped.

'OK, OK,' he said, reaching for his mobile. He checked his phone book and pressed the button. She watched as he waited.

'It's his voicemail,' he said, as he put away the phone. 'I will try him later or first thing in the morning.'

She drank some champagne and left saying she had an early shift the following day. She wasn't sure why she hadn't told Mo about her pregnancy, or why her initial elation had subsided so quickly. Even stranger, she didn't know why she failed to tell him about her earlier conversation with Pat O'Hara. But the sooner Mo contacted the solicitor the better, for her own piece of mind.

thirty-eight

It was late on Wednesday morning when Garda Tina Fanning, who was working in the Communication Room at Dun Laoghaire Garda Station, took the call on the Garda Confidential Line. The voice was muffled, and difficult to distinguish. In any event the message was brief and the caller quickly hung up. She scribbled the message on a pad.

The killer's souvenirs are to be found at apartment 17 Miltown Heights.

She tore out the page and placed it neatly on top of the other seventy-five tip-offs she had received that morning. At 1 p.m. she despatched the pile of messages up to the incident-room, where two sergeants and three gardai were working around the clock collating the various statements and information that had been gleaned by detectives doing the donkey work on the ground. A detailed report from the pathologist had also come in. Other than the fatal wound to the neck there were no other injuries. This was significant and the absence of defensive type injuries strongly suggested that the victim knew his attacker, or else was taken completely by surprise. The fact that his clothes had been removed before the attack also suggested the victim had stripped for consensual sex and was then murdered. The presence of his mobile phone and seventy euros in the pocket of his jeans ruled out robbery as a possible motive. A conference was held at four, and Cummins outlined the developments. The incident-room team had prepared a brief report on the confidential information that had come in from the public. Sergeant Marty O'Halloran delivered this to the meeting. First, there was a report that a man had been seen at 1 a.m. in a petrol station on the Rock Road at Booterstown. He drove a large motor cycle. When he paid for the petrol the Chinese attendant noticed what appeared to be blood on front of his leathers. Security footage covering the garage forecourt had been viewed, and the number of the bike noted. It was a Lithuanian-registered bike and enquiries were ongoing with Europol in order to identify the owner. In the meantime, the traffic corps were to stop the vehicle, if spotted, and interview the rider. The sergeant then detailed a number of crank calls, one of which identified a motor bike garda, who was known to the locals in the Dun Laoghaire area as *the enforcer*, as the culprit. This nugget of information was greeted with laughter.

'And then there is this,' the sergeant said inspecting a piece of paper. 'For what it's worth,' he added.

He then read Garda Tina Fanning's note.

Immediately Cummins reared up. 'When did that come in?' he barked.

'Sometime this morning,' the sergeant replied.

'For heaven's sake,' he snapped, as he stormed from the room with the piece of paper in his hand, Brannigan in tow.

In the superintendent's office he rummaged around the drawers until he found a block of standard form search warrants. He took one from the block and began to fill it in. Brannigan intervened.

'What the hell are you doing, Jack?'

'That's Barouche's address on the note. We are going to search it.'

'Steady on,' Brannigan cautioned. 'It's probably a hoax.'

'A hoax? Are you joking me, Noel, or what?'

'Take it easy, will you? You can't issue a warrant unless you have a reasonable suspicion. How can you base your suspicion on a one line statement from an unknown informant?'

Cummins looked at him, his face flushed. 'Do you not see the significance of this?'

'Not really.'

'Whoever rang in with this information knows four things: firstly they know Barouche's address; secondly, they know he is a suspect; thirdly, they know the O'Shea murder is linked to this one, and fourthly, they know that he took some hair from both bodies.'

Brannigan rubbed his forehead.

'But how could they know that?' he asked.

'They couldn't, Noel, that's the point. We never made public the fact that O'Shea's murderer took a souvenir.'

'But wasn't it in the pathologist's statement of evidence?'

'Yes it was, but she never gave evidence because the case collapsed.

The only people who knew what was in that report was us and the defence team.'

'I see,' Noel mused.

'And nobody knows that a similar souvenir was taken from Peter Hegarty, except, of course, the killer or, at the very least, someone very close to him.'

Brannigan raised an eyebrow. 'Or someone on the inside,' he added. 'What are you driving at, Noel?'

Brannigan rested his arm on a filing cabinet and inspected his nails. 'Jack, don't tell me that O'Hara hasn't spoken to you.'

Cummins sighed heavily. 'You really have it in for him, don't you?'

Brannigan shook his head. 'I know his form that's all, and I smell a rat.'

Cummins placed his hands on the table. 'OK, Noel, spell it out.'

"You told him about the eyelash, didn't you?'

'I might have.'

'And that we had no sample from Barouche to compare it with?'

Cummins nodded.

'And he wanted you to arrest him, but you told him we couldn't bring him in without a reasonable suspicion.'

'Yes, so what?'

'And fortuitously the reasonable suspicion lands in our laps from an unidentified source.'

'What are you getting at, Noel?'

'My bet is that O'Hara is the source of that information,' he said flatly, looking at the note that was lying on the desk in front of Cummins.

Cummins tapped his fingers on the desk. He took out his mobile and rang Pat.

'Hello,' Pat said.

'Pat, it's Jack. There has been a development and I need to talk to you urgently. Can you come to Dun Laoghaire Garda Station?'

'I'll be there in twenty minutes.'

Brannigan looked at Cummins. 'He'll deny everything,' he said.

Cummins shook his head. 'He won't lie to me. In the meantime, send a car out to Miltown, I want Barouche watched and bedded down for the night. If Pat's not involved in this, we move at dawn. In the meantime get everything ready. I want the same boys as last time to interview him, and I want the forensic department on standby to provide us with a DNA comparison as soon as we have a sample from Barouche.'

'Shouldn't we at least wait until you hear what O'Hara has to say?'

'Do it now,' barked Cummins.

Fifteen minutes later, Barouche was sitting in darkness on the balcony of his fourth-floor apartment. It had begun to drizzle, so he took his glass of wine from the small wooden table, and was about to move inside. His attention was drawn to a navy-blue Toyota Carolla as it quietly rolled into the car-park below. The car stopped and its lights were turned off. With the aid of a streetlamp Barouche could just about make out two figures sitting in the front seats. Neither got out of the car. He went inside and filled the dishwasher. After tidying the kitchen, he showered and returned to the living room in a dressing-gown and slippers. He went back to the balcony. The car and its occupants were still there.

Cummins shook hands with Pat as he entered the office, and gestured him to sit down. Cummins leant against the windowsill looking down at him.

'This is strictly off the record and goes no further. Is that clear?'

Pat nodded in agreement.

'Read that,' he said, pointing to the piece of paper sitting on the desk.

Pat read it and glanced up at Cummins.

'Pat, you and I go back a long way. We've been through the wars together and I regard you as a friend. I want to know if you have anything to do with this.'

Pat didn't answer and shuffled nervously in his chair.

'Well, did you?' Cummins pressed.

'Jesus, Jack, you're going to kill me.'

Cummins let out a sigh of exasperation. 'Pat, have you lost the plot completely? I never thought you could stoop to this level, regardless of how much you believed in this bastard's guilt.'

A look of bemusement crossed Pat's face. 'What do you mean?'

'Sending in confidential information,' Cummins snapped.

'I didn't send it in,' Pat protested.

'Then what did you do wrong?'

Pat took a deep breath. 'I picked up Barouche's girlfriend on Tuesday morning and gave her a good talking to. I told her all about his past, and how she was being used. I wasn't sure I got through to her but obviously I did,' he said, looking down at the note.

Cummins looked bewildered. 'You think she is the anonymous caller?'

'She must be. I told her about the hair being taken as a souvenir and to keep her eyes peeled. She must have found it.'

'Did you give her your number?'

'Yes.'

'Then why didn't she ring you?'

'Betraying him mustn't have been easy for her. I reckon she was too embarrassed.'

Pat felt Cummins's eyes upon him.

'You're not lying to me, are you?'

'On Nicola's grave, that's the truth.'

'That's good enough for me. We are going to lift Barouche in the morning, and I want you to take the day off. Do I make myself clear?'

Pat smiled. 'Crystal clear. Am I off the hook for this?'

Cummins laughed and waved an arm. 'Get out of here.'

When Pat had gone, Cummins sat down and filled out the search warrant. When he was finished, he called Brannigan into the room and handed it to him.

'It's over to you, Noel,' he said. 'And good luck.'

'Is O'Hara clean then?'

'I'm satisfied he didn't make the call and that's all you need to know. I am going home for some well-deserved sleep.'

thirty-nine

The following morning the gardai swooped in force, four cars and eight detectives. The first Barouche knew of it was when he answered the door to his apartment. Brannigan handed him the warrant as the other detectives brushed by him and into his home. Barouche protested, but was handcuffed by a detective and led into the living room where he was told to sit in a chair and shut up. The detectives immediately commenced a methodical search. Brannigan stood over Barouche with a supercilious grin on his face. Within minutes a detective searching the bookcase declared he had found what they were looking for. Brannigan placed the small silver box in a handkerchief and closely inspected the contents: two small locks of hair, each bound with what appeared to be darning thread. Brannigan looked at Barouche and told him to stand up. He then placed his hand on Barouche's shoulder.

'You are under arrest for the murder of Peter Hegarty.'

Barouche nodded. 'I want to contact my lawyer,' he said.

'You can do that down at the station.'

Barouche was brought to Pearse Street Garda Station where he was detained. Dermot Kenny was summoned and arrived in short time. He sat across a table from Barouche in a tiny consultation room.

'What have they got?' Dermot asked.

'I have no idea.' Barouche replied.

'Well they must have something. My advice to you is to refuse to answer their questions.'

Barouche shook his head. 'I have nothing to hide, Mr Kenny, I will tell them what they want to know.'

Dermot breathed a heavy sigh. 'We have been through all this before, and look what happened. This time say nothing, and don't sign anything.'

'With all due respect to your advice, I have nothing to hide and I will answer their questions. Can you tell Mary where I am? I don't want her hearing about it on the news.'

Dermot nodded.

'And I don't mind if the police want to interview her.'

'Are you sure about that?' Dermot asked.

'Very sure,' Barouche replied firmly.

Barouche was supplied with breakfast in his cell, but was unable to eat. At 9 a.m. he was brought from the cells to the medical room where a doctor introduced himself as Dr Zuharry. He proceeded to take a sample of blood from Barouche. The sample was then whisked off to the forensic science laboratory at Garda Headquarters in the Phoenix Park. Barouche was taken to the same interview room where he had been interviewed on his last visit to the station. Detective Sergeant McAllister and Detective Garda Coyne were sitting on the far side of the table when he entered the room.

'Hello, Doctor,' Detective Sergeant McAllister said. 'We meet again.'

Barouche looked both detectives in the eye. 'You have got the wrong man.'

McAllister raised an eyebrow.

'Well, you know the procedure. I am going to caution you and I have to advise you that the interview is being videotaped.'

Barouche nodded. 'Why am I here?' he asked.

McAllister smiled. 'We ask the questions,' he replied.

As McAllister started asking questions, Coyne was busy writing on a sheet of paper.

'Where were you last Saturday night?'

'I was working in the hospital.'

'Until what time?'

'I was there until the following morning.'

'So, you have witnesses who can verify you were there?'

'Yes, most of the staff on duty would have seen me at some time or another.'

'Whereabouts were you working?'

'In the A & E Department.'

'All night?'

'No, at around nine o'clock Nurse Coughlan suggested that I get some sleep. I was exhausted.'

'And did you?'

'Yes.'

'Where?'

'I went up to the Radiology Department on the first floor. I wanted to consult with Dr Williams, but he wasn't there.'

'Where did you go then?'

'I had a very sick patient downstairs and I was worried about her.'

'So you went back to the A & E?'

'No, when I was up in Radiology I lay down on a trolley and fell asleep.'

'Why didn't you go to the doctors' quarters?'

'I only intended to rest for a short time. I had my bleep with me and I told Nurse Coughlan to contact me if the patient's condition worsened.'

'And did she?'

'No, I understand her condition stabilized and I wasn't required.'

'How long did you remain in the Radiology Department?'

'I woke at five.'

'Where did you go then?'

'I went back down to A & E, checked on the patient, and then went home.'

McAllister sat back in his chair. 'What you're really telling me, is that from shortly after nine p.m. until five a.m. you were alone.'

'That's right.'

'And there are no witnesses who can verify where you were between those hours.'

'I suppose not; what time was the young man killed?'

'You tell us, Doctor,' McAllister said drily.

'I don't know anything about his death,' Barouche protested.

'Well, unfortunately for you he was murdered sometime between midnight and two a.m..'

Barouche frowned.

'The silver box that was found in your apartment, does it belong to you?'

'No, it doesn't.'

'Where did you get it?'

'It arrived in the post on Tuesday morning.'

McAllister smiled. 'What did you think when you saw the contents?'

'It contained some locks of hair; I had no idea what to make of it.'

'Come now, Doctor, did you not appreciate the significance of the package?'

'No, I had no idea.'

'Did you bring this strange event to anyone's attention?'

'Yes, I told my girlfriend.'

'And what did she make of it?'

'She thought it was highly suspicious, she wanted me to contact my solicitor.'

'And did you?'

'Yes, I rang him.'

'And what was his advice?'

'I didn't get to speak to him; I got through to his voicemail.'

'And did you leave a message?'

'No, I rang him the following morning. His secretary said he was in Naas doing a case and that he would phone me back.'

'And did he?'

'No.'

'So the only person who can verify your story about receiving this strange package in the post is your girlfriend.'

'Yes, but she will tell you all about it.'

'Like she provided you with an alibi in the last case.'

Barouche became agitated. 'What's this about?'

'You know full well.'

'I don't know. What has the hair got to do with anything?'

'Doctor, we believe the hair found in your apartment was taken from the scalps of Johnny O'Shea and Peter Hegarty.'

Barouche began to tremble.

'What's wrong, Doctor?'

'I don't believe this; it's like a nightmare. What the hell is going on?'

'You tell us.'

'I have nothing to tell you,' Barouche snapped.

'As we speak, the hair is being forensically examined in the laboratory. You appreciate that if we are right, you are in serious trouble?'

'I am being framed,' Barouche protested loudly. 'You're framing me for a crime I didn't commit.'

'And why would we do that?'

'I don't know, but someone is framing me. How did you know that the silver box was in my apartment?'

'We can't tell you that.'

Barouche buried his head in his hands and appeared deep in thought.

'The only person who knew it was there was Mary and she would never have told you.'

Just then the door of the interview-room opened and McAllister was called outside. Barouche looked at Coyne. 'I am being framed,' he protested.

Coyne shrugged his shoulders. 'Whatever you say, Doctor.'

McAllister returned to the room and sat down. Barouche felt the detective's eyes upon him, and shuffled nervously in his chair.

'Doctor, I have some bad news for you. The report is back from the lab and the hair found in your apartment matches the DNA profiles of the victims.'

Barouche stood up and placed his two hands on the table. He said something in a language the detectives thought was Arabic.

'Please sit down,' McAllister said pointing to the chair.

Barouche slumped back into his chair.

'Why did you kill him?' Coyne asked.

Barouche glared at him. 'I told you already that I didn't do it. Someone is framing me.'

McAllister changed the direction of the questioning.

'You own a large motor bike don't you?'

'Yes, a BMW, why?'

'Were you ever in the park at the entrance to Dun Laoghaire pier?'

'No, I was never near the place.'

'Are you sure about that?'

'Yes, I am positive.'

'Have you ever loaned anyone your bike?'

'No I wouldn't trust anyone with it. Why are you asking me this?'

'Where was your bike when you slept in the hospital?'

'In the multi-storey car-park.'

'And was it there the following morning?'

'Yes. Why are you asking me these questions?'

'That's enough for now. Detective Garda Coyne is now going to read over the notes of our interview with you.'

Detective Garda Coyne did just that. When he finished he asked Barouche if he agreed they were correct. Barouche nodded.

'Will you sign the notes?' Coyne asked.

Barouche shook his head. 'My solicitor told me to sign nothing.'

'Very well. We are going to sign the notes in your presence and then you will be taken back to your cell. You should think long and hard about your position. We will see you later.'

McAllister was called into the detective superintendent's office where Cummins and Brannigan were waiting for him.

'Any luck?' asked Brannigan.

'No, he claims to have received the silver box in the post.'

Brannigan laughed. 'A likely one; has he an alibi?'

'He says he was asleep at the hospital, but there are no witnesses to back up his story. Any word on the eyelash, so I can nail this down?'

Cummins looked at Brannigan and then back at McAllister.

'I'm afraid the eyelash is a bit of a red herring, the DNA profile doesn't match up with Barouche's.'

'That's unfortunate,' remarked McAllister. 'And the tyre tracks?'

Cummins shook his head. 'No match there either. But we have him with the hair, he's in trouble.'

'Will I ask him about Pender?' McAllister enquired.

'Why not, you never know what you might turn up,' Brannigan replied.

Later that morning McAllister and Coyne returned to the interview room where they went over the same ground. However Barouche stuck to his story.

'How can you explain the silver box?' McAllister asked again.

'I already told you. Listen, do you think for one moment that if I had killed those poor young men and kept what you call souvenirs, that I would leave them lying around my apartment?'

'Why not? You weren't expecting us.'

'That's where you're wrong, Detective. I knew I would be a suspect after the last time and it was only a matter of time until you came.'

McAllister appeared thrown by the answer.

'Did you kill Dan Pender?'

'What?' Barouche exclaimed. 'Who is Dan Pender?'

'He's the witness who found your watch at the scene.'

Barouche raised his arms in the air. 'Why would I kill the only witness who saw the murderer? Why would I kill the very man who could establish my innocence?'

'You claim to have been set up. Have you any idea who would want to frame you?'

Barouche looked them squarely in the eyes.

'It's the same one who framed me the last time: Pat O'Hara. He hates my guts.'

Later that afternoon Barouche, a blanket over his head, ran the gauntlet of press photographers who had descended on the Bridewell Courthouse. Inside the dilapidated district court, reporters were corralled in the press box. Mary sat, ashen-faced, in the public gallery, as the charge was read over to Barouche.

'For that you the said accused, did on the 15th April 2006 at Dun Laoghaire Pier in the Dublin Metropolitan District murder Peter Hegarty. Have you anything to say?'

'I am innocent,' Barouche protested.

He was remanded in custody and led away by the prison officers. Outside, Mary fought her way through the reporters. Suddenly she felt a firm hand take her by the arm, and she was bundled into the back of a car parked outside the gates.

'What's going on?' she asked the lone detective who was seated in the driver's seat.

'It's OK,' O'Hara said, as he clambered in beside her. 'I'll get you away from here.'

She tried to open the door, but it was locked.

'I don't want your help,' she protested. 'Let me out.'

'Calm down, Mary. That was a very brave thing you did.'

She looked at him in bemusement. 'What the hell are you talking about?'

Pat looked at her and smiled. 'Phoning the Confidential Line.'

She started to scream. 'What are you trying to do, you bastard? I didn't phone anybody. Why are you doing this to us? Why can't you leave us alone?'

O'Hara appeared thrown by her response.

'I thought after our talk the other day, you came to your senses.'

'No. Mo told me everything. He told me all about the goings on in Canada, and what you did to him the last time. Now let me out, you bastard,' she roared.

Pat instructed the driver to pull over, which he did, and she leapt from the car.

'I'm sorry,' Pat called after her, as she hailed a passing taxi.

forty

Pat visited the Eircell offices in Clonskeagh where an attractive blonde-haired woman, wearing a dark suit, approached him and introduced herself as Susan Collins, a line support manager in the Technical Operations Department. She brought him through her analysis of the telephone records of Barouche's mobile phone.

'First let's deal with the records of the mobile telephone number assigned to Mohamed Barouche. I have listed the calls made from this number on the 14, 15, 16, 17, and 18 of April. I have also identified the numbers that he phoned. There are several calls made to Mary O'Toole on the 17 April and several to St Vincent's Hospital during the entire period.'

'Are there any others?'

'Only one. On the 18 April at 9.30 a.m. he made a call which lasted three minutes twenty-three seconds.'

'Whose number is that?'

'The subscriber is Kenny and Company solicitors.'

'I see,' Pat said.

'There are no other significant calls, but he retrieved his voicemail messages on Sunday at 2.36 p.m.

'The first telephone number is assigned to Mary O'Toole. There are a total of ten calls made by her to Barouche between 8.30 p.m. on Saturday the 14 April and 3.30 a.m. on Sunday the 15 April. These calls vary in duration from three seconds to fifteen seconds. All the calls were diverted to voicemail. There is one call made at 9.03 p.m. on the Saturday night. That number is assigned to the account of one Fidelma Matthews.'

'That's very helpful, Ms Collins. So when is the first call that Barouche actually took from Mary O'Toole?'

'On the Sunday morning at 11.47 am, it lasted two minutes and thirteen seconds.'

'Any luck with the cell identification?'

She smiled. 'Of course, Sergeant. The GSM network consists of thirteen central exchanges; we call them MSCs, which is short for Mobile Switching Centres. These centres are connected to sixteen Base Station Controller Exchanges, or BSCs for short, and these in turn are connected to in excess of eight hundred base stations, which are dotted around the country. Each of these base stations covers a specific geographical area and essentially they provide coverage for most of the country. Once a mobile is switched on, it immediately sends out a signal that locates the nearest base station and once this is done, the phone is registered as being *attached*.'

Pat nodded indicating that he understood.

'What happens when someone makes a call?'

'Once a number is dialled into the handset and the send button is pushed a radio link is established with the caller's nearest base station. The caller's identity and the dialled number are transmitted to the base station, which then forwards the information to HLR, which is short for the Home Location Register. Here it automatically requests routing information, which will enable the network to contact the number dialled so that a connection can be made between both parties. If the person who is called has their mobile phone switched on, it will be attached to its nearest base station and the HLR will be able to locate it by sending a paging signal to all cell phones within its area. When the phone picks up this paging signal, it will ring, and if answered or diverted to voicemail, a connection will be made. Once this occurs a call data record is generated at a serving MSC station and is then automatically sent over a data link to a billing centre for processing.'

Pat rubbed his brow and looked somewhat bemused.

'What does all that mean?'

'There are three base stations that are relevant in your case. One is located in Drimnagh, one at RTE in Donnybrook, and one in Dun Loaghaire. The Donnybrook station has a radius of three miles in all directions, and St Vincent's Hospital is within its coverage. The Dun Loaghaire station has a similar radius and St Vincent's Hospital falls outside that radius. All the calls made by Mary O'Toole were transmitted to her base station in Drimnagh and forwarded through the Home Location Register, to the Donnybrook base station, which then paged Mr Barouche's number. The fact that the calls were then diverted to his voicemail means that when he received those calls Barouche was in a three-mile radius of Donnybrook station.'

Pat thought for a moment.

'So if Barouche says he was in St Vincent's Hospital between midnight and two o'clock, it would appear that he was there.'

Ms Collins shook her head. She picked up the list containing Mary's records.

'It means that between 8.30 that night and 3.30 the next morning his phone was within a three-mile radius of the Donnybrook base station.'

'Which gives him an alibi.'

'Not necessarily.'

'What do you mean?' Pat asked.

'His calls were all diverted to his voicemail. All that can be established from our data is that his phone wasn't outside the area during those times. Where he was is an entirely different matter.'

O'Hara stood up and thanked her for her co-operation. He then drove down Aylesbury Road in the direction of St Vincent's Hospital. A brief shower of rain had carpeted the tree-lined road with pale-pink cherry blossom. Spring was very much in the air. Having parked his car in the multi-storey car-park at St Vincent's Hospital, he made his way to the newly built reception area. He marvelled at the marble floor that lay beneath a vast atrium, and after obtaining directions from a porter he found a room that housed the security department. There he spoke to Daniel Murphy, who had been on duty the previous Saturday night/Sunday morning.

'Do you know Dr Barouche?' Pat asked.

'Doesn't everyone,' came the reply.

'Do you recall seeing him last Saturday night?'

Murphy shook his head.

'Would you remember if you saw him?'

'Not particularly, we never take much notice of the staff, it's strangers who stand out with us.'

'I can understand that. But he claims to have gone up to the Radiology Department at 9 p.m. and remained there until 5 a.m. Did you have any reason to inspect that area of the hospital between those times.'

'The department is closed after 6 p.m., I never have reason to go up there.'

'Is it locked?'

'The public don't have access, but hospital staff do.'

Pat asked Murphy to show him the area. They got the lift to the first floor and walked around a balcony that overlooked the reception area.

Then they proceeded through large double doors, into the Radiology Department. A small waiting area housed some chairs, and there were two trolleys up against a wall.

'Are trolleys normally left there?' Pat asked.

'No idea, sure aren't they scattered all over the hospital.'

Pat found Murphy's attitude unhelpful and he noted the smell of alcohol from his breath. He glanced up at the ceiling and noticed a wide-lens security camera.

'Does that work, or is it a dummy?' he said pointing to the camera.

'It's real, we have monitors downstairs in the security office.'

'Are they on a timer?'

'Yes, each area is checked automatically every thirty seconds.'

'I presume everything is recorded.'

Murphy nodded.

'Where are the tapes for last Saturday night?'

'Downstairs, you're lucky we only keep them for a week.'

Pat followed Murphy down to the security office and retrieved the tapes, which he signed for. He then drove to the technical bureau at Garda headquarters.

Mary sat on a hard wooden bench in the barren wasteland that was the visiting area of Cloverhill Prison. The noise of crying babies and their cackling mothers was deafening. Eventually she was shown into a small cubicle where Barouche sat on the far side of a vinyl topped table. He was strangely pale; his eyes sunken and the blue prison overalls two sizes too big for him. She felt overwhelmed by a deep sense of sadness, but bravely fought back the tears.

'How are you bearing up?' she asked.

He looked at her and smiled. 'Well, it's not the Four Seasons, and room service is slow, but I will get by.'

'Are they feeding you?'

'Yes, and it's not all that bad. I got a job in the library.'

'That's good, it will keep your mind occupied until the trial.'

He nodded.

'Have you seen the lawyers yet?' she asked.

'No, Mr Kenny phoned and said they will be out to see me early next week,' Barouche replied.

'That's good.'

'I need you to ring my father to tell him what's going on. He will have to send Mr Kenny some money.'

'Do you need me to help you out, I have some savings and my dad said he could borrow money from the credit union.'

Barouche smiled. 'Thanks Mary, and thank your father for me, but it won't be necessary.'

'We are all behind you, Mo, we know you didn't do it.'

'I really appreciate your vote of confidence, but will a jury believe me?'

'Of course they will.'

'I believe O'Hara sent that package to me. How else could they have known it was there?'

She hesitated. 'Do you really think he is capable of doing that?'

'Yes, I think he is obsessed with me. He must have gone crazy after the last trial, and now he is trying to frame me again.'

'Don't worry, your lawyers will expose him at the trial.'

'They did a good job the last time. I hope they can pull it off again.'

'Is there anything you need?'

He shook his head. 'You have given me the only thing I need.'

'What's that?'

'Your love.'

Mary felt her eyes welling up inside and shuffled off the seat.

As the huge steel gate slid back, she felt a warm breeze blow the hair from her face. She glanced up at wispy white clouds racing across the evening sky. She should have told Mo about O'Hara picking her up at the bus stop, she thought. Why had O'Hara thanked her for tipping off the Gardai? It made no sense if O'Hara was behind all this. As she sat in the back of the taxi, her mind raced back and forth. Every question bred another, until eventually she was swamped with doubts about almost everything.

forty-one

'What do you mean, the warrants are defective?' Cummins roared into the phone.

'They don't recite the statute that authorises the search,' Superintendent Tom Shortt replied.

'Why in God's name did you leave them in the draw of your desk then?' Cummins barked.

'I was going to destroy them, but I never got around to it. I forgot the damn things were there.'

'And how the hell was I to know they were faulty?'

'You never asked.'

There was a moment's silence.

'Look Tom, I'm sorry for raising my voice; it's not your fault, I should have checked the warrant myself.'

'What are you going to do?' asked Shortt.

'I haven't got a clue,' Cummins replied wearily.

Cummins summonsed Brannigan to his office, and told him to bring the search warrant with him. He stood at the window watching a Luas tram gliding up Harcourt Street. Brannigan, with the original warrant in his hand, entered the room.

'Jack, what's up?'

'Just give me the thing,' he said snatching the warrant from Brannigan's grasp.

Cummins sat down at his desk, put on his reading glasses and inspected the document closely. He then slumped back in his chair.

'I don't believe it,' he said under his breath.

'What's up?' Brannigan asked cautiously.

Cummins glanced up at him and handed him the warrant.

'I think it's defective.'

Brannigan examined the warrant. 'Is the deficiency fatal?' he asked gingerly.

'How do I know? I'm not a lawyer. If it is our case goes out the window. You had better get it over to the DPP and get his views on it.'

Brannigan, the warrant in hand, paced up and down the room in silence.

'Jack, is that such a wise move?' he eventually said.

'What do you mean?'

'We have another option.'

Cummins placed his hand to his mouth and sighed heavily.

'Noel, are you suggesting what I think you're suggesting?'

'Why not? We can't let this guy off the hook again. You could easily fill in another search warrant and no one will ever know.'

Cummins opened a drawer in his desk and took out a bottle of Bushmills whiskey and two glasses. Having poured two large ones, he handed one to Brannigan.

'Noel, I am going to forget what you just said. Now when you have knocked that back, bring the warrant over to the DPP's office.'

Brannigan knocked the glass back in one go.

'Jack, I'm sorry, I didn't really mean that.'

Cummins waved his arm towards the door. 'Just get out, I want to be alone.'

Pat sat in a small room in the technical bureau watching a monitor. The recording was in black and white and the quality poor. The screen flashed every ten seconds to different locations in the hospital. A digital clock at the bottom of the image recorded the time and date. At the recorded time of 9.20 p.m. Pat observed a figure pass under the camera located in the Radiology Department, but he could only make out the top of the head. The figure vanished into an adjacent room. Several minutes later the figure walked up and down the waiting area. He could make out that it was a man and he appeared to be wearing jeans and a dark sweater. Minutes later the camera returned to the area, and the man was perched against a trolley. The tape then switched to a different location. At 10.05 p.m. the screen returned to the radiology department and the same man was lying on the trolley, with his back to the camera.

O'Hara stopped the tape and went to make himself a cup of coffee. Shortly after he returned to the screen and made himself comfortable. He pushed the play button. The screen switched back and forth, but every time it returned to the Radiology Department the man was lying in the same position. O'Hara struggled to remain awake, but when the tape reached 5.06 a.m. the man sat up and appeared to inspect his watch. He then stood up quickly and walked under the camera. Again, all that was visible was the top of the man's head. Then suddenly the man glanced up at the camera, but almost immediately the screen moved to a different location. O'Hara stopped the tape, rewound it and played it again. The man sat up looked at his watch, walked towards the camera and glanced up. O'Hara rubbed his eyes. He was exhausted. He rewound the tape again but this time froze the image so he captured the face of the man looking up at the camera.

He pushed the eject button and placed the tape in a brown envelope and sealed it. He then turned off the lights and closed the door. In the corridor outside he glanced at his watch, it was 2.30 a.m. He drove along the winding coast road towards the fishing village of Howth. It was raining heavily and he felt mesmerized by the constant beat of the windscreen wipers. When he arrived at Howth harbour, he parked the car, took the brown envelope from the seat and sauntered down the rain swept pier. It was pitch dark and the place was deserted. The sea was choppy in a westerly wind and only the sound of fishing boats straining against their moorings or the odd clang of bells chiming high up on swaying masts distracted him from his thoughts. He reached the end of the pier and turned the collar of his trench coat against the wind and rain. His mind wandered back to the countless cases he had investigated: the murders, the rapes and the kidnappings. And the twisted faces of the perpetrators were there again. But this time the pleading faces of their victims made an appearance. Johnny O'Shea's face was there, alongside Darren Pender's and Peter Hegarty's. Were they trying to tell him something?

He looked down at the envelope he clasped in his left hand and sat on a low granite wall gazing across the sea towards Lambay Island. He took a naggin of whiskey from his coat pocket, slowly unscrewed the cap and slugged back a mouthful. He coughed and dragged the sleeve of his coat across his mouth. Why had he bothered, he thought. All those years wasted in the pursuit of evil men and women. Maybe he had got too close to them. Had he become one of them? Could there be any greater evil than the distortion of the truth? He placed his head in his hands and his huge frame began to shake as though with fever. Then he sobbed, uncontrollably.

forty-two

Carmen was sitting on her bed painting her long fingernails, when she heard a heavy thud on the hall door. She stood up, wrapped her pink dressing-gown around her lithe body, and walked into the hall. As she peered out the spy hole, she saw a tall man she didn't recognize as a client. Another thud startled her and she took a step back.

'Gardai, open the door,' the man roared.

Before she had time to pull the safety chain across the lock, she heard the sound of splintering wood and the door crashed in on top of her.

'What's going on?' she screamed, as the intruder thundered into the small hallway.

She was grabbed by the arm and forced into the sitting room, where she was unceremoniously thrown on to the sofa.

'Stay there, you stupid bitch,' he roared.

She went to stand up, but as she did he swung his arm and struck her across the face with the back of his hand. She slumped back on to the sofa and felt blood trickle from her mouth. She watched in horror as he ransacked the room, scattering her belongings in all directions. Eventually he pulled up the carpet and retrieved a small plastic folder that contained her passport, a large quantity of cash and her bank statement. He sat opposite her examining the documents.

'You've been a busy little girl,' he observed as he held up her deposit account statement, which showed a balance of 43,000 euros.

Carmen leapt forward and attempted to grab the documents from his hand, but he pulled away and laughed. She felt uneasy as his eyes wandered up her exposed legs and settled on her cleavage. Wrapping her dressing-gown tightly around herself, she folded her arms across her breasts.

'Don't worry, babes, I'm not going to touch you, you're not my type,' he said as he reached inside his tweed jacket. 'I'm more interested in this man,' he said as he handed her a photograph.

She glanced at the photograph of Gerry and shook her head.

'I don't know him.'

'Don't lie to me, we have had this place under surveillance for months and he's one of your regulars.'

A startled look crossed her face.

'Now, before I drive you to the airport and put you on the next flight back to Prague, I will ask you one last time. Do you know him?'

She wiped the blood from her mouth, and nodded.

'He told me his name was Gerry,' she muttered.

'And what's he into.'

She hesitated, but as the man gathered her passport, money and documents together she reluctantly answered.

'S and M.'

'Bondage and all that sort of stuff?' he asked.

She raised her head and looked at him. 'We talk a lot as well, he is a nice man.'

He let out a mocking laugh. 'I'm sure he is, babes, and a hefty wallet too, no doubt.'

She lowered her head again. 'He looks after me,' she muttered.

The man smiled, then scribbled a mobile number on a piece of paper and handed it to her.

'This is the story. Next time your pal Gerry rings, tell him your apartment was raided and you have to see him in the Herbert Park Hotel. Then phone me at that number and book a room in the hotel. Is that clear?'

A look of bemusement crossed her face.

'Why?'

'Don't ask why, just do as I tell you,' he said firmly.

She didn't answer him. He reached forward and grabbed her by the throat and lifted her to her feet. She felt his spittle as he roared into her face.

'It's your choice, babes. You can do what I tell you or else you leave the country with nothing but the clothes on your back. Do I make myself clear.'

'OK, I'll do it. Let me go, you're hurting me.'

He released his grip. 'Sorry about the mess,' he said as he walked out the door, taking her passport with him.

Later that afternoon Carmen received a call from Gerry looking for an appointment. She told him she would see him in the Herbert Park Hotel at 7 p.m. After the call Carmen paced up and down with the mobile in her hand. She opened her purse and took out the piece of paper given to her by the policeman. She hesitated before dialling the number.

'Hello, it's Carmen.'

'Hello, babes, have you any news for me?'

'Yes, he rang me.'

'Are you seeing him?'

'Yes.'

'When?'

'Seven o'clock tonight.'

'The Herbert Park Hotel, as I told you?'

'Yes.'

'OK babes; book a room under your own name. I will pick you up in your apartment at half six. Is that clear?'

'Yes. What are you going to do to him?'

'Never you mind. I'll see you at half six and give you your instructions then.'

Dermot Kenny and Gerry sat at the counter in the Porter House bar on Parliament Street. It was 4.30 p.m. and the traffic outside was already in gridlock.

'When can you see Barouche?' Dermot asked.

'Friday evening if that's all right with you.'

Dermot nodded. 'Have you read the papers?'

'From cover to cover.'

'Is he in trouble?'

'Maybe, but I don't like the look of the warrant.'

Dermot looked surprised. 'Is there a defect?'

'It doesn't state on the face of the warrant the statute authorizing the search.'

'So, the doctor strikes it lucky again,' Dermot quipped.

'I'm not so sure. Any news on who the judge is?'

'McBride.'

'He could swing either way.'

Dermot looked at Gerry. 'Have you no remorse?' he asked.

'Remorse for what?'

'If you hadn't done such a good job the last time, Peter Hegarty would still be alive.'

'Jesus, Dermot, why do all your clients enjoy the presumption of guilt?'

'I'm cynical by nature, can't help it.'

'If your clients only knew what you were saying behind their backs.'

Dermot laughed. 'That's why I have do-gooders like you in my stable.'

'I don't know about that. Look at Darren Walshe, I didn't do much for him.'

'Are you still beating yourself up over that? It wasn't your fault he committed suicide. He'd have gone that way eventually, all those druggies are the same, nothing to live for.'

'Dermot, don't be so hard. Those guys put you on the map.'

'That's about all they are good for, providing work for the likes of me.'

Gerry supped his pint and decided to change the direction of the conversation.

'Tell me, Dermot, do you not think there is something strange about this case?'

Dermot shook his head. 'The only thing odd about this case is that we are getting paid so much loot for doing so little. And on that very point, you will be glad to hear I got a banker's draft this morning from Barouche senior covering our fees. And there is a promise of a bonus if we get him off.'

'That's good news.'

'So, you can buy me another bloody pint, my glass is empty.'

forty-three

Gerry arrived by taxi at the Herbert Park Hotel. He rang Carmen on her mobile phone and she instructed him to come up to room number 312. He took the lift to the third floor and gently knocked on the door. Carmen opened it and stood in front of him, wearing a red leather jumpsuit, high-heeled black leather boots, and a black leather cap. Gerry felt a surge of excitement, which he fought.

'Carmen, I'm not here for that,' he said, looking over her shoulder at the rope lying across the bed.

She placed her hands on her hips. 'What are you here for then?' she asked incredulously.

'I wanted to say goodbye to you in person. I have to go away for a very long time.'

She cocked her head. 'What do you mean, go away? Where are you going?'

'Back to my wife and family,' he answered.

'Is that right,' she said, as she moved towards him.

Gerry pulled away. 'No, Carmen, I'm serious about this. I came to say goodbye. I know this is business for you, but I still respect you and consider you a friend.'

She studied him closely. Her blue eyes carried more than a hint of sadness. She closed them for a moment, as if soaking in his words. Then she threw back her head, laughed and looked at him mischievously. Grabbing his arm with purpose, she twisted it behind his back and forced him face down on the bed. He struggled, but before he knew it, his wrists were tightly bound together behind his back. She ripped open his shirt, and dragged his trousers to his ankles.

'Carmen, what are you doing?' he pleaded.

She ignored him, tied his ankles together and rolled him over on his back. He looked up at her and saw tears in her eyes.

'I'm really sorry, Gerry, I have to do this.'

'Do what?' Dismay was evident in his tone.

She took a small camera from her bag as he struggled violently to break free.

'No, Carmen, please don't do this.'

She ignored his plea and proceeded to take four photographs of him from different angles. Her body trembled as she hastily threw the camera in her bag and put on a full-length coat. Opening the door to the room, she stopped and turned.

'I'm really sorry,' she said. 'They forced me to do it; please believe me, I had no choice.'

And she was gone.

forty-four

'Pat, it's Cummins here, where have you been?'

'You told me to do some work on the alibi and the cell identification, I have been working full time on that.'

'Any luck with the phone records?' Cummins asked.

'No, nothing of any great significance,' Pat replied.

'What about the alibi?'

Pat hesitated. 'It doesn't stand up.'

'That's good news. We met prosecuting counsel and he is very upbeat about the case.'

'What about the warrant? I thought you were in some difficulty with it?'

'We are, but we might be able to find a way around it. Are you all right, Pat, you sound a bit down.'

'I'm tired, that's all.'

'Why don't you take some leave?'

'I just might do that. I'm glad the whole thing is coming to an end.'

'That makes two of us.'

'Jack, did Brannigan advise you against issuing the search warrant?'

'Yes, he did.'

'And did he blame me for providing the confidential information?'

'Yes, why do you ask?'

'Just curious that's all. He knew you would confront me with his concerns, didn't he?'

'Yes, but after I spoke with you, I put his mind at rest and he seemed happy enough.'

'That's what I guessed.'

'Why are you so concerned about it?'

'No reason; as I said I am just curious.'

As Gerry collected his post from his pigeonhole in the Law Library his hands began to shake. The unfamiliar white envelope, his name and address handwritten on the front, and sellotape across the flap, all spelt disaster. He looked furtively around the busy library, placed the envelope inside his jacket pocket and headed downstairs to the toilets.

He sat in a cubicle and, with trepidation, opened the envelope. It was as he suspected. Four photographs, and they weren't pretty. He felt a shiver run along his spine and then a hot flush. He started to sweat and thought he was going to pass out. A few deep breaths later he had settled himself. He looked inside the envelope for a note. How much was this going to cost him? he thought. He found a piece of paper and inspected it closely.

If Barouche walks, the press get these.

He turned the sheet over, but there was nothing written on the back. He read the note again, and rubbed his brow. What the hell was this all about? Having put the photographs back in the envelope, along with the note, he left the cubicle and wearily climbed the stairs back up to the library. As he reached the top he saw a group of young barristers huddled together gossiping. Something was said and they all laughed uproariously. He thought he saw one of them look in his direction and immediately avert his gaze. He left the library for fresh air. As he sauntered along the pavement, hands buried deep in his pockets, he didn't notice the throngs of tourists or the drizzle that had settled on the city. He'd assumed that Carmen had done the dirty on him for some mafia-type thugs and they were going to take him to the cleaners. But the note clearly indicated a different and more sinister motive. The prosecution knew their whole case depended on a dodgy warrant. Presumably the guards got to Carmen. Was O'Hara behind all this? What the hell was he going to do? He rang Sarah on his mobile.

'Hello, Gerry.' She sounded delighted to hear from him.

'Can you meet me for dinner tonight?'

'I could think of nothing nicer. What time and where?'

'Browne's on the Green, half past eight, is that OK?'

'I'm looking forward to it already,' she replied enthusiastically.

forty-five

Browne's on the Green was unusually quiet for a Thursday night. An elegant restaurant, with rich velvet furnishings, crisp white table cloths and sparkling chandeliers. Gerry was already on his third gin and tonic when Sarah was escorted to his table by the headwaiter.

She looked striking in a taupe cashmere dress that caressed every inch of her body. She slid into her chair, seductively crossed her legs and, with a sweep of her hand, brushed her thick, dark hair from her face.

'Nice to see you, Gerry.'

'And you, you look stunning.'

She threw him a coquettish smile. They ordered from the extensive menu. When the waiter departed, Sarah sensed Gerry's unease.

'What's wrong, have you bad news?'

He glanced furtively around the restaurant, leant forward and spoke in a half whisper.

'Sarah, I'm really sorry for bothering you with this, but I had no one else to turn to.'

'What is it?'

He took the white envelope from his pocket and passed her the photographs. She glanced at them and then put them face down on the table beside her.

'I thought you were going to give that up?' she asked, the disappointment palpable in her voice.

Gerry shook his head. 'It's not what you think, I called to see Carmen the other day because I decided to say goodbye; then she sprung this on me.'

'So what's it all about?'

'I'm being blackmailed.'

'By that lousy slut?' she replied angrily.

'No, I don't believe she had a choice in the matter. I think someone was leaning on her.'

'How much do they want?'

'It's not about money.'

'Then what?'

'I am defending Dr Barouche.'

She sat back and glared at him. 'That homophobic murderer, why are you defending him?'

'It's my job, I don't get to pick my clients.'

'So, what has that got to do with kinky photographs of you?'

'It's a high profile case and the gardai are determined to convict Barouche at all costs.'

'That's fair enough, that's their job too, but what's that got to do with this?'

'They have serious difficulties because they screwed up on the search warrant.'

'And?'

'I believe they are blackmailing me into throwing the case.'

A look of incredulity crossed Sarah's face. 'Jesus, Gerry, are you serious?'

'Very serious, and I don't know what to do.'

'If it is them, would they really send those photographs to the press?'

'The detective I suspect is behind all this is half mad. I have no doubt as soon as I raise the issue of the warrant, those pictures will be rolling off the presses of some tabloid newspaper.'

'Well, you have no choice then, throw the case,' she said firmly.

Gerry sat back, a look of astonishment on his angst-ridden face.

'Just like that? What about my duty to my client and my professional integrity?'

'Integrity my arse,' she snapped. 'Life is about survival. If those photographs are published you will be the laughing stock of the town; you'll be ruined, socially and professionally.'

'And if I throw the case, I will never be able to look myself in the mirror again.'

Sarah sighed heavily. 'Gerry, cop yourself on. You got yourself into this stupid mess, and there is only one way to extricate yourself from it; do as they say. Didn't he murder that young man anyway?'

'Yes, it certainly looks that way,' he conceded reluctantly.

'So, if he gets off on some technicality, he will probably go off and do it again.'

'There is that possibility.'

'To hell with him then, that's where he belongs. And to hell with your so-called professional integrity.'

'But …'

She leant across, and took his hand in hers.

'But nothing, you asked my advice and I'm telling you what to do. Is that clear?'

'Yes, Sarah, perfectly clear.'

As the waiter approached she picked up the photographs and slipped them into her handbag.

'Have you spoken to your wife recently?'

'About this?'

'No, about anything.'

He shook his head. 'I left a couple of messages for her to contact me, but she hasn't responded.'

'That's just as well. It's over between you two, and you have to accept that.'

'Do you really think we're finished?'

She winked at him and smiled. 'I know so,' she said as she ran her shoe along the inside of his calf.

forty-six

Gerry was staring out of the window of his office at the grey clouds rolling ominously over the city. Sarah's advice had been from the heart, but in truth his decision had already been made. The phone rang.

'You bastard,' a voice roared down the phone.

'Who is this?'

'It's your ex-wife, you creep,' Emily screamed.

'Hold on, Emily, what do you mean *ex-wife*? What's the matter?'

'What do you mean *what's the matter*? What could possibly be wrong with me?' she replied, her voice loaded with sarcasm.

'I don't know. I was going to ring you, we need to talk.'

She laughed. 'About what I have in my hand?'

'What are you talking about?' he asked in trepidation.

'These nice holiday snaps of you,' she said flatly.

There was a long silence as Gerry struggled for words.

'Emily, I can explain everything.'

She cut across him. 'You can explain it to my lawyer in court. I honestly don't know how you could do this to me. Whoever, or more accurately, whatever you have become, I want you to know I am going to make you pay for ruining my life.' She slammed down the phone.

Gerry hung his head and tears rolled down his cheeks. Why had the bastards done this to him? Why had they involved his wife? The phone rang again.

'A Detective Sergeant O'Hara is here to see you,' the receptionist said.

There was a long pause before Gerry replied, 'Send him up.'

He wiped the tears from his eyes, and took a few deep breaths. Pat rumbled into the room, with a bundle of papers under his arm. He looked down at Gerry, who remained seated behind his desk.

'Thank you for seeing me, Mr Hickey,' he said, as he placed the bundle of papers on the table.

Gerry glanced at the papers and then at Pat. 'What's this?' he snapped.

Pat placed his hands on the back of a chair and shifted towards it. 'May I sit down?' he asked.

Gerry glared at him. 'No, you may not. What have you left on my desk?'

Pat appeared taken aback by Gerry's aggression.

'They are some additional statements in the Barouche case.'

'Why didn't you serve them on my instructing solicitor? You have no business being here,' Gerry said firmly.

'I thought they were important. The trial is on Monday and I didn't want you to be at a disadvantage.'

Gerry laughed mockingly. 'Oh I'm sure you didn't. Now get out of here.'

Pat took a step back towards the door, then stopped.

'You will read those statements, won't you? They are important.'

'What evidence have you fabricated now?' Gerry replied.

Pat shook his head dismissively. 'I'm sorry you have that attitude, Mr Hickey, but I urge you to read those statements.' He turned to leave, but hesitated again. 'And one other thing, it's not for me to tell you how to run your case, but it might be in everyone's interest if you didn't raise the issue of the defective search warrant.'

Gerry placed his hands on the table and hauled himself to his feet. 'Detective Sergeant, I think you have already made that pretty clear. Now get out of my office, you blackmailer,' he roared, as he pointed to the door.

Pat shrugged his shoulders, looked mystified and left. Gerry paced up and down his office seething with anger. How blatant O'Hara had been, he thought. The cheek of the man. Eventually he sat down, settled himself, and commenced reading the additional evidence.

Later that evening, heavy rain was beating down on the flat roof of the consultation room in Cloverhill Prison. Barouche sat on the far side of the table from Gerry, Dermot and Patricia Quinn, the junior counsel in the case.

'All set for the big trial on Monday, Doctor?' Gerry asked.

Barouche appeared unimpressed at his lawyer's cheerful demeanour.

'I didn't do it, Mr Hickey, you have to believe me,' he said firmly.

'Oh, I believe you,' Gerry answered without hesitation.

Dermot glanced at Gerry, a bemused look on his face. What was he up to?

'I am glad, Mr Hickey, it is important to me that you believe right is on your side. Can you persuade a jury that I have been framed?'

'Well, I'll certainly give it my best shot. Your fiancée wants to meet us to discuss your case. Have you any objections to us seeing her?' Gerry asked.

'She has been a great support to me and I don't want to hide anything from her this time. You can tell her everything.'

Dermot nodded and scribbled a note of what Barouche had said. Gerry sat back on his chair and folded his arms.

'Well, Doctor, you know the procedure by now. Have you any questions?'

Barouche leant forward. 'Yes. Mr Kenny mentioned to me the other day that there may be some technical point on the warrant which might win my case.'

Gerry shook his head. 'No,' he answered flatly. 'I think we will concentrate on the merits of the case. Now, if there is nothing else, we have to prepare ourselves for the trial.'

Barouche looked mystified, but couldn't think of any questions. Gerry stood up, shook his hand and was gone.

Outside the main gate of the prison Dermot turned to Gerry. 'Are you not going to raise the point on the warrant?'

'No, I will explain it to you later,' he answered as he turned to Patricia. 'Can you give me a lift back into town?'

forty-seven

Doyle's Bar on Drumcondra Road was packed to the rafters with Kerry football supporters, who had enjoyed yet another success on the playing field of nearby Croke Park. Pat and Eleanor sat at a small table in the corner, drinking.

'Eleanor, are you coming down to the trial tomorrow morning?' Pat asked.

'Wild horses couldn't drag me away from it. I can't wait to see Dr Barouche finally get his comeuppance.'

Pat rubbed his brow. 'I wonder if that's such a good idea,' he replied.

'What do you mean?'

'All those cameras and reporters, it might be upsetting for you. Perhaps it's best to stay away.'

She looked at him suspiciously. 'Pat, is there something you're not telling me?'

He hesitated before answering. 'Eleanor, I have been a guard for thirty years. We do our best to get things right, but sometimes for one reason or another mistakes are made.'

'What are you trying to tell me?'

'I don't want you to be in court if Barouche gets off the hook again. I'm not sure you will be able to take it a second time.'

A look of dismay crossed her face.

'I don't understand, how could he get off?'

'I don't know. There are a million things that can go wrong in a prosecution and I think you should prepare yourself just in case.'

Her eyes narrowed. 'There is something else you're not telling me, isn't there?'

He shook his head defiantly.

'Pat, what do you know?' she persisted.

199

He leant across and gently took her hand in his. 'I told you, we do our best, but sometimes our best just isn't good enough.'

She pulled her hand away. 'You know something don't you? And you're not going to tell me.'

He took a gulp from his Guinness, and wiped his mouth. 'OK, I'll pick you up in the morning and we'll go together,' he said, batting her off.

Eleanor could plainly see the troubled look on Pat's face and decided to change the subject.

'Pat, what are you going to do when this is all over?'

His face suddenly lit up. 'Funny you should ask that question, I wanted to talk to you about that.'

'To me?' she said with surprise.

'Yes, an aunt of mine passed away last Christmas and left me a beautiful stone farmhouse overlooking Slea Head.'

'That was nice of her.'

'I was always her favourite, God only knows why. Anyway, I was thinking of converting it into a small guest house and moving back home.'

A look of disappointment crossed Eleanor's face. 'What about your job?' she asked.

'To hell with that, it's time to call it quits.'

She started to fidget nervously with the gold chain that adorned her neck.

'Does that mean you'll be moving down to Kerry for good?' she said, in a near whisper.

'Yes, I have had enough of the city; it's time to return to my roots.'

She lowered her head. 'I see. So I won't get to see you then?'

He smiled. 'Well, that's very much in your hands.'

She raised her head and looked at him. 'What do you mean?' she asked.

He searched her eyes, and then smiled. 'Eleanor, I want you to come with me.'

She gasped and placed a trembling hand to her lips.

'Well?' he pressed.

Tears welled in her eyes as she looked at him lovingly. But the look on her face carried more than a hint of sadness.

'What's wrong?' Pat asked.

'I'm a married woman and I have lived here all my life. What business have I got running off with you to the West of Ireland?'

He stood up and looked down at her. 'I thought it was a good idea but obviously I was wrong. I'll get you another drink,' he said.

She watched him at the bar ordering the drink. After a few minutes he returned with a broad smile on his face.

'What are you smiling about?' she asked.

'Oh nothing much, just having a giggle at myself and my silly dreams.'

'Listen, Pat, you took me by surprise with your proposal. I need time to think about it.'

'So, there is a chance you might come with me?' he asked, enthusiastically.

'I don't know. I had resigned myself to living out my days in Whitworth Road.'

'With that excuse for a husband of yours?'

'I didn't think there was much else left for me, that is until you came along.'

He smiled. 'There is so much more left for you, Eleanor, and believe me your next step is going to be the most important one you are ever going to take.'

'You think I don't know that?' she replied.

He knocked back the Guinness.

'Why are you so scared? Has that bastard come near you again?'

She shook her head. 'I don't know what you said to him, but I haven't seen or heard from him since.'

She glanced down at her drink. 'Pat, it's nothing to do with him.'

'What is it then?'

'It's my home, where I reared Johnny. If I left the house I would feel I was letting go of the past, of all my memories.'

'That's understandable, but you can take them with you, you know.'

She looked up and smiled. 'Pat, you're a wonderful man. I don't know what I would do without you.'

He reached over and wrapped his hand around hers. 'Whatever you decide, I will always be here if you need me. After all it's Kerry I am going to, not bloody Australia.'

'Can I give you my decision in the morning?'

Pat sat back and thought for a moment.

'I'll tell you what, if the answer is yes, wear a flower in your hair. That way you don't have to make a long speech about how much you would love to, but can't.'

She leant across the table and squeezed his cheek.

'Only you could come up with a silly idea like that, you big oaf.'
'Well, is it a deal?' he asked.
'OK, it's a deal,' she replied.

forty-eight

Mr and Mrs Hegarty and their teenaged daughter ran the gauntlet of press cameras as they climbed the steps of the entrance to the Four Courts. Once inside the busy rotunda, they searched for a familiar face. Brannigan, who was standing under a pillar talking to Cummins and Mr Dempsey, spotted them, and excused himself. He had reserved seats for them and ushered them into the packed courtroom. The large courtroom, heavily panelled in oak, had a distinctly Victorian feel to it. The jury had already been selected and were sitting on the right-hand side in the raised jury box. To their right, and at a higher level again, green velvet curtains flanked the judge's throne. Directly below, the registrar was busy checking the files and ensuring the paperwork was in order. Below him, Dermot was sitting in the solicitors' bench struggling with the *Irish Times* crossword. Gerry, wigged and gowned, sat on the far side of a wide table facing Dermot. On the other end of the table Dempsey was flicking through his barrister's notebook, fine tuning his opening speech. Patricia Quinn, Gerry's junior, and Edward Blake, Dempsey's junior, occupied the bench behind, and Cummins and Brannigan the one behind again.

To the left, in the dock, Barouche sat alone. Despite the dark Armani suit, crisp white collar and pale-grey tie, he looked gaunt and unwell. The gallery in the main body of the courtroom was packed with journalists and members of the public. Eleanor was seated beside Pat. She looked elegant in a dark-brown suit, her hair tied neatly in a bun and graced with a small carnation. She saw Barouche glaring over at Pat.

The court fell silent when the tipstaff, carrying papers and a chunky legal textbook under his arm, came out the door leading to the judge's chambers. He placed the papers and the book neatly on the judge's desk, turned on a reading light and pulled back the throne-like chair. He then returned to the judge's chambers. A sense of anticipation hung in the air. Shortly afterwards, the tipstaff returned, called out *All rise*, and Mr Justice McBride entered centre stage.

Mr Justice McBride, according to himself, was one of the few remaining *characters* on a rather grey and uninspired Irish Bench. In truth, he modelled himself, transparently so, on Mr Justice Bullingham, the fictitious character of *Rumpole of the Bailey* fame. True, he possessed much of Bullingham's boorish demeanour, but any flicker of intellect was sadly missing. A tall man, with a keen face and hawkish eyes, he sat erect, poised to pounce on any departure from his own unorthodox rules of engagement. The registrar somewhat theatrically read over the indictment.

'Mohamed Barouche on the 15 April 2006 within the State murdered Peter Hegarty; how say you in answer to the charge, are you guilty or not guilty?'

Barouche, chest out and shoulders arched, glanced across the court-room at the jury. 'Not guilty,' he replied defiantly.

Eamon Dempsey rose to his feet, adjusted his wig and commenced his opening speech. His arguments were succinctly delivered, yet full of compelling logic. Barouche couldn't offer any reasonable explanation as to how the locks of hair came into his possession. Yes, he claimed to have been framed by an unscrupulous police officer but this didn't stand up to scrutiny. Though Barouche had been acquitted of the murder of Johnny O'Shea and couldn't be tried again, nevertheless the evidence in that case could be given if it supported this one. The locks of hair were DNA profiled and without doubt came from both victims. This unquestionably linked Barouche to the murders. Quite independently Barouche's watch was smeared with Johnny O'Shea's blood and had been found close to the place where he met his death. This evidence rebutted any theory the police had framed him since there was no suggestion that Barouche's watch had been planted at the scene of the first killing. Dempsey told the jury that on hearing all the evidence they would be left in no doubt that Barouche was the murderer. When Dempsey had finished his speech and resumed his seat there was a long silence as the hostile eyes of the jurors settled on Barouche. Mr Justice McBride suggested that it would be a convenient time to adjourn for lunch.

Gerry and Dermot strolled along Inns Quay under a warm sun. Dermot turned to Gerry.

'There goes our bonus.'

'What do you mean?'

'Barouche is going to be convicted, and you know it,' Dermot replied flatly.

'O ye of little faith, always the pessimist, Dermot.'

'You would want to be an imbecile to think otherwise.'

'Perhaps.'

Gerry stopped in the shade of a large tree and glanced down at drift-wood floating aloft the swollen waters of the Liffey.

'Must be all the rain we had over the weekend,' he remarked.

Dermot took his hands out of his pockets and leant against the low granite wall.

'Gerry, is there something you're not telling me?'

Gerry turned to him and smiled. 'Dermot, how long have you been briefing me?'

'Since you started at the bar, why?'

'In all that time I have never known you to show the slightest interest in any of your cases. Why all of a sudden are you interested in this one?'

'I don't know, and before you ask, it's not the promise of a bonus.'

'Mmm, and it certainly isn't out of any love for your client.'

'Perhaps not. I find it better to remain detached. It means my judgment isn't impaired.'

'So, why are you so interested in this case?'

'Because I have been thinking about it and there's something not quite right.'

'How do you mean?'

'The tip-off, it doesn't make any sense. Do you think O'Hara is behind it?'

'I have my view on that, and all will be revealed later.'

'What about the warrant? It's not like you to let a technicality slip by. You always said, no challenge, no appeal. Have you reconsidered raising it as an issue?'

'No, I'm not going to challenge it,' Gerry replied firmly.

'And, as your instructing solicitor, would it be too much to ask why not?'

'Dermot, I have a lot on my mind at the moment. I will explain everything later. Now let's get back to the court.'

forty-nine

The court resumed after the luncheon recess and the first witness was Garda Pat Dillon from the mapping section in Garda Headquarters. He had prepared a number of maps for the benefit of the jury. A general location map showed Dun Laoghaire Pier and the area immediately surrounding it. He had marked all the relevant locations on the map and highlighted them in yellow. He also produced a map that zoomed in on the actual *locus delicti* and he had highlighted where the body was found. The next witness was Garda Muldoon of the photographic section. He produced photographs of all the relevant locations, including where the body had been found, close-ups of the blood splatters on the outer pier wall, and the tyre tracks in the area nearby. He then produced photographs of the corpse, both at the scene and in the morgue.

Dr Carmel Hudson, the State Pathologist, was then called to the witness box. An attractive woman in her early forties, she gave her evidence with considerable authority. She stated that she had examined the body at the scene and quickly determined the cause of death. Having measured the temperature of the body, she believed the time of death to be approximately 1 a.m. Her estimate, she conceded, was not precise and death could have occurred an hour either side of that time. She stated that the corpse was then removed to the morgue where she conducted a detailed post-mortem. Her initial observations at the scene were confirmed, and her final opinion was that Peter Hegarty died from a single laceration to his throat.

Gerry rose to his feet to cross-examine.

'Doctor, did you examine the body for any other injuries?'

'Yes, I did.'

'And did you find any?'

'No, there were no other injuries.'

'Is that not unusual?'

'Yes it is. Normally one expects the victim to resist an assault, to fight back. When this happens, the victim often receives defensive type injuries.'

'Can you give us an example?'

'Certainly. It is common for victims attacked by someone wielding a knife to raise their hands in an effort to ward off their attacker. In the process one expects to find injuries to the hands or arms.'

'What does the absence of such injuries suggest to you?'

'It strongly suggests that the victim was taken by surprise.'

'During the course of your examination did you discover anything of evidential value?'

'Yes; when I was examining the deep laceration to the neck I discovered an eyelash.'

'Where exactly did you find it?'

'Deep in the wound.'

'And did you form any opinion as to how it might have got there?'

'I thought the location of the eyelash was strange. Its location strongly suggests that it was either lying on the skin prior to the attack and was picked up by the knife and carried into the wound, or else that it was actually on the blade of the knife.'

'Could you please explain to the jury what leads you to express that opinion?'

'The eyelash couldn't have made its own way into the wound. If anything one would expect it to be carried out of the wound by oozing blood.'

'I know it's not your area of expertise, but are you aware that the eyelash was DNA profiled and was found not to have come from my client?'

'Yes, I am aware of that.'

'And it wasn't the victim's either.'

'So I believe.'

'Was there any possibility that it might have been deposited there accidentally, by yourself or your assistant?'

'No, in order to rule out the possibility of contamination our own DNA was compared with that of the eyelash, and neither matched it.'

'Had anyone else gone near the body?'

'No. I remember Detective Superintendent Cummins and Detective Inspector Brannigan being at the scene, but I ensured that they remained a safe distance away.'

'In any event, your findings strongly suggest that the eyelash was deposited during the course of the attack.'

'Yes, that's my opinion.'

'Thank you very much, Doctor.'

Detective Superintendent Cummins was then called to give evidence.

'Is it correct to say that you were the officer in charge of this investigation?' Mr Dempsey asked.

'Yes, sir, that's correct.'

'And on the 18 April did you have cause to issue a warrant to search the home of the accused, Mohamed Barouche?'

'Yes, as a result of—'

Before he had a chance to finish, Gerry was on his feet.

'No issue arises in relation to the issue of the warrant, My Lord.'

Mr Justice McBride appeared surprised. 'You're not challenging the admissibility of the warrant?' he asked.

'No, My Lord.'

'Well, if that's the case, we won't be needing the superintendent then.'

'No, I don't require him.'

The judge looked at Cummins. 'We don't require you, Superintendent, you may step down.'

'Thank you, My Lord.'

Cummins couldn't disguise the grin on his face as he made his way back to his seat. He was off the hook. He resumed his seat beside Brannigan and whispered, 'They didn't spot it, we're home and dry.'

Just then Dempsey announced that the next witness was Detective Inspector Noel Brannigan.

'Good luck, Noel,' Cummins said, as Brannigan squeezed past him.

'Luck has nothing to do with it,' he replied.

Dempsey examined him. 'I think you obtained a search warrant from the last witness?'

'Yes I did.'

'And as a result did you go to the home of the accused?'

'Yes, myself and a number of other gardai called to his apartment.'

'What happened when you arrived?'

'I knocked on the door of the apartment and after a short time the accused opened it. He was dressed in his night attire, so I presumed he had been in bed.'

'Did you speak to him?'

'Yes, I showed him the search warrant and explained the reason for our visit.'

'Did he offer you any resistance of any description?'

'No, Doctor Barouche invited us in and sat quietly in the living room whilst the search was being carried out.'

'What happened next?'

'A few minutes into the search, Detective Garda O'Brien approached me and showed me a small silver box which he had found hidden amongst some books on a cabinet.'

'Could the witness be shown exhibit number 8?'

The exhibits officer handed the detective inspector a see-through evidence bag, which contained a silver box.

'Is that the box?'

'Yes, it is.'

'Was there anything inside the box when you examined it?'

'Yes, there were two pieces of hair tied together, with what I thought was twine.'

'What did you do with the box and its contents?'

'I handed them back to Detective Garda O'Brien and instructed him to place both items in evidence bags. I then arrested the accused for murder.'

'Did you caution him?'

'Yes, I gave him the usual legal caution.'

'And did he make any reply?'

'Yes, he said he wanted to see his solicitor.'

'I think he was taken by other detectives to Pearse Street Garda Station.'

'Yes, that's right.'

'And you had no further dealings with him.'

'No, I didn't.'

'Thank you very much, Detective Inspector.'

Brannigan was leaving the witness box as Gerry slowly rose to his feet.

'Just a minute, Detective Inspector, I have a few questions.'

'Sorry, sir, of course.'

'Detective Inspector, you were involved closely in this investigation, were you not?'

'Yes, I was.'

'As you were with the O'Shea investigation.'

'Yes.'

'The locks of hair match perfectly the bald areas on both victims, do they not?'

Brannigan thought for a moment. 'I don't fully understand the question, sir.'

'We know the DNA matched up with the victims, but more than that, the actual clumps of hair also fitted the area on the scalps where hair was missing.'

'Yes, I understand what you are saying. The pieces of hair fitted the areas where hair had been removed from the victims.'

'Precisely,' Gerry responded.

'Yes, that is correct; they matched.'

'So the hair found in my client's apartment must have been the hair that was taken from the victims?'

'Yes, I suppose so.'

'There is no supposing about it, they fitted like pieces of a jigsaw puzzle, did they not?'

'Yes, they did.'

'So, the jury can take it, if someone sent that hair to my client, he must have been the killer.'

Brannigan appeared puzzled. 'I don't understand. Exactly what are you driving at?'

'I am merely pointing out the obvious, an unscrupulous police officer couldn't have retrieved samples of hair from the victims' corpses and sent them in the silver box, because the hair fitted like pieces of a jigsaw puzzle to the scalps of the victims.'

Brannigan nodded. 'I see, yes, that's right.'

'Indeed, so we can exclude the possibility of anyone other than the killer planting this evidence in my client's apartment.'

'Yes.'

Barouche looked at Dermot with a look of bemusement on his face. What side was Gerry on?

'Am I right in thinking, Detective Inspector, that no trace evidence was found at the scene of Johnny O'Shea's murder.'

'No, there wasn't.'

'That's unusual, isn't it?'

'Somewhat.'

'It might indicate that the murderer knew what he was at?'

'I don't understand the question.'

'I suggest to you the absence of trace evidence strongly suggests that the perpetrator took steps to ensure that he didn't leave anything behind.'

'Yes, you could say that.'

'That he had a knowledge and understanding of the significant advances in forensic science.'

'Perhaps, but there are plenty of amateur sleuths out there.'

'Tell me, Detective Inspector, where were you on the night of Johnny O'Shea's murder?'

Mr Justice McBride leant forward and intervened. 'Exactly what are you suggesting, Mr Hickey?'

Gerry glared at the judge. 'I have the right to cross-examine without interruption; if Your Lordship feels obliged to advise the witness of his right to refuse to answer questions that might incriminate him, I have no objection. But I have no intention of showing my hand to this witness at this point in time.'

A murmur rose from the public gallery.

The judge narrowed his eyes, and then turned to the witness.

'I am sure, Detective Inspector, you of all people, will appreciate you don't have to answer that question.'

Brannigan smiled. 'I have no difficulty, My Lord. I was at home when I got a call advising me of the death.'

'Do you live alone?'

'Yes.'

'In Portobello, I believe.'

'Yes, that's right.'

'Which is a less than two miles from where Johnny O'Shea was murdered.'

'Yes, about that.'

'Are you are sure you received such a call?'

'Yes, I am positive.'

'I have a statement here from Detective Garda Jim O'Mahony who says you rang him at 12.06 precisely.'

Brannigan appeared surprised. 'That might be right, I don't remember.'

'And indeed his phone records confirm that.'

'I will accept what you say.'

'He goes on to state that you requested him to collect you at your home.'

'So?'

'And on the way he heard from communications that there had been a killing.'

'I must have learnt about the killing from someone else,' Brannigan replied dismissively.

'Are you sure about that?'

'I can't think of any other explanation.'

'You see, the first report of the death was received in communications at 12.08, and was immediately passed on to units on the ground.'

'It's a very small margin, sir. I cannot be sure at this time who phoned me.'

'Are you sure the phone call, you claim to have received, concerned the killing?'

'I am almost positive, why do you ask?'

'Because Detective Garda O'Mahony goes on to state that when he collected you, you were unaware of the homicide.'

'Well, I must have called him about something entirely different, and he advised me of the killing, I thought I already knew about it.'

Dempsey interrupted the cross-examination.

'Mr Hickey has referred to a statement made by Detective Garda O'Mahony, I don't see his statement in the Book of Evidence. Can I ask where he got it?'

'Yes, Mr Hickey, where did this statement come from?' the judge asked.

Gerry stood up and addressed the judge. 'It was served on me by the prosecution last Friday, by way of disclosure. If Mr Dempsey hasn't yet received it from his own camp, it certainly isn't my fault.'

Dempsey turned to Cummins with a bemused look on his face. Cummins looked at him and shrugged his shoulders.

'So let's get this right, Detective Inspector, when I originally asked you where you were on the night of the Johnny O'Shea murder, you told me you were at home and you received a call advising you of the homicide. When confronted with the statement of Detective Garda O'Mahony and his phone records, you changed your mind and told us you received a call from an unidentified person who informed you of some unknown crime.'

'I don't see what you're getting at, the sequence is unimportant to me.'

'Indeed. Do you recall arriving at the scene?'

'Yes, I do.'

Brannigan asked the usher for a glass of water. As he sipped it slowly his eyes wandered to the back of the court where Pat was seated.

'Detective Sergeant O'Hara was already there.'

'Yes.'

'And he had a witness in the back of his car who had discovered the body and may have seen the killer leaving the scene.'

212

'I believe so, yes.'

'Did you speak to the witness?'

'No I didn't.'

'Why not, Detective Inspector?'

'He was drunk.'

'How do you know that?'

'O'Hara must have told me.'

Gerry picked up a document in his hand and appeared to read it. Brannigan shuffled in the witness box.

'That's strange, Detective Inspector. I have a statement from Detective Sergeant O'Hara in which he states, that when he met you he advised you that he had a witness in the back of his car who may have seen something. He doesn't mention anything about telling you the witness was drunk.'

'He's mistaken,' Brannigan said firmly.

'Is he also mistaken when he says you turned your back on him and told him to *get the witness out of here and down to the station*?'

'I don't remember saying that, but it wouldn't be unusual. It's desirable to have statements taken from witnesses as soon as possible, when things are fresh in their minds.'

'Surely not when they are drunk, Detective Inspector.'

Brannigan took another sip of water.

'On reflection, perhaps Detective Sergeant O'Hara didn't tell me that the witness was drunk. I may have found it out after.'

'Am I right in thinking that the witness, whose name was Dan Pender, later made a statement to the gardai claiming to have seen the killer fleeing the scene?'

'Yes, I believe he did.'

'Did you consider that to be a significant development?'

'Potentially, yes.'

'Were you present in Pearse Street Garda Station when Dr Barouche was detained there?'

'Yes, I was.'

'Were you aware that Dan Pender was present in the station for the purpose of trying to pick out the man he saw fleeing from the alley shortly after Johnny O'Shea was killed?'

'Yes, I knew he was there.'

'Why didn't you supervise the identification parade?'

'I had other business to attend to.'

'Like what?'

'I can't remember at this stage.'

'But he was an important witness, was he not?'

'Yes.'

'Did you speak to him?'

'No, I didn't.'

'Why not?'

'I told you I had other business to attend to.'

'Was there some reason why you were avoiding one to one contact with Pender?'

'None whatsoever,' Brannigan replied, indignantly.

'Dan Pender was to attend court on the day of the trial, wasn't he?'

'Yes.'

'As you were?'

'Yes, naturally I would have been there.'

'So he would have come face to face with you?'

'Possibly.'

'Not possibly, Detective Inspector, he could not have avoided you.'

Brannigan smiled. 'OK, we would probably have met at some stage.'

'The gardai were unsure if he would turn up in court, isn't that right?'

'I believe so.'

'So Detective Superintendent Cummins instructed members to track his movements during the day before the trial, watch him all night and pick him up first thing the following morning.'

'Yes, I understand that the detective superintendent gave those orders.'

'So you knew where he was sleeping that night?'

'I am not sure that I did.'

Gerry picked up another document and examined it closely.

'Again your answer intrigues me, Detective Inspector. I have a statement in my hand from Detective Garda James O'Malley. He states that he kept you personally informed of Pender's movements on the eve of the trial, and that shortly before midnight you phoned him and asked him where Pender was. He goes on to state that he informed you that Pender was asleep in an alley off Dawson Street, and appeared to be there for the night. He further states that you told him to abandon the surveillance, to return at six and then pick Pender up. What do you say to that?'

Brannigan looked at the judge. 'What can I say? I don't remember that, but if Detective O'Malley says I gave him those orders, he must be right.'

'Why did you instruct Detective Garda O'Malley to abandon his surveillance of Pender?'

'Because he said he was bedded down for the night. It was a waste of resources to leave two members on him all night.'

'Is that your only explanation for overriding the instructions given by your detective superintendent?'

'Yes, but I think my decision was justified in the circumstances.'

'Yet a moment ago you couldn't even remember your conversation with Detective Garda O'Malley.'

Brannigan's eyes narrowed as he glared at Gerry.

'What are you driving at, Mr Hickey?'

'Less than an hour after your conversation with Detective Garda O'Malley, the unfortunate Mr Pender met his death.'

'Yes, at the hands of Darren Walshe, who was a vagrant like Pender.'

'You also took charge of that investigation, didn't you?'

'Yes, I did.'

'Was Darren Walshe ever tried for the murder?'

'You know full well, Mr Hickey, that he committed suicide shortly before the trial. He had over seventy previous convictions.'

'Were any of them for violence?'

'I don't know.'

Gerry offered the detective inspector a computer printout.

'I think, Detective Inspector, you will find from an examination of this list of his convictions, that he didn't.'

Brannigan waved his hand dismissively. 'I will take your word for it, I don't see how that is relevant.'

'So, despite being under garda surveillance, Mr Pender never came face to face with you at the trial, did he?'

'That has nothing to do with me.'

The judge intervened. 'Can you come to the point, Mr Hickey? I can't allow a meandering, pointless cross-examination; you're wasting the court's time.'

Gerry glared at the judge. 'I can assure you that my cross-examination is aimed at undermining the prosecution case.'

'By suggesting that the detective inspector had something to do with it,' the judge snapped. 'I hope you are acting on instructions. I may be forced to report the matter to the Bar Council.'

'Report me to whoever you like,' Gerry snapped.

The judge's face became flushed with rage. 'How dare you address me in that fashion; now get on with your cross-examination.'

Gerry ignored the rebuff and continued, 'Next you were involved in the investigation of this case.'

'Yes, I was.'

'What led you to my client's apartment.'

'We received confidential information.'

'From whom?'

'We don't know; it was from an anonymous caller.'

'Male or female?'

'I'm not sure.'

'Those calls are taped, aren't they?'

'Yes, I believe so.'

'I have heard the tape, Detective Inspector, and it's clearly a male caller, but his voice has been disguised.'

Brannigan looked surprised. It was becoming clear that Gerry had done his homework.

'Again, Mr Hickey, I'll take your word for it.'

'Have you any inkling who the caller might have been?'

'No, I haven't a clue.'

'The information the caller left was to the effect that the killer's souvenirs were to be found in my client's apartment, isn't that right?'

'Yes, I believe so.'

'So, can we exclude my client from the list of possible suspects?'

'That's not unreasonable.'

'And his girlfriend can also be excluded, since the caller was male.'

'Yes.'

'At that stage, who was aware that a souvenir, or a trophy as Mr Dempsey called it in his opening speech, had been taken from Peter Hegarty's body?'

'The state pathologist, her assistant, Detective Superintendent Cummins and myself.'

'Anyone else?'

Brannigan hesitated and appeared deep in thought.

'I believe that the detective superintendent also told Detective Sergeant Pat O'Hara.'

'So which of those people do you believe made the call?'

'I don't know what you mean?'

'Nobody else knew about the souvenir. It must have been one of those five people.'

'I resent that suggestion.'

Gerry allowed himself a sardonic smile that seemed to unsettle Brannigan.

'What was your reaction when Detective Garda Masterson informed you that an eyelash had been found in the wound to Peter Hegarty's neck?'

'It was a major breakthrough.'

Gerry leant forward towards the witness box and fixed Brannigan with a hawkish eye. 'Answer the question, what was your reaction?'

Brannigan looked away. 'I don't remember.'

'Let me remind you, Detective Inspector,' Gerry said, as he picked up another document.

'Detective Garda Masterson says, and I quote, *When I broke the news to Detective Superintendent Cummins and Detective Inspector Brannigan, the superintendent was pleased at the breakthrough, the detective inspector on the other hand immediately sought to undermine the significance of it.* What do you say to that?'

'So, I am cautious by nature, there is always the possibility of contamination.'

'Was it at that point you decided to frame Dr Barouche?'

Brannigan leant forward and glared at Gerry. 'I reject that suggestion, Mr Hickey. It's outrageous.'

'Because you realized that there was physical evidence linking you to the murder.'

A murmur rose from the public gallery.

'That is an absolutely preposterous suggestion. Your client murdered Peter Hegarty and you know it.'

'Where were you between midnight and three o'clock on the morning of the killing?'

'I was at home.'

'Alone?'

'Yes.'

'Do you own a Yahama V series motor bike?'

'You know I do, Mr Hickey.'

'Did you ever bring your motor bike to the park beside Dun Laoghaire pier.'

'No, I didn't.'

'Were you present along with Detective Superintendent Cummins when Detective Garda Kieran Doherty pointed out tyre marks which he found in the park?'

'Yes, I was.'

'What make were the tyres?'

'Pirelli Diablos, I think.'

'Did you share Detective Garda Doherty's confidence that if a match was found, he could identify the tyres?'

'Yes, and I hoped it was a breakthrough.'

'Is that why you changed the tyres on your own bike the following day?'

A murmur rose from the public gallery. Beads of sweat glistened on Brannigan's face as he reached into his breast pocket for a handkerchief. Gerry held aloft a piece of paper.

'I have here a statement from Pat Donnelly, who is the proprietor of Donnelly Tyres in Ranelagh. He states that on Monday the 16 April 2006 you purchased a new set of Dunlop tyres at a cost of three hundred and seventy-five euros.'

'So what?'

Dempsey rose to his feet to make an objection but the judge looked down and waved his arm.

'Sit down.'

He then turned to the witness. 'Detective Inspector, do you accept that you bought a new set of tyres on the 16 of April?'

'I honestly cannot remember the date I changed my tyres, My Lord, but if Mr Donnelly says it was on the 16 of April I won't quarrel with him.'

'It seems an odd coincidence. Have you an explanation for it?'

'I found the Pirellis performed poorly in the wet, My Lord, so I decided to change them; it's purely a coincidence.'

'How long had you been driving on them?'

'About nine months, My Lord.'

'I see, you will agree it seems a little strange that you chose that moment to change them.'

'Yes, but perhaps my conversation with Detective Garda Doherty and his reference to damaged tyres, focused my mind on my own tyres. I honestly don't know, but I can assure you there is nothing sinister in it.'

The judge made a note in his notebook and glanced down at Gerry.

'Carry on, Mr Hickey.'

'I wonder if you would like to reconsider your answer.'

'There is nothing to reconsider.'

'Very well. Fortunately Mr Donnelly left the tyres lying in his yard.'

Brannigan reached forward and poured himself more water with an unsteady hand.

'And Detective Garda Doherty compared them with the cast he had taken from the scene. I will read a portion of his statement: *One of the tyres was damaged, the damage caused a distortion in the thread and this was mirrored in the cast taken from the scene. As a result I can state it is highly probable that the tyre I examined left the tyre track found at the scene.* What do you say to that, Detective Inspector?'

Brannigan sat forward in the witness box. 'That form of identification is notoriously unreliable. His conclusion is based on the balance of probabilities, which, Mr Hickey, you well know is valueless in a criminal trial.'

He sat back and folded his arms defiantly.

'Could the witness be shown exhibit 21?'

The exhibits officer handed the detective inspector a see-through evidence bag that contained an envelope.

'Detective inspector, do you recognize that envelope?'

'Yes, it was taken from your client's apartment.'

'Do you notice anything missing?'

The detective inspector examined the envelope.

'Yes, the stamp is missing.'

'Would it surprise you to know that it was sent to the forensic science laboratory at Garda Headquarters?'

'Not really.'

'Well, would it also surprise you to learn that on close examination the stamp yielded traces of saliva?'

Brannigan squinted his eyes and placed a hand to his forehead.

'Are you all right, Detective Inspector? You look unwell.'

'I am fine, Mr Hickey.'

'The forensic scientist was able to construct a DNA profile. Have you any idea what he compared it to?'

Brannigan shook his head.

'He compared it with the DNA extracted from the eyelash found on Peter Hegarty's body.'

Some of the jurors sat forward in their seats, as a sense of anticipation gripped the courtroom.

'And?' Brannigan asked tentatively.

'They match,' Gerry declared.

Mr Justice McBride called for order, as the public gallery became unruly. When the noise subsided, Gerry continued, 'So, Detective Inspector, it appears that Peter Hegarty's killer decided to frame my client. He posted the hair to my client and then phoned the Garda

Confidential Line. And he did so in the certain knowledge that my client's apartment would be raided and the incriminating evidence found. Have you any idea who that person was?'

'I don't know; I can only speculate.'

'Feel free, Detective Inspector.'

'Detective Sergeant O'Hara fitted up your client the last time and he appeared to me to have a pathological hatred for him. It is possible that he has done the same thing this time.'

'But you agree that whoever sent the letter to my client must be the killer?'

'Yes, it certainly looks that way.'

'Are you suggesting that Sergeant O'Hara is the killer?'

Brannigan sat back and looked into the body of the public gallery to where Pat was sitting. He hesitated and then looked at the judge.

'Yes, I am reluctantly forced to that conclusion.'

As the public gallery erupted Eleanor tightened her grip on Pat's hand. He looked down at her and smiled.

'Order in court, order in court,' the judge barked.

After the commotion had settled, Gerry continued, 'So, Detective Inspector, O'Hara is the killer; it's his eyelash that was found at the scene, and his saliva on the stamp. He murdered Johnny O'Shea and Peter Hegarty and the war he has waged against Dr Barouche stems from a desire to cover his own tracks. Is that what you are saying?'

'I am reluctant to condemn a fellow police officer, but the evidence you have pointed to, forces me to agree with your proposition.'

Gerry leant down and picked up a statement of evidence. He slowly turned the pages. The detective inspector glanced at the judge and smiled, his gesture wasn't reciprocated.

'Detective Sergeant O'Hara was requested to check out my client's alibi, was he not?'

'Yes he was.'

'So if my theory is right, he would have suppressed any evidence that pointed to my client's innocence?'

'Yes, I would expect that he would.'

'I am going to read you a portion of a statement made by Detective Sergeant O'Hara: *On the 18 April 2006 I called at St Vincents Hospital and secured video footage which covered the area in which Dr Barouche claimed to have fallen asleep sometime after 9 p.m. on the night of the killing. I brought the tape to the Technical Bureau where I examined it closely. The tape has a built-in timer. On viewing the tape*

I saw a man enter the Radiology Department, lie down on a trolley and fall asleep. He remained asleep until shortly before 5 a.m. On close examination I recognized the man as Dr Mohamed Barouche. I had the tape examined by garda technical experts. They found the tape and the timer to be in working order and there was no evidence that the tape had been interfered with. As a result I am left in no doubt that Dr Barouche has a cast-iron alibi and could not be responsible for Peter Hegarty's murder.'

'Can I see that statement?' asked Brannigan.

Gerry handed the statement to the exhibits officer, who in turn handed it to the witness. He examined the statement closely. He then handed it back. A look of dismay crossed his face.

'I have never seen that statement before. It should have been drawn to my attention.'

'There is an explanation for that, Detective Inspector.'

Brannigan raised an eyebrow.

'After Detective Sergeant O'Hara viewed that tape, he realized my client was being framed by someone close to the investigation. As a result of his concerns he went directly to the Garda Commissioner and sought permission to conduct his own investigation. Having viewed your telephone records and received expert evidence of cell identification, he concluded that you were the murderer. Would you like me to go through your telephone records?'

Brannigan sat erect in the witness box and took a deep breath. He then turned to the judge and said. 'I am refusing to answer any more questions on the grounds that the answers may incriminate me.'

The judge glared down at him. 'You should have done that some time ago,' he said, his tone heavy with sarcasm. 'You may step down.'

There was silence in court as Brannigan wearily left the witness box. As he passed Barouche, a slight grin crossed his face. When he reached the back of the court, members of the public moved aside to let him through. He glared at Pat as he passed him. Outside in the round hall Detective Superintendent Cummins and another detective approached Brannigan. Cummins placed his hand on Brannigan's shoulder and said, 'I am arresting you for the murders of Johnny O'Shea, Dan Pender and Peter Hegarty, you are not obliged to say anything but anything you do say will be taken down in writing and may be given in evidence. Do you understand?'

Brannigan hung his head. 'I understand,' he muttered.

Back in the courtroom, Dempsey declared that he was offering no further evidence. Mr Justice McBride directed the jury to find the defendant not guilty and rose quickly.

Journalists rushed from the court as Barouche embraced Mary. Cummins looked shell-shocked as he approached Pat.

'Why didn't you tell me?' he asked.

'I couldn't, Jack, in theory you were on the suspect list.'

'And Brannigan, how did you know it was him.'

'As soon as I found Barouche's alibi stood up it had to be someone on the inside. I ran a check on his phone records and they placed him in Dun Loaghaire at the time of the killing.'

'I don't understand; he was hell bent on us not going near Barouche from the beginning.'

'O'Shea was to be the first of many and Barouche's confession scuppered his plans. Pender was simply an eye-witness who had to be disposed of.'

'But after Hegarty's murder, Brannigan was adamant that we didn't go near Barouche.'

'Sure, up until the discovery of the eyelash. From then on Barouche had to be convicted and the case closed because he knew there was evidence linking him to the murder. He sent Barouche the hair, made a call to the confidential line and the rest is history. He even tried to blackmail Mr Hickey into throwing the case.'

'Blackmail, with what?'

'We don't need to go into that.'

'But he didn't want me to issue a warrant.'

'Reverse psychology, Jack, he knew you had to act on that information, and he knew you didn't believe I was responsible.'

'But why didn't you arrest him before the trial?'

'He would have clammed up and refused to answer any questions. I knew the arrogant bastard wouldn't have backed away so quickly in public, Hickey did a fine job.'

'And you provided him with the ammunition,' Cummins observed.

'Yes, Jack, it was the right thing to do.'

'Fancy a pint? I'm pretty shook,' Cummins asked.

'I'm sorry, I have a date with a certain little lady.'

Cummins glanced over towards Eleanor. 'I see, very nice too.'

Pat excused himself and approached Barouche, who was enthusiastically clapping Gerry on the back. Pat took a deep breath.

'Doctor, after everything I have done to you, what I'm about to say will sound very shallow. Nevertheless, I want to apologize to you for intruding on your life the way I did, and for putting you through hell. I hope one day, when the dust has settled, you will find it in your heart to forgive me.'

Barouche looked at him and smiled. 'It takes a brave man to admit the error of his ways. Your actions in exposing Detective Inspector Brannigan more than atone for anything you may have done in the past. Sergeant, I don't need the dust to settle, I accept your apology and forgive you here and now.'

Pat looked down at Barouche's extended hand, and grasped it.

'Thank you, Doctor.'

Gerry ushered Pat aside. 'Sergeant—'

Pat cut across him. 'There's no need, Mr Hickey. You must have been under horrendous pressure.'

Gerry looked at him quizzically.

'She is back in Prague. I found the disc of photos in Brannigan's locker and destroyed them.'

Gerry breathed a sigh of relief. Words eluded him, so he shook hands with Pat and hurried from the courtroom. Pat turned to the public gallery where Eleanor sat alone. He threw her a beaming smile but she lowered her head. She opened her handbag and appeared to rummage for something. Removing a photo of Johnny she placed it to her lips and kissed it. She regarded it closely, and then placed it back in her bag. She stood up slowly and moved towards the door of the court where she stopped, turned and looked at Pat.

'Are you coming or what, you big oaf?'

epilogue

Under questioning Brannigan broke down and confessed to all three killings. He claimed that a Christian brother had sexually abused him as a schoolboy and this gave rise, so he said, to his pathological hatred of homosexuals. He was remanded in custody to the Central Mental Hospital for psychiatric assessment. It was there that he claimed to hear voices in his head telling him to do evil things. A week before his trial a warder found him hanging in his cell.

Pat O'Hara and Eleanor run a small guesthouse overlooking Slea Head on the Dingle Peninsular. They spend most of their leisure time hill walking in the Kerry Mountains.

Dr Mohamed Barouche and Mary married in September that year. Shortly afterwards she gave birth to a baby girl. They emigrated to Australia.

Gerry Hickey moved in with Sarah and still practises as a barrister. He remains unaware that his new partner sent the embarrassing photographs to his ex-wife.